The Vultures

The Vultures

Mark Hannon

Apprentice House Press
Loyola University Maryland

First Edition

Casebound ISBN: 978-1-62720-311-1
Paperback ISBN: 978-1-62720-312-8
Ebook ISBN: 978-1-62720-313-5

Printed in the United States of America

Design by Vanessa Gleklen
Editorial development by Annabelle Finagin, Elizabeth Leik and Mary Kokoski
Promotion plan by Annabelle Finagin

Author photo by Jeremiah Hannon
Stadium photo on back cover by John Boutet

Apprentice House Press
Loyola University Maryland
4501 N. Charles Street
Baltimore, MD 21210
410.617.5265
www.ApprenticeHouse.com
info@ApprenticeHouse.com

"*Public diversions at home, wars abroad; some-times terror, sometimes torpor, or stupid sloth; this is thy daily toil.*"

The Meditations of Marcus Aurelius, Book X

"*The worse things got downtown; the more people, businesses, and stores left; the more grandiose, ambi-tious, outrageous, and removed from reality became the plans advanced for its renewal.*"

-Mark Goldman, *City on the Edge*

To my little family

BUFFALO, NEW YORK
(1970)

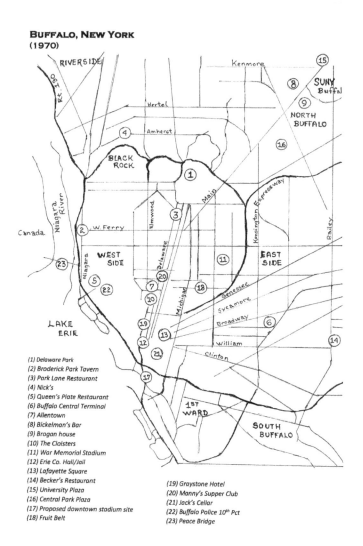

(1) Delaware Park
(2) Broderick Park Tavern
(3) Park Lane Restaurant
(4) Nick's
(5) Queen's Plate Restaurant
(6) Buffalo Central Terminal
(7) Allentown
(8) Bickelman's Bar
(9) Brogan house
(10) The Cloisters
(11) War Memorial Stadium
(12) Erie Co. Hall/Jail
(13) Lafayette Square
(14) Becker's Restaurant
(15) University Plaza
(16) Central Park Plaza
(17) Proposed downtown stadium site
(18) Fruit Belt

(19) Graystone Hotel
(20) Manny's Supper Club
(21) Jack's Cellar
(22) Buffalo Police 10th Pct
(23) Peace Bridge

M. Kokoski

1.

The black and white police car drove across the shopping center parking lot, its tires crunching on the ice just before dawn on a February day. The driver stopped next to a cluster of unmarked cars where a group of young men dressed in hooded sweatshirts and blue jeans huddled around a tall man carrying a portable radio. An officer with captain's bars on his dark blue overcoat stepped out of the black and white and addressed the man carrying the portable.

"Going out with a bang, eh, Patrick?" the Captain said, shaking hands with the tall man.

"Big kick at the finish, Captain," Lt. Pat Brogan said with a smile.

"Got everything you need?"

"Yes sir," Brogan said. "I called Judge Casper at home, and he signed the warrant. I've got a crew of good men ready to go, and the uniforms from 17 are ready to back us up."

"Ah, the ever-helpful Judge Casper. All right, good work." To Brogan, the Captain added, "Nobody gets hurt." Then, to the assembled police raiders, "Good hunting, men."

Brogan looked around at his men. "Hammer's moving out," he said quietly into the portable radio. The young plainclothesmen slammed car doors and four old Plymouths rolled quietly uphill following Brogan through the Central Park Plaza lot and into the neighborhood of wooden houses.

Brogan keyed his radio, and a uniformed Lieutenant several blocks away answered, "Anvil's moving," signaling several marked police cars to head into the neighborhood. Brogan unbuttoned his corduroy car coat and slid his holster forward on his belt. He looked over at the mustachioed driver and said, "Ok, Sal, drive past the house and stop at the corner." The car glided past a two-story house with a rotting porch and flaking brown paint and stopped behind a beat-up Ford Fairlane. The man in the Ford got out, rubbing his hands together.

"Hammer 2, 3 and 4 in position," Brogan's portable squawked. Brogan and Sal got out of their car and stood with the chilled detective.

"Morning, Mel, everything quiet?" Brogan asked.

"They're all asleep, Lieutenant," the detective said. "They were partying until about an hour ago, but all's quiet now."

"Any deals during the night?"

"Not that I saw," Mel said, stamping his feet in the cold. "Probably wanted to get happy with the shipment first."

Brogan nodded and heard the uniformed Lieutenant's mike key again.

"The uniforms are coming in now. Ok, men. Sal, you and Mel are with me, going in the front. Aloysius, Weisbeck and O'Conner have the place surrounded."

The three detectives approached the house, and Brogan nodded as one of the younger men drew his pistol and the other racked a round into a shotgun. Three black and white police cars slid silently down the street behind them.

"Hammer 1's going in," Brogan said into the portable, then jogged up the creaking steps and kicked in the front door with a grunt, sending it swinging.

"Buffalo Police! This is a raid!" Brogan shouted. He heard glass shattering, wood breaking and "Police!" shouted at the back of the house as he looked around the living room where Sal and Mel were dragging groggy youths off sagging couches and forcing them face down onto ragged carpets littered with beer cans and wine bottles.

Meeting the raiders coming from the back at the staircase, Brogan pointed them up the stairs and then descended into the basement, his sidearm held high. Stopping at the bottom of the stairs, he swung the pistol from left to right until he spotted a frizzy haired boy in a t-shirt trying to squeeze out a basement window. Walking forward, Brogan said, "Buffalo Police, stay where you are!"

The boy slid back onto the floor and reached to his pants. Brogan stepped up to him and put his revolver to the frizzy head. Please don't do anything stupid, kid, he thought. Not on my last day. The kid's hands shot up, and a bag of pot flipped out onto the cement floor.

"Don't shoot! Don't shoot!" the kid screamed, and Brogan figured he couldn't be more than eighteen, Tommy's age. Brogan patted him down quickly then handcuffed him as two uniformed policemen came down the steps. He dragged the kid by his belt to the uniforms, nodding at the bag on the ground.

"Got it, el-tee," the first uniform said. Going to the back of the house, Brogan followed the wreckage of the plainclothes raiders into the kitchen, where policemen were turning over the chairs and tables and emptying cabinets. Sal came into the kitchen from the front of the house.

"Looks like Mel was right, Lieutenant. They were partying with the shipment before they moved it. There's three kilos wrapped up and one busted open. Found six people here, the guys from the 17th are getting them loaded up now."

Brogan nodded, then spotted an Army field jacket hanging on a chair. Gesturing with the portable, he said, "I'll be right back," and rushed to the front of the house, where the raiders were bending the suspects into police cars. He went from car to car looking in the back seats and exhaled when he'd observed all the prisoners.

Thank God he wasn't here, he thought.

2.

The owner of the Buffalo Bills, Paul Eigen, sat in the middle of the banquet table and looked over its occupants. A well-fed bunch, they were finishing up coffee and lighting cigarettes, one frozen food company owner firing up a Dominican cigar. The right mix, Eigen thought, as he looked over the collection of businessmen, politicians and reporters, for maximum impact. Eigen remembered C.P.O. Shober at Great Lakes. When he wanted 100% of your attention, he would kick things. Kick open doors. Knock over bunks. Send footlockers flying. It worked, every time.

"All right, gentlemen," Eigen said, "shall we proceed to see the new, improved Civic Stadium?" The Mayor of Buffalo nodded and smiled at that old name for War Memorial Stadium, buttoning his suit coat like he was getting ready for a graduation picture. The score of men rose and exited into the suburban parking lot as Eigen signed the bill for the meal and stuck a few twenties into the hand of the headwaiter who shook hands with him.

"Share this with the staff, Joe."

"Always a pleasure, Mr. Eigen."

The men approached the private bus and got on board, Eigen watching to make sure they didn't head for their own cars and away from his control.

"Not your basic school bus, eh, Paul?" the county executive said, running his hand over the plush upholstery on the seats.

"I got the top of the line for this crowd, Mr. Burgos," Eigen answered.

Sitting next to Eigen up front, the mayor turned around to talk to the reporters.

"The Press Box has been completely overhauled," he said, "new phone lines, air conditioning installed and heat reworked."

"Thank God," the football writer from Sports Illustrated said quietly to a compatriot from the Buffalo Courier Express. "I was glad they didn't make the playoffs last year. The thought of covering them in December makes me cringe."

"The windows," said a reporter from the Daily News. "I remember you could barely get them open when it was hot, and they didn't keep the wind out when it was cold."

"The new draft choices will love the bigger lockers," the mayor added, smiling as the bus rolled down Broadway, passing commercial occupancies, some open, some closed with graffiti covered roll up doors. As they turned on Jefferson, the reporter from The Rochester Democrat and Chronicle pointed his chin at an empty lot.

"Used to get good rolls and sandwiches at the bakery that was there."

When they pulled into the weedy parking lot, the Herald-Journal's rookie reporter said to a dismayed city councilman, "This place looks like some old Roman ruins."

Once off the bus, the mayor led the way, trotting eagerly up the concrete steps under the Bison friezes on the towering concrete gateways. Inside, he led them down to the home team locker room that smelled of the new royal blue paint covering the concrete block. The guests crowded around the two scarred wooden benches in the 30' room. Spreading his hands wide once everyone was inside, the mayor said, "New lockers, new paint," and gestured towards the dimly lit shower room where a man in white coveralls looked up from his work on the floor, "and new tiles in the showers."

"What's that smell?" the Democrat and Chronicle said.

"You mean the paint?" the Plain Dealer asked.

The tile man looked up. "Nah, he probably means the shit smell," pointing at the shower drain. "We're right above the sewer here. Been smelling it all week."

The reporters laughed. The mayor forced a smile and blinked.

When they left the locker room and began to trudge up the long, wide ramp towards the press box area, the group fell silent except for the mayor.

"I remember walking up this ramp the day we won the AFL Championship in '64," he said. "There was electricity in the air. Standing room only. Thousands of excited fans, everyone anticipating the game. What a day that was!"

As they approached the press box, Eigen stood on the ramp waiting for them, his arms folded across his chest.

"Gentlemen. Before you look in on the new remodeled press box, I'd like to point out a few items. Firstly," he said, pointing to puddles emanating from the rest room to his right, "the plumbing in this place is shot. Hasn't been overhauled since they put it in in '37. Second," he said, kicking the wall as hard as he could and dislodging large chunks of concrete, "the concrete walls are spalling. The weather has been at work on it for over thirty winters and is winning. Thirdly," he said, looking at the open-mouthed mayor, "there's only enough parking in the lots for about a third of the stadium's capacity, and everyone else either takes at least two buses to get here or parks in people's driveways and yards out there," nodding his head in the direction of Jefferson Street with its boarded up and burned out businesses.

"We need a new stadium, my friends, and we need it now," Eigen announced. "I've just come from Seattle, where a group of investors is ready to build a football-only stadium on the order of the Astrodome in Houston," which got all the reporters scribbling furiously. "I hope we can save the football franchise here in Buffalo, but if not, other places have the welcome mat out. With that, Eigen walked through the crowd and down the ramp to a car that awaited him, leaving the mayor and the other politicians open mouthed as the reporters crowded up the narrow stairway to the press box to grab the newly installed phones.

3.

When Tom got home from classes, he dropped his books on the dining room table and started looking through the mail.

His mother called out from the kitchen, "Hi Tommy. How'd it go at school today?"

"Ok," he said, finding a blue envelope with his brother Rory's writing on it.

"Rory sent us two letters, Tommy," she said over the sound of sizzling pork chops on the stove. "Did you find yours?"

"Yeah, Mom," he said, opening his letter as he sat down in the den where the five o'clock news was on.

"Three more weeks until he gets out of there," she said, grabbing the medal of St. Michael around her neck and saying a quick prayer.

Tom looked down at the pale blue stationery.

> *Tom,*
> *Just one month to go. I've finally earned my short-tim-er's stick. I cut a notch in it every day until I get out of here.*
>
> *The patrols have picked up a lot since we got mortared twice last week. Two guys got hurt, nothing really bad, but with the three guys out for malaria, we're down five in the platoon, and only two guys came in to replace them, and they don't know shit. They say the NVA has moved a lot of people in around here and are terrorizing the*

*villes by night. A few of the local headmen disappeared,
and a couple of them got found dead in a ditch just outside camp. After that a lot of the local men disappeared,
too. We figure they got "drafted" by Uncle Ho, the dink
bastard. Remember how Dad used to talk about how the
French and Belgians were happy to see the Americans
show up during WWII? Well, nobody's friendly to us
anymore. When we went through this one ville, we
searched it for weapons but didn't find any. The ARVN
scout found a cache of rice he said was for the NVA, so
we set the cache and a bunch of hooches on fire and left.
These people get their asses kicked no matter which way
they turn. I'll be glad to get the hell out of here. I don't
know if we're doing any good for anybody.*

*I've been saving up my money, and when I get home, I
should have enough to buy a car. A few months after I
get back to the states I'll be out of the Army – that will
be before the end of the summer, and we can go to the
beach whenever we want.*

*Send me a letter, you bum! It reminds me that the whole
world isn't 110 degrees and full of bugs. I swear to
God, when I get home I'll never complain about the
snow in Buffalo again.*

Your Big Brother (and don't you forget it!),
Rory

When Tom looked up from the letter, a reporter on TV was
standing in a road outside a village. American soldiers in green were
walking in a line away from the camera towards the village, and there
were several contorted bodies in black pajamas lying on the road.

Tom couldn't make out what the reporter was saying as he thought, Dead bodies and they just walk past them, and Rory's part of this craziness?

4.

Heading out through the wire at dawn, Rory Brogan felt better about going on patrol. Since Lieutenant Keenan and Sergeant Washington had taken over the platoon, Rory had watched the squad tighten up. Weapons were at the ready, noisy gear was taped down or left behind and the men kept their intervals. Crossing through the free fire zone, they used hand signals, keeping their mouths shut and eyes open as they entered the bush.

Gervase was walking point, two men ahead of Rory. He was moving slowly, then even slower. About a klick in, he flashed a closed fist and dropped to one knee. Sergeant Washington moved up and knelt next to him, stared into the bush, then stuck his arm out to the side, his hand in a fist. The squad fanned out to form a skirmish line. Rory's pulse quickened as he flanked out to his left, toward the edge of a muddy stream. His eyes jumped back and forth from where he put his feet to the bush ahead. With every snap of a twig or swing of a branch, the blood pulsed louder in his ears. Bugs landed in the sweat on his face and neck and in his ears. Rory fought off the urge to swat them, keeping his hands on his rifle, index finger tapping just outside the trigger guard. He swung the M-16 in a narrow arc in front and kept pace with the others. To his right, Isada looked to the Sergeant, who stopped and raised a closed fist. They waited and listened. Nothing. Washington turned toward Rory and Isada and swung a raised hand back and forth. The squad started falling back into line on the trail. Rory exhaled as he flanked off behind Isada and stepped back towards the trail.

Rory heard the metallic ping and Isada spun around and looked wide eyed at him. The roar of the mine's explosion blew him sideways through a mass of bamboo branches. He landed on his back feeling as light as air, amazed at a force that could drive him through such dense bush. He heard unintelligible shouting and thought, Goddammit, keep quiet in the bush. He saw Sgt. Washington staring down at him. Grimacing, the sergeant reached out and removed Rory's bloodied helmet and carefully laid his head on a flak jacket.

Oh shit, I must be really fucked up, Rory thought. I can't see anything to my left. Voices approached, and he could hear the PRC 77 operator speak loud and fast, the radio squawking back. Rory kept blinking his right eye to see what was happening, but something wet kept blocking his vision.

The last thing he remembered was watching Doc Wilson pull one of the big field dressing bandages out of his bag, being picked up, and then everything went dark.

5.

Rita heard the DJ on WBEN start to read the noon news and stood up. Lunchtime, she thought, then, but it's just me today, as she looked in the refrigerator. The doorbell rang. She went to the steps and saw a man in a brown jacket waiting there. Who's this? she wondered. He rapped on the door.

"Western Union," he said.

Oh no! She remembered Pat saying, "They always send a soldier now if a GI's killed in action."

"Yes?" she said, slowly opening the door.

"Telegram, Ma'am," and he handed her an envelope.

"Let me get some change..."

"No need for that." He turned and left.

She turned the yellow envelope over and opened it. Leaning against the doorframe, she read,

```
FROM: MILITARY NOTIFICATIONS BUREAU
DEPARTMENT OF DEFENSE
WASHINGTON, DC
REPORT DELIVERY    DO NOT PHONE
DO NOT CALL THE SECRETARY OF THE ARMY
TO: MR AND MRS PATRICK BROGAN
    75 CORDOVA AVENUE BUFFALO, NY 14214

THE SECRETARY OF THE ARMY REGRETS TO
INFORM YOU THAT YOUR SON PRIVATE
FIRST CLASS RORY BROGAN WAS WOUNDED
IN ACTION BY AN EXPLOSIVE PLACED BY
```

A HOSTILE FORCE. HE HAS BEEN PLACED
ON THE SERIOUSLY ILL LIST AND IN THE
JUDGEMENT OF THE ATTENDING PHYSICIAN
HIS CONDITION IS OF SUCH SEVERITY THAT
THERE IS CAUSE FOR CONCERN. PLEASE
BE ASSURED THAT THE BEST MEDICAL
FACILITIES AND DOCTORS HAVE BEEN MADE
AVAILABLE AND EVERY MEASURE IS BEING
TAKEN TO AID HIM. HE IS HOSPITALIZED
IN VIETNAM. ADDRESS MAIL TO HIM AT
THE HOSPITAL MAIL SECTION, APO SAN
FRANCISCO 96347. YOU WILL BE PROVIDED
PROGRESS REPORTS AND KEPT INFORMED
OF ANY SIGNIFICANT CHANGES IN HIS
CONDITION.

JAMES H ONEILL MAJOR GENERAL USA
C 114-140 THE ADJUDENT GENERAL
DEPARTMENT OF THE ARMY WASHINGTON DC

Rita spun inside the hallway and stumbled to the phone, gripping the telegram. Staring at the envelope, she started dialing the number for the 17th Precinct, then stopped. No. Dial Pat's number at the DA's office. She tried again.

"Good afternoon, District Attorney's office."

"Pat. May I speak to Patrick Brogan, please?"

"Mrs. Brogan? Are you ok?"

"Rory. Something's happened to Rory. Pat, where's Pat?"

"He's out of the office, Mrs. Brogan. Wait on the line, I'll try to find him."

Rita's legs gave out and she found herself sitting on the floor while she waited. She tried to read the telegram again, but the words made no sense.

"Mrs. Brogan, this is District Attorney Butler. Pat's on the street right now, but we're tracking him down."

He could hear Rita sobbing on the other end. He covered the speaker and said to the secretary, "Get a deputy over to Brogan's house now."

Then, to Rita, "Mrs. Brogan, we're sending a deputy over to your house to assist you, and we'll have Pat home as soon as we can get in touch with him. Are you ok?"

"It's our boy, Rory. Something happened to him in Vietnam. This telegram says... I don't know what happened," and she dropped the phone.

Pat Brogan was tipping back a Pepsi in the Mayflower Restaurant and looking over the cup when he spotted her walking to a table. Amy? No, it's Arlene, that's it. Arlene Wagner. Wow, she still looks great. Jon Roth turned around, glanced and said, "Know her?"

"Went to school with her at St. Mark's, long time ago."

Pat took in the short black hair, the way she curved herself into the chair and he put down his cup.

15

"You just about finished?" he said to the lawyer.

"Yeah, just about."

"Ok, I'm just going to go over and say hello to my old classmate. I'll meet you at the car."

He had just gotten to Arlene's table and their eyes lit up in recognition.

"Arlene?"

"Well, Pat Brogan, it's been years!"

"Pat!" Roth shouted from the restaurant's exit.

What the hell is it now?!

Roth stood by the door with a perspiring deputy. "Pat, there's some kind of family emergency. You've got to get home now!"

Rory! It's got to be Rory...

"I'll drive," Jon said. "The DA got a phone call from Rita, she got a telegram about Rory. There's a deputy at the house now. He says the telegram says Rory's alive, but has been hurt overseas."

...and I'm trying to chat up some gal. What the hell was I thinking?

Jon pulled into the driveway right behind the sheriff's car, and Pat jumped out. Inside, Rita was sitting at the phone stand in the hallway wiping her eyes and face, and the deputy stood next to her, hand on her shoulder. Pat knelt before his wife.

"Can I see the telegram?" he asked quietly. He took it from her gently and read the dreadful report.

"He's alive, Rita. Our son is alive."

She looked up, clenching the handkerchief and said, "How badly is he hurt? When will we know? Will he be coming home?"

Resting his hands on her knees, he looked in her reddened eyes. Absolute honesty now, boyo, he thought.

"We don't know yet, Rita." He looked at the telegram again. "I'm not sure how they update the families now."

The deputy nodded and said, "They send telegrams when he's moved." Pat stood and both parents looked at the young deputy. He put out his hand to Pat. As they shook, he said, "Rick Kania, Mr. Brogan. I got back from there two years ago. They usually send a telegram when he's moved from place to place and give you a status report."

Pat nodded and put his arm around Rita.

"If he's in a hospital, he's probably going to make it. The dust-off choppers... that's the medevac helicopters, do a good job," Kania said.

"Can we call someone before that and find out how he's doing, what his injuries are?" Rita asked. Pat and the young veteran looked at each other.

"Uh, no. The Army doesn't have any procedures for that, ma'am."

Jon asked from the foyer, "What do you need?"

Pat and Rita looked over at the lawyer. "Uh, nothing right now, Jon, thanks. Just tell them I'm taking the rest of today and tomorrow off."

"Ok, Pat," he said. They shook hands all around.

"Anything you need, Mr. and Mrs. Brogan, just let me know," Kania said.

"You've got my numbers, Pat, call anytime," Jon said.

When they had left, Pat helped Rita stand up and they hugged. After a while, Pat said, "C'mon Rita, let's go sit in the kitchen."

He got her a glass of water and held her by the shoulders as she sat at the table.

"It's better than before," he said. "It took a lot longer to get to a field hospital. A lot of guys didn't make it. During the war it could be weeks before you found out anything except that the guy was hurt." Rita nodded and stared at the table.

Goddamn Army, he thought.

I never should've let him go, she thought.

6.

"All right, I think that will be enough of Plato's government by timocracy for today," the professor said.

"Boy, is it," Tom whispered, putting his pencil in his pocket and closing his notebook. HR leaned over to him and whispered, "Stop by College A, Artie scored last night."

Tom nodded, and the two of them walked across the frozen lawns of the campus to Main Street, where the experimental College A was housed in a storefront. Inside, the walls were covered in posters advertising student events around the neighborhood, including several sponsored by the Students for a Democratic Society. Bushy haired Artie waved them to a back room past a bespectacled older man stacking flyers.

"Take some, spread them around, fellas. We're mobilizing against the ROTC on campus," the older man said.

"Ok, professor," HR said, taking a handful.

"That guy's a teacher?" Tom asked quietly.

"You know it. That's professor Fred and that's what College A is all about." Pointing to a sign over the door, he spoke the motto: "Self and Community."

In the back room, Artie, HR and Tom shared a joint.

"How about a beer next door, guys? I'd like to check that place out," HR suggested.

"Gotta help Fred," Artie said.

"Gotta get home," Tom said, picking up his books. As he shuffled down the ice-covered sidewalk towards home, Tom thought about

Rory. He remembered his older brother crouching behind cars in the wintertime, hanging on to the bumper, "pogeying" as the cars drove down the icy street and smiling back at him as his feet slid over the pavement.

"Don't tell mom and dad," he'd say when he hopped back onto the sidewalk a block or two later. Now he's in the jungle in Vietnam fighting this insane war, he thought, shaking his head.

When he got onto his street, Tom saw the sheriff's car and another vehicle pull away from the house. He ran inside to find his mother crying at the kitchen table and his dad holding her shoulders from behind. When his dad looked up, Tom could see he had been crying too.

"What happened?" Tom shouted.

His dad wiped his eyes and his mom sobbed.

"It's Rory, Tom. He's been wounded," his dad said.

Tom dropped his books and stared at them, trying to choke out some words.

"What...how...is he going to be ok?"

"He's in a hospital now over there. He's alive. That's about all we know right now, son." His dad nodded towards the telegram on the table.

Tom picked it up and read it. "Don't call? What's this bullshit, don't call? We gotta find out, dad!" Rory never should've listened to dad's bullshit about duty. He'd be ok now.

7.

Bill Correlli sat in his office at W.D. Correlli Development looking at all the piles of paper on his desk. There were maps of Buffalo and its suburbs showing proposed highways and sites circled in red. There were articles and drawings of the Astrodome in Houston, plans to expand the University of Buffalo campus, there were biographies of prominent businessmen in the Buffalo area, financial reports on local banks, and, on top, the latest financial report on his own businesses.

He couldn't sit still thinking about the possibilities.

Correlli looked at the maps, turning them this way and that with calloused bricklayer hands. The city of Buffalo, so long an industrial powerhouse, was shrinking. Industries were going out of town and overseas. The once-crowded port had died, killed by the St. Lawrence Seaway ten years ago, the facilities crumbling along the lake and Buffalo River. Business people downtown were afraid to look over their shoulder at the ruins nearby that were creeping towards them. They were afraid when the promise of urban renewal bulldozed the old but found nothing to replace it except subsidized housing, leaving them with instant ghetto projects and empty lots. They were moving to the suburbs, where Correlli had prospered, first laying brick, then building houses and shopping centers. Not bad for a guy who graduated with a vo-tech diploma from Kensington, he thought. He had kept away from the Mafiosi and their easy money, ducked the political schemers when he could and stayed when others were running for the Sun Belt.

Now Correlli saw opportunity in the city. The people downtown were grasping at anything, and he had a plan.

When his secretary buzzed, Correlli answered, "Not now, Cindy." He focused on three items on his desk – the article that announced the Astrodome as the "Eighth Wonder of the World" showing a picture of developer Rex Yarborough, President Johnson and several Apollo astronauts smiling at its dedication; the profile of Titus Webb, that outlined his family's bringing of art, music and architecture to Buffalo, of how he was the city's greatest citizen and a man of vision; and the headlines from the Buffalo News – "Eigen Considers Moving Bills."

Now's the time, he thought. Now's the time for me to make the leap, to bring it all together and make a mark that will last forever. Picking up the phone, he made the call to the Webb Family Foundation.

8.

Pat put the long barreled and the snub-nosed Colt revolvers into an old bowling ball bag and put four boxes of .38 special ammunition on top of them. That should be more than enough. He considered putting the bag in the trunk of the Chevy but thought, You never know, and put the bag on the seat next to him. He intuitively scanned the cars and people as he headed down to police headquarters on Franklin Street, parked in a "Police Only" spot, and went into the yellow brick building. Walking down to the shooting range in the basement, he noticed a young patrolman's quizzical look at the bowling bag. "Newest incentive, kid, bowling balls for shooting excellent on the pistol qualifications. Part of the latest union contract," he said, smiling as he left the stairwell.

Listening to the pow-pow-pow coming from the range, Pat opened the metal fire door and matched smiles with Marty "Fatboy" Meegan as he entered.

"Well, Marshal Patrick Brogan. I heard you turned in your badge," the gray haired Meegan said, reaching over the desk to shake hands.

"Yup pardner, I figger it's time to leave the streets of Dodge to the young lawmen," Pat said, nodding towards the gun range where the shots continued to bang away. "But I still gotta qualify for the County Investigator's job."

"I wouldda been gone myself, Pat, if they hadn't got me this cush job," Meegan said as he put the target sheets in front of Pat.

"It's like they say, Meegs. Some men are qualified for the job, others are born in South Buffalo."

"Hah! Jealous!" Meegan answered, "By the way, what'll you be carrying in the DA's office?"

"The Detective Special."

"Not as accurate as the 4 inch, but hell, you won't need it there."

Pat nodded, picking up the paper targets. The two veterans shook hands again.

"Keep 'em straight, Lt. Meegan."

"Show 'em how it's done, Patrick. Deputy Zelinski'll be running the shoot," he said, introducing him to a young Erie County Sheriff's Deputy in a black turtleneck and a badge attached to his belt.

They walked to the shooting alley, and once the deputy had inspected his weapons, he loaded the .38 special and placed it in the holster.

Pat asked, "I guess we'll have to do the S.R.T. Test first?"

The deputy shook his head. "Nope, no Slow, Rapid and Timed Test."

"Just the Practical Pistol Course? Barricade? Left and right hand?"

"Nope, not that either for your job. Here's the qualifying test for your position: put six shots on the silhouette at 7 ½ feet, reload, repeat. Do the same with the detective special and you qualify.

"Seven and a half feet? No distance shooting?" Pat asked. "The last time I qualified with the police special we started at 7 yards and worked out way up to 50 yards."

"I heard you would score 280 or better out of 300 on the P.P.C. test," the deputy commented.

"Yeah, I did. Now it's all at close range, huh?"

"They did some studies. FBI, New York, LA. Says most shoot-outs happen up close and in low light conditions – gotta be ready, shoot, reload, shoot."

"Sounds right." Pat said.

"We'll do the police special first, but we can leave the lights all the way up," Zelinski said, as the target whizzed up in front of the booth. Pat took a deep breath, settled his feet in the combat position, slowly let his breath out and squeezed off the six rounds. While he reloaded, he noticed they all hit the ten ring. He fired another six rounds, again all in the ten ring. I wish they were the commie bastards who set that mine, he thought.

He repeated the procedure with the snub-nosed revolver, but this time two rounds missed the ten ring, one hitting the Bar X ring and the other landing in the 9 ring.

"Good shooting. You qualify," the young deputy said as he filled out the paperwork.

"I had good teachers," Pat said, thinking about the noise and shouting of the instructors at Fort Dix. He also thought about the adrenalin pumping through his system when he fired at real people, Krauts in Europe who were trying to kill him with everything from grenades to machine guns and where a fraction of a second, a single misfired round meant death. "Yeah, good teachers," he said, thinking of the bloodied bodies of those a shade too slow, and his son, far away in a hospital.

He put the pistols away in their cases and put the remaining bullets in the bowling bag with them. Clean the pieces when I get home. Reload them, put them in the holsters and forget about it, he thought.

As he walked up the steps, Pat looked at his watch. Hell, it's early, he thought. I'll just head over to County Hall and hand in my qualifications. Walking outside, he saw a patrolman looking at his car and pulling out his ticket book.

"Don't waste the paper, young man." The blue shirt looked up.

"Oh, I'm sorry, lieutenant. I didn't recognize your car."

"No problem, officer. I'm riding off into the sunset anyway."

The patrolman touched the brim of his cap and smiled. Pat started the car up. As he backed out, he thought how he'd miss the respect, the camaraderie and the friends over here. Time to move on, he thought as he drove. Take the pension, make another salary to help pay for Tommy's college and... the ache came into his stomach and forehead as he thought again about his shattered Rory. What can we do, what can we do? What can money do for my boy?

The car behind him blew his horn when the light changed. Pat clenched the steering wheel and drove. He pulled into a deputy's spot behind the county court house and grabbed the paperwork. He spotted a gray uniformed sheriff's deputy coming out of the county hall and waved him over.

"What's up, pal?"

"My name's Pat Brogan," he said, putting out his hand. "New Investigator in the DA's office. Ok if I park here?"

"Hey, you're the sheriff's old partner in the city, right?" he said, gripping Pat's hand. "Welcome aboard. I'm Rocco Buscaglia, work outta the jail. Don't worry about the parking, boss. Just tell 'em at the desk, and it'll be fine."

Pat nodded, relieved at the easy transition. It was just as easy in the Hall where he got his parking pass, met the lieutenant on duty and turned in his shooting qualifications to the bureau chief's secretary.

That's done, he thought as he drove home. Just keep the detective special on my hip and lock the rest of this stuff up.

9.

HR looked out the storefront window of College A at St. Joseph's School across Main Street at dismissal time. As nuns and lay teachers stood watch, the patrol boys with their white and orange belts dispersed and took up their posts while a few parents gathered at the end of the driveway on Main Street to meet the littlest ones. Children streamed from the school in orderly lines carrying bookbags and lunch boxes, their breath visible on the cold day. When they hit the street, shouts of joy erupted and the kids scattered running or waited for friends behind them.

Tom watched too. He remembered hoping to arrive on the sidewalk in front of the school just at the right time to meet up with a girl named Linda, perhaps to exchange a greeting that might lead to walking home with her in that incipient mating ritual.

"The Catholic Church is probably the biggest institution of fascist indoctrination in Buffalo," HR said, standing just behind Tom. "Look at those kids. All in nice lines, learning to conform. Learning imperialism – they teach those kids Columbus discovered America, the annexation of the Southwest and the massacre of Indians as Manifest Destiny, and overrunning the Philippines as liberating the Filipino people. It's really going to take something to wake these people up to it – direct action against the ruling class to show them the powers that be are using every facet of society to keep power and make money, waging war on the Vietnamese people to do it."

Tom thought about Rory's letter—so we set the cache and a bunch of hooches on fire and left. HR stepped a little closer to Tom and lowered his voice.

"We trashed the room where Dupont was doing recruiting over in Lockwood Library last night. They've got the contract from the Defense Department to make napalm. Shit, all they say on the news is 'vandals attack library on campus' and give the estimated cost of the damages. It's going to take something bigger than that to make these people," he said, nodding towards St. Joseph's, "realize how they're being used."

They continued to look out the window for a few minutes more as the school children exited.

"I just heard they might be shutting down the experimental colleges," Artie said from behind them. "The townies are complaining we're a bad influence on the local kids, some of the faculty objects to the self-grading policy, stuff like that. It's a mess, man."

"Hey, that would make you eligible for the draft!" HR laughed, pointing where Artie was pinning up a poster for a Buffalo Draft Resistance Union Rally. Tom and Artie looked at the names of the speakers.

"Martin Teeley, Vietnam vet. He went to school with Rory," Tom said.

"Jake Cross," Artie said. "He's the guy with all the connections underground in Canada."

"That might come in handy if I don't keep my grades up," Tom chuckled.

"Hey, let's go get a beer at the place next door," HR said. "I'd like to check out the townie bar."

"I gotta close up," Artie said.

"I'll go with you," Tom said as they walked out the back door of College A, avoiding the stares and comments of the parents and children on Main Street. Walking down the alley, they entered the back entrance to Bickleman's Lounge. As they approached the bar, two regulars turned on their barstools, their eyes narrowing when they spotted the long hair.

"Hey Tommy, long time no see, my man," the white aproned bartender greeted as the regulars continued to stare.

"Hi Harley," Tom said, taking off his Army field jacket.

"Paul, Joe," Harley said, "You remember Tommy, don't you? Pat Brogan's younger boy."

Paul and Joe looked again, their faces eased, and Paul said, "Oh, sure, sure. Hiya, Tommy. I didn't recognize you with the hair. Get Tommy and his friend a beer on me, will you, Harley."

HR stood stock still, his hands in his pockets.

"A couple of Schmidt's drafts, Harley. Thanks, Mr. Paulino."

"Cheers, boys," Paulino said, raising his bottle of Genesee.

"How's the family, Tom?" Paulino asked, "I haven't seen your dad in here in a while."

Tom froze, fearing Mr. Paulino would mention his dad's occupation in front of HR.

"Ok, Mr. Paulino. He doesn't get around much these days, I guess."

"Yeah, that's terrible about Rory," Paulino said. HR looked on, fascinated as Tom interacted with the locals.

"Yeah, thanks," Tom said, putting down his beer.

A few silent moments passed, then HR said, "Well, I gotta go, Tom, you coming?"

"Yeah. Thanks for the beer, Mr. Paulino."

"Sure, Tommy, say hi to your folks for me, and we'll keep Rory in our prayers. Don't worry, kid, it'll work out, I'm sure."

Tom nodded as they went out the back door into the fading daylight. HR stopped in the small parking lot in the alley and Tom stood still, his head down, thinking about his wounded brother. Cause for concern, the telegram said. What the fuck does that mean?

"Imperialism, Tom, that's what did it. LBJ and the other politicians, whipping up the people's fear of communism to play on their loyalty to start a war in Asia to get control of the resources, make sure they keep the markets to shore up the capitalist economy. That's what got your brother hurt."

Tom looked up, his eyes flaring. HR took a step back. "The whole country got taken in, Tom, all of us. The domino theory bullshit, make the people afraid and they'll seek security, even go to war. We've got to make them see, Tom. The National Liberation Front is our brother, not our enemy. We've got to stop the war against the downtrodden people, stop the wars against the worker states, stop fighting wars for the corporations. Then none of us will get hurt for unjust causes."

Tom shook his head and the two were silent for a moment. A Ford station wagon pulled into a spot next to them. Two short-haired men wearing ties got out.

"This place here, Al," one said, gesturing with the keys. Al got out of the car, looked at the two long-haired students and glanced at his partner.

"I have the keys, Al, let's get the stuff unloaded."

Tom and HR walked down the alley towards HR's car.

"I wonder who those guys are," HR said.

"Dunno," Tom said. "Looks like they're moving stuff into the empty store next to the bar."

"Look!" HR said. "Those boxes. Some of them have DuPont on them. They're from the place we trashed last night. They must be moving their location off campus!"

"Huh. They're moving it right into the old Chicken Delight. The university must be renting a bunch of these places."

They got into HR's Volkswagen and started driving downtown.

"That's another target for us, Tom. One of the three Rs – Recruiters, ROTC, Researchers. We chase 'em off campus, then we'll run them right off Main Street, and show them the movement is growing, striking back.

"Say, you tell your folks about moving into the apartment down in Allentown with me and Nancy yet? It'll be great – you already got a job downtown and you can ride up to school with us or take the bus. You've got your own room and you can come and go anytime. All the action down there – it isn't like the bourgeois neighborhood around here, it's more like Greenwich Village in New York. And it's cheap, too – you can swing it on your salary from the warehouse job. You said it yourself, they like you and'll have you running a forklift any day now for a raise."

Tom thought about his moving out of the house, the only place he'd ever lived. No more getting woken up for Mass on Sunday morning. No more lectures about drinking or smoking pot. I've got my own money from the warehouse job and the last roommate left all his furniture. HR's got a decent stereo, too. Just bring my clothes, books and some other stuff. Yeah, and best of all, no more having to sneak around with a girl.

10.

The next telegram arrived as Rita was pulling laundry out of the dryer. She rushed up the stairs at the doorbell and had change ready for the tip by the door. She sat down at the phone stand as she read,

> ...HE HAS SUSTAINED TRAUMATIC AMPUTATION OF THE LEFT ARM BELOW THE ELBOW AND THE LEFT LEG BELOW THE KNEE. HIS LEFT EYE AND JAW HAVE BEEN SERIOUSLY DAMAGED. THESE WOUNDS HAVE BEEN STABILIZED. HE IS CURRENTLY IN CLARK AIR FORCE BASE HOSPITAL IN THE PHILIPPINES AND WILL BE TRANSFERRED TO WALTER REED HOSPITAL, WASHINGTON, DC ON TUESDAY MARCH 28 FOR FURTHER TREATMENT...

What have they done to my boy? she thought, looking over at the little cabinet in the coat closet where they'd kept mittens and hats for the boys. He's lost an arm and a leg. What about his eye! His jaw? "Who do I call to find out!?" she screamed into the empty room.

When Pat came home half an hour later, she was curled up on the couch in the living room, rosary in hand.

11.

Pat scooped another shovelful of the wet, heavy snow, threw it onto the front yard and looked behind him. It's March already. Gotta be the last snowfall of the year, he thought, another fifteen feet to finish shoveling the driveway. The streetlights came on, and he looked up into the darkening sky as another few snowflakes fell onto his face. He wondered if it would stop soon. He tugged the skier's headband down farther over his ears and leaned on the shovel. I wonder where Tommy is, he thought, he should be home by now. Pat smiled, thinking about how the boys used to help him shovel the driveway. They had their own tiny orange shovels and would fling snow everywhere. Snowballs thrown and angels made, runny noses and Rita calling them inside for hot chocolate when they were cold and soaked. Rory will never shovel anything again, he thought, as a tear dropped onto his old leather glove.

The side door opened. Rita stuck her head out and, seeing him leaning on the shovel, waited.

"I've made some hot chocolate, Pat," she said after a few moments.

Pat turned and looked at his wife, their eyes meeting. "Ok, mom. Just let us...I'll finish the driveway and I'll be in for some." She waited a few seconds, watched until he turned back to the driveway and returned inside. He took a breath, gripped the shovel and resumed shoveling, the snow flying off the driveway now, faster and faster as he approached the street.

When he finished, Pat straightened up, leaned back to stretch and took a deep breath. Hearing footsteps crunching towards him,

Pat looked over and saw his younger son Tom approach down the sidewalk, eyes downcast.

"Hi," Tom said. They looked at each other in the dark, Pat taking in his son's long black hair and unearned GI field jacket. Not carrying any books either, he thought.

"Mom's just made some hot chocolate."

"Uh-huh."

They went inside silently, Pat stowing the shovel in the hallway, unzipping his rubber boots and putting them on a mat. Tom kicked the snow off his construction shoes and went through the door into the foyer hallway.

"Pat? Tom?" Rita inquired, knowing their sounds.

"It's both of us, mom." Pat said, unbuttoning his long brown overcoat and hanging it up on a hanger in the closet. He reached to take Tom's coat.

"I got it," Tom said, putting it on a hook.

"Dinner should be ready in five minutes," she said. "And I've got hot chocolate for the both of you."

"Great," Pat said, following Tom through the dining room back towards the kitchen.

"Well," Rita said, handing Tom a cup of hot chocolate. "How was philosophy today?"

"Irrelevant," he answered, jutting his chin towards the TV playing in the den, where Dan Rather spoke into a microphone as GIs rushed across a rice paddy in the background. Pat thought about bringing up a story about a war correspondent he'd met in Europe during the war but figured it wouldn't help and sat down at the kitchen table with the Buffalo Evening News sports page.

As Rita put the plates on the table, Tom sat down and Pat folded the paper and put it away.

"Ah, meat loaf, great for a cold night," Pat said. Pat and Rita said grace quickly while Tom sat still. Knives and forks in hand, the parents began to eat while Tom poked at his meal.

"Everything ok at school, Tommy?" Rita asked.

"It's ok. Classes are going fine."

"How about your friends? We don't see the kids from high school much anymore."

"Yeah," Pat said. "What's Joey from the wrestling team doing these days? And how about Carmine and young Paul? It seemed like they used to live over here when you guys were in high school."

"Mmmm, Joe's working out in Hamburg now at the Ford Plant and those other guys are in school out of town."

"You could bring some of your new friends over here from UB for dinner sometime, Tommy. They probably get sick of the cafeteria food at school," Rita said.

"A lot of them live off campus in apartments around town." He hesitated, then said, "I've been meaning to tell you, I'm going to be moving into an apartment with some friends. HR's roommate George moved out last week and he's got an empty room. They're going to be coming by in a little while to help get some of my stuff."

"Gee, Tommy. This is quick. Is anybody else living there?" Rita asked.

"Move? Move where, Tom?" Pat said.

"On Mariner Street, in Allentown. It'll be my friend HR and his girlfriend Nancy. It's cheap, but they could use some help with the rent."

"Where on Mariner Street?" Pat asked, thinking of recent drug raids in that neighborhood.

"Near Virginia. It's a brick apartment building, even has a fireplace."

"Gees, Tom, are you sure you want to do this? You're walking distance to school here, you don't have to fix your own meals, you've got your own room..." Rita asked.

"Nah, I'll be able to swing it. I've got the job at A.M. & A's and can catch the bus up Main to school."

"There's a lot of junkies down there these days, breaking into houses and cars, mugging people just for what's in their pockets," Pat said.

"I know, dad, I can handle it."

"Does this place have a laundry room, Tommy?" Rita asked.

"Yeah, it does," he said, thinking of the old washer he'd seen in the basement which HR said never worked.

The doorbell rang, and Tom jumped up to get it.

"Hey man, you ready?" the tall, blonde-haired kid at the door asked.

Pat and Rita got up and walked to the door.

"Hey, howya doin'? I'm HR," the blonde-haired kid said with a smile, sticking out his hand. Rita shook it, then crossed her arms in front of her chest.

"Pat Brogan."

"Good to meet you!" the kid said. Pat gave him the once over. Hair parted down the middle, hooded sweatshirt with jean jacket, black dungarees and Army boots. Reddened eyes.

"So, HR, you live down on Mariner Street?" Pat said.

"Yeah, right in the heart of Allentown."

"You from Buffalo, HR?" Pat continued.

"No...my folks live in White Plains."

"I see. What do you take at UB, HR?" Rita asked.

"History."

"You working?" Pat said.

"Uh, not right now. I'm lining up a job over at Markel Electric."

Tom came down the stairs, an olive-green duffel bag thumping behind him. HR picked up a cardboard box filled with books.

"Mom, dad, I gotta go. I'll be back for some more of my stuff later. Bye!" and he went out into the driveway, throwing the duffel bag into the rear of the Volkswagen bug.

"Tom! Have you got your all your books?" Rita shouted.

"Yeah mom, I got enough. I'll get the rest later," Tom shouted back as the VW backed out.

"I don't think I like this idea, Pat."

"That HR kid's high," Pat answered. "I'll go over there tomorrow, check the place out and talk to Tommy. If we're paying for his schooling, he can't be sitting around getting high with a bunch of doped up hippies."

"And who's this girl that's living there? Tommy says it's that HR's girlfriend."

"Yeah. He's been getting good grades, he's got the job over at the warehouse, but this could really foul him up. I'll go over there and lay down the law to him."

As Pat and Rita returned to the table, they caught another report on the TV.

"Communist rockets today destroyed a C-130 landing supplies at the air force base at Pleiku..."

The draft will get him if he doesn't pass his classes, Rita thought with a shiver.

In the car headed over to the west side, HR couldn't stop talking.

"This is going to be great, man. We can all ride to school together and hang out in Allentown."

"Yeah," Tom said. "It'll be great. I should have brought my albums with me." Tom thought about the records and the clothes his parents had bought him this last Christmas, all smiles as he opened his packages. The Stones' "Let It Bleed" and Jefferson Airplane's "Volunteers" albums. They didn't have clue what they were about.

HR waved his hand. "Don't worry about that, man. Between Nancy and me we've got plenty of music. You can get that stuff later."

"Yeah, later," Tom said, thinking when and how he could get in and out of the house without seeing his father. He was glad they got out of there as quick as they did, if HR and dad had gotten talking, and HR had found out his dad was a cop...

"You ok with your folks on this, Tom?

"Ennh, not great. They'll get used to it."

"What's your old man do, anyway?"

Tom stiffened. "Uh, he used to work for the city. Now he works for the county."

"Huh. Petit bourgeois, like my folks. I guess it'll take some time to get them to understand the world's changing," HR said, digging a joint out of his pocket and passing it for Tom to light. They toked carefully as they negotiated traffic downtown.

"When are you going to join the party, man?" HR asked.

Holding the smoke in his lungs a moment more, Tom replied, "Ahh, I'm not into the politics so much," thinking HR and the World Worker's Party were pretty far out there. "But I'm with you on stopping the war, man. It's just insane," he said, the images of the bodies at My Lai coming to mind and... I wonder what Rory looks like, what he's feeling now? They got him into this with all the talk about duty and now he's hurt bad. He used to show me all the moves on the basketball court and got me into wrestling. Now he's a cripple, and for what?

12.

After a week at Clark Air Force Base Hospital the cycle of Rory's morphine injections was still every four hours, but the pain dulling effects only lasted half that. Within two hours of an injection, he started sweating, drenching the bedsheets. Then the shakes and the nausea would start, and when he vomited, they would have to suction out his mouth, replace the feeding tube and clean him up. The room would start to rotate, and Rory would grab on to anything, a bed railing, an orderly's arm, anything, to stop the spinning. The nurses and orderlies never complained, they just held him down until he passed out, and then the nightmares came.

He was getting sent out to play right field in Little League when a left-handed hitter came up in the ninth and they were up 3-2. Mr. Myers was sitting on a lawnmower that looked like a combine at the edge of the field, smoking a cigarette, waiting for the game to end. The left-handed kid went for the first pitch, hitting the ball right over the first baseman's head. Rory charged it, slipped, but caught it off his chest. He held the ball up to show he had it and everyone charged out and Mr. Meyers started coming forward on the lawnmower.

"Hey! Stop!" Rory shouted, but Mr. Meyers just kept coming forward, and everyone else was celebrating.

"Stop!" he screamed, but he couldn't get up, he couldn't get out of the way. The lawnmower kept coming forward, and Mr. Meyers tossed away his cigarette. Rory closed his eyes as the blades started chopping into his arm and leg.

"Can't anybody hear me?!" he screamed.

13.

Pat drove over to Allentown after work the next day. He went down Allen Street slowly and looked around. A couple of used book stores, a bar with opaque windows. Queer hangout. A sub shop. A four-story men's club. The University Club, former D.A. Stone's hangout. Two guys with long hair stared into the open engine compartment of a rusting Ford Falcon. Haven't got the slightest idea how to fix it, do you? A blonde hooker in a plastic raincoat smiled at him as he waited for the light at Elmwood. Phew. Head to the clinic if you get with her, brother. The Greek diner on the corner and another bar next to it with a sign featuring the Lone Ranger. Dope deals in there. A small department store that sold everything from shoes to brooms. Two more bars, one brick, been there forever, one a wooden cottage painted black. Always trouble in that joint. What the hell does Tommy want to live down here for?

Pat found a parking spot up the street from Tommy's apartment house, locked the car doors and walked back to it. Looking over the mailboxes, he saw three names taped to the mailbox for Apartment 3 – H. Roberts, N. Molla, T. Brogan. He tried the front door, locked. Good. At least they got it locked. He pushed on the doorbell but heard nothing. He pushed again and waited. Nothing. He went back to his car and waited, watching the street. After an hour, he saw HR's Volkswagen go by, gears grinding. He waited another half hour, and the two boys were walking back towards him from Allen Street. In the bars. While they were still twenty feet away, he got out of the car and stood on the sidewalk. Both boys stopped. HR blinked and Tom said, "Uh, hi, dad."

"I tried the doorbell, nobody answered," Pat said.

"Yeah, we stopped for a beer after school," Tom said.

No books.

"Well, I'm heading up," HR said to Tom. "Nice to see you, Tom's dad," and he trotted back to the apartment house.

"Tommy, I want to talk to you about this new place. Your mom and I are concerned..."

"C'mon, dad. I'm eighteen years old, I'm working and going to school. I can pay for my rent with what I make at the warehouse."

"It's not that, Tommy. We're worried that you won't keep up with your studies, and with all the bars and the dope around here..."

"Look, you didn't think Rory was too young when he went off to Vietnam, did you? You thought that was ok, he could take care of himself, and look what happened! Now I've got a crippled brother and you guys just go to church and pray that it'll all go away!"

Head down and hands in his pockets, Tom brushed past his father.

"Tommy, wait! That isn't true..." but Tom was already going up the steps with his keys out and into the building. Pat heard the door slam shut.

14.

Tom heard the sound of the Rolling Stones' "Street Fighting Man" getting cranked up in the living room. He shut the copy of Plato's Republic and swung his legs off the bed, kicking over his Krober's *Anthropology* and Paine's *The Rights of Man*. Shit, didn't get to them tonight, he thought as he sheathed the wide leather belt to his jeans.

HR was nodding his head to the music as he passed a joint to Artie.

"Hey, Tom, c'mon in, have a toke. Artie and I were just getting ready to go out for a beer. Come along, my man."

Artie nodded, took a deep drag and passed it to Tom, who took the joint carefully and got two short puffs off the roach.

"Yeah, let's finish the joint and head out to the Silver. There's always cool people in that joint," HR said.

"It's cheap, too," Artie added, chuckling.

The three of them walked up Mariner St., hands in their pockets. When they turned onto Allen Street, HR pulled his hands out and gestured at the street.

"This is so cool. All kinds of people here. Black, white, working people, artists, thinkers, all coming up with new ways of seeing things. Really free in their minds. That's what's going to change this country, and we're right here at the beginning of it. So cool... like in 1848. All the ideas came together and changed Europe forever. It's time for that to happen in America."

HR led the way, opening the door to the bar, and jukebox music, noisy talk and the smell of spilt beer wafted over them as they entered. HR smiled as he looked over the crowd, nodding to a couple of regulars, his eyes bright and his hands in his pockets.

Tom pulled out some singles. "Pitcher of Schmidt's, please," he said to the bartender, a big guy wearing an untucked Buffalo Braves jersey.

"Three glasses?" the bartender asked.

"Yeah, for now," HR said. "We may need more later."

The three stood at the bar, Tom carefully pouring the beer. A dark-complexioned man with curly hair smoking a cigarette turned to them. "Hello, HR."

"Hey, Jimmy. How are you?" HR replied.

"I am fine," Jimmy answered, holding up his Pall Mall. Tom noticed an accent. Middle East. Israeli?

"I see the Zionists are attacking the Palestinians again," HR said.

"The Jews are exterminating the Palestinian refugees with their American weapons," Jimmy said, waving his cigarette.

Looking over Jimmy's shoulder, Tom spotted a guy in a Bills' cap and plaid shirt look up from his beer and stare at Jimmy with glazed eyes.

"Jimmy's a real source of the truth about what goes on in the Middle East," HR said. "He's a student like us. Came here from North Yemen." HR signaled the barman for another glass, and Tom poured another beer for Jimmy.

"How'd you get here from North Yemen, Jimmy?" Tom asked, putting the glass before Jimmy.

"Scholarship. We are a new country and will need leaders," Jimmy answered.

"That's cool," Artie added. "They pay the full ride?"

"They must. In America, there is no sharing."

"Huh," Artie said, looking down at the floor as the guy in the plaid shirt got off his stool.

"Yer one fuckin' nasty Arab," Plaid Shirt said.

Jimmy's eyes went wide as he turned, stood up and backed off his stool.

"Hey man, take it easy," Tom said, shaking his head and mouthing "DRUNK" to HR and Artie.

"Yeah, well, fuck you and fuck him," Plaid Shirt said, swinging a round house right. Tom blocked the looping punch with his left as HR backed away. Jimmy threw himself against the wall and Tom threw a right hand, going straight from his shoulder to Plaid Shirt's chin. The man staggered back, falling into his stool. The bartender came around the bar and got between them.

"Ok, that's it," the barman said, glancing at Plaid Shirt hanging on the bar. He turned to face Tom.

"Fuck him," Tom said. "He insulted Jimmy and threw the first punch."

"I don't give a shit who started it, all you guys need to call it a night," the bartender said, eye-to-eye with Tom.

HR clapped Tom on the shoulder. "Easy there, young Ali. We'll just get some more beer someplace else. It'll all be ok tomorrow."

Tom picked up his change and headed for the door, HR and Artie following.

"What an asshole," Artie said.

"Never seen that in Jake before," HR said.

"Who's Jake?" Tom asked.

"The guy you hit. He's a regular there. Just sits there watching TV and drinking Gennys from the time he gets off work on the trash trucks until after the eleven o'clock news comes on, then he goes home. Weird."

"Hey, where'd Jimmy go?" Artie asked.

"I dunno. Maybe he'll meet up with us later at Birdie's. He usually goes there late," HR said.

"What's Jimmy's real name?" Tom asked.

"Gamil," HR said. "He calls himself Jimmy in case the Zionists on campus attack him." HR led them up wooden steps into a one-story cottage painted flat black with a sign that read Birdie's 19th Hole and Hens' Roost.

"Looks like the place is jumpin' tonight," Artie said.

"Yeah," HR said, clapping Tom on the shoulder. "Let's do some shots to celebrate the victory of the people's champion and see what else we can score here."

15.

Pat kicked the Barca lounge chair's footrest out and laid back. "Tonight," the announcer said, "the ABC Movie of the Week features Darren McGavin in 'Challenge.'" Hmm, he's usually pretty good, I wonder what this is about, he thought.

"Darren McGavin stars as a veteran soldier sent to a jungle island to fight an enemy commando..." Nope, don't need to watch any fighting in the jungle... I hope Rory's sleeping ok... what else is on? Columbo's on Channel 2. Ahhn, phony cop show. A lieutenant who solves crimes in LA by himself. Hell, a Lieutenant spends all his time trying to get his guys to show up on time and do their job.

Pat jumped up as the phone rang. "I got it," he said, even though no one else was home. Rita was at a meeting over at St. Joes and Tommy...

"17th Precinct, Lieutenant Bro..."

The laughter that came over the line could only be Marty Meegan's.

"Take the harness off already, Pat, your first retirement check should be rolling in any day now."

"Jesus, Meegs, I wonder how long it's going to be until I break that habit."

"I give it six months. By that time, the guys at the County will have you broke in with your new title, Mr. Special Investigator. Hey, the reason I'm calling is there's this guy, a doctor out in Amherst who's been by the range and is interested in shooting. He belongs to the Northtowns Rod and Gun Club and wants a real combat shooter to help him. I mentioned your name, told him what a dead-eye shot you were, ex-Army, had a couple of shooting incidents on the job, like that. He seems a good guy, young fella, knows a lot about guns."

"He's not some kind of cowboy gun nut, is he? Wants to hang out with the police, get into a shootout in a liquor store or something?"

"Nah, he seems all right to me. Just interested in shooting at targets. Who knows, he may pay you for lessons, pal, buy your ammunition for you or something. I'd give him a call at least, see what's up."

Pat wondered what kind of doctor he was. Maybe he could help... "Ok, Meegs, gimme his number. I'll give him a holler and see what he's about."

"Yeah, good, Pat. Like I said, he came down to the range a couple of times to watch. I talked to him, he seems ok. Number's 836-8941. Lives out in Eggertsville."

Pat wrote the number down. "What's his name there Meegs? I gotta have that, too."

"Oh, yeah. His name's Kraft. Dr. Charles Kraft."

"Ok, Meegs, I'll give him a holler. Anything else going on?"

"Well, it looks like Beasom's going to get the job at the 6th."

"Beasom! That eejit couldn't tie his own shoes! How'd he get through the Captain's test?"

"Weeelll, it seems there was this study group put together that included some of the Commissioner's softball team..."

"Ahhhgh. Now you're making me glad I retired."

"That part'll never change, partner," Meegan said, laughing. "Forget all that shit and have some fun teaching the good doctor to shoot, Pat. I'll talk to you later," and he hung up, still laughing.

Beasom, he thought. When I was in a car with him, hmm, had to be around 1949, '50? He'd disappear 'to put away some equipment' and I'd have to write all the reports because they got kicked back when he did them, the dummy. Now he's going to be a captain in the busiest precinct in the city. Ah, hell, he thought, glancing at a slouching Peter Falk on the TV, let me give this doctor a call, see what he's like.

Pat dialed the number, and, after one ring, a teenage voice answered, "Kraft residence, Donald speaking."

"Yes, may I speak to Dr. Kraft please?"

"Yes, I'll get him. DAD! The phone's for you..."

"Thanks, Donnie. Hello, Dr. Kraft speaking."

"Dr. Kraft, this is Lieu...Pat Brogan. Lt. Meegan from the police department asked me to call you, said you were interested in doing some shooting."

"Oh yes, Mr. Brogan, I'm glad you called. Lt. Meegan said you were the man to see about combat shooting. Would you be interested in going as my guest to the club and giving me a few pointers?"

"Well, yeah, I think I could do that. How much experience do you have with firearms, Doctor?"

"Well, growing up in Machias, I did a lot of target shooting and hunting as a boy, but I've never had much experience with handguns."

Good, Pat thought. A country boy, been around guns before and not some nut job. Sounds young. "Ok, Doctor..."

"Call me Charlie..."

"Ok, Charlie, I'm Pat, by the way. So, do you have any handguns of your own?"

"I've got a .45 automatic that was my dad's in the Army, and a state police issue .38 Special."

"Interesting. How'd you come by the state police weapon?"

"It was given to me by a state trooper out of the Batavia Barracks after I operated on him in the ER."

"Huh. When was that, doc?"

"Four years ago, in the summertime."

"Trooper Van Dyke?"

"Yes, it was."

Brogan remembered. Phil Van Dyke got into a confrontation with a Road Vulture way out on 33 in Corfu, and the biker pulled a gun. The biker died, but Phil laid there a long time before anyone came by and found him.

"Phil finally came back to work two years ago. He was lucky to be alive."

"He'd lost a lot of blood when they got him to us. You guys lined up to give. I think we went through...ninety-six pints before it was all over."

There was a pause, then Pat said, "Yeah, but he made it. Anyway, are those the weapons you want to shoot with?"

"Yes, yes, I would. I'll bring ammunition for them, of course. I'd like your advice on their cleaning and care, Pat, especially as they're both gifts. Will you be bringing any guns?"

They're weapons, not guns, Pat thought, this guy's never been in the service. "Yeah, I'll be bringing my service weapon, a .38 Smith and Wesson snub nose. I can always use the practice."

16.

HR brought Tom into the used bookstore, his blonde hair bouncing with enthusiasm as he approached the old man in the worn suit.

"Hey man, c'mon over and meet Carl Vincent! He's the founder of the World Worker's Party."

The older man nodded at them and continued speaking to three other students, "The party was in the right to support the USSR's invasion of Hungary in 1956 and the Warsaw Pact's occupation of Czechoslovakia in 1968. It is the responsibility of worker's states to fight the capitalist revanchists, just as the Vietnamese are fighting American imperialism today."

Vincent looked over at the two youths. "Well, hello. From your picture in the World's Worker paper you must be HR, the party's leader on campus," he said, shaking hands with HR. "And this man?"

"Tom Brogan, sir. I'm a friend of HR's."

"Well," Vincent said, "I'm glad to see the movement is so active on the U.B. Campus. You know, I used to live and work in Buffalo, years ago. I worked at Wickwire Spencer in Tonawanda. Where do you two work?"

"I'm a warehouseman at A.M. & A's downtown," Tom said.

"I'm a writer," HR said.

"I see," Vincent said. "We've got to expand our membership amongst the workers. Although it's great that the students are responding to the party's message, the only thing that will bring down capitalism is victory in the workplace. The idea must come from the shop floor. You must get me some of your writings, HR, while I'm in town.

"When I was working at Wickwire, there was a dispute about Korea. I had worked there for two years and I was making headway among the steelworker's local there. When Truman invaded Korea, the bosses whipped up the McCarthyites in the plant and they ran me out for handing out pamphlets about the real reasons the U.S. was at war. Your writing, young man, must always tell the truth about the capitalist motives if we are to get anywhere with the working people, particularly in this town where so many send their sons overseas."

Tom thought about the other guys at work. Most of the older ones were all for the war, even agreeing with the "bomb them back into the Stone Age" rhetoric. The younger ones were worried about getting drafted, getting killed. They didn't say much in front of the older guys, and they sure weren't going to any protests. He didn't know about these World Worker's Party guys, but this war was so fucked up. Maybe those guys destroying the draft records were right. Maybe if Rory...Tom dropped his head and promised himself to call his parents to see how Rory was doing.

17.

Pat pulled into the parking lot at the Northtowns Rod and Gun Club and saw a guy in his late thirties in khakis and a plaid Pendleton shirt removing two black boxes from his trunk. Gotta be him. Brought both weapons, really wants to get into this, he thought. The man shut the trunk and, spotting Pat, smiled and waved. Pat picked up the two boxes of shells from the front seat and got out.

"Dr. Kraft?" Pat asked.

"Charlie Kraft," the man said with a smile as he put out his hand. "Glad you could make it today."

"Pat Brogan," the policeman said. "I see you've already got your shooting glasses on," he said, nodding towards the yellow tinted safety glasses as they walked into the range.

"Yeah, I figured they were worth the money as much as I like to shoot."

The doctor showed his pistols and ammo to the clerk and paid for them both. When asked for id, Pat showed his new County Investigator's badge and pulled the .38 snub nose off his hip.

"Aisle 6, gentlemen," the clerk said, and handed them their targets. Once in the stall, the doctor carefully opened up the box with the .45 in it and placed a box of ammunition to the side on the table.

"Ok if we shoot the .45 first?" Charlie asked. "I've only fired it once, and I couldn't hit anything until I moved the target within 10 feet."

"You probably won't hit anything until you get real close," Pat said with a small shiver. "When they're brand new, they're fairly accurate, but after firing around 50 rounds the barrel starts to get loose. You could put a .45 in a vice and still miss at just about anything but point-blank range."

"I've read that. Always made me wonder why the Army would equip soldiers with such an inaccurate gun."

"Stopping power. They first issued them during the Moro Uprising in the Philippines around the Turn of the Century. Used them to stop drugged up guerrillas their .38s wouldn't bring down."

Pat looked down, thinking, as the doctor loaded the .45's clip. The lieutenant shot him in the shoulder and blew his arm off, he thought, remembering a German who charged them in a hallway with a bayonet. Blood, muscle, cloth all went flying and he went flat on his back. Then we bashed his head in with our rifle butts.

"No, the .45 will stop whoever you hit with it, wherever you hit him, Charlie."

"Ok, I've loaded two clips. Why don't you go first, Pat, and show me what works best?"

Pat stepped up to the table, put on the earmuffs and picked up the .45.

"Move the target as close as possible, Charlie. Good." Pat gripped the pistol tightly, aimed for center of mass and fired off two rounds rapidly. One just nicked a corner of the target's elbow and the other the edge of the paper on the left. Pat looked again and adjusted, firing two more rounds, which ripped big holes in the paper to the silhouette's right. Taking a deep breath and letting it out slowly, he fired the last three rounds, one of which hit the outline of the head, another the neck and the third drilled the target's mid-sternum.

"Wow," the doctor said. "Just like you said, not accurate, but big holes." Hard to fix those wounds, even if they were on the periphery, he thought.

"Yeah. Take your time, use a two-hand grip and fire a couple of rounds, see what you've got, adjust and fire again." Put out rounds until they stop coming at ya, Sergeant Dunaway used to say.

They shot for an hour, comparing the three pistols for accuracy. When they showed the target sheets to the range clerk, he nodded in admiration. As they left, Pat asked, "Want to get a beer, Doc?"

Checking his watch, Charlie said, "Ok, but I can't stay long."

"No problem, I got stuff to do, too. Follow me."

Pat led them out of the suburban parking lot down to a bar near the city limits with a giant black horse hanging over the front entrance. Inside, it was dark and cool, and Pat was relieved there wasn't anyone who might be a student inside. The doctor carefully poured a Michelob into a pilsner glass while Pat sipped a Schmidt's draft.

"That was good Pat," Charlie said. "I know it's not real combat shooting, but I appreciate you showing me how you guys do it."

"Yeah," Pat said, a flood of sudden skirmishes during the war coming to mind. "Sometimes your mind gets so sharp you think you can hit a mosquito on a branch, and sometimes, nothing goes where you aim it... it all happens so fast."

"Hmm. I guess I'll probably never know."

"You're not missing anything," Pat said. "Hell, if you've worked on shooting victims, you've had to keep your wits together under pressure."

"Yeah, the ER can get pretty hectic when they bring a shooting victim in."

"Where'd you work in emergency rooms, Doc?"

"Columbus Hospital downtown and Sister's on Main Street. Sister's used to get a lot of stabbings on weekends, especially when it was hot."

"You ever work at the VA, Doc?"

"I did a rotation there when I was in med school."

"See any guys in there come back from Vietnam?"

"No. This was several years ago," the doctor said, thinking of the men Pat's age who were long missing limbs and eyes.

"My oldest boy got wounded over there. He's in the Philippines now, at Clark Air Force Base Hospital." Pat watched the bubbles rise in his glass. "They say he's going to Walter Reed next."

"How... badly was he hurt, over there?"

"A commie mine got Rory," he said, turning the base of the beer glass.

"What are his injuries, if I may ask?"

"His left eye's gone. They, they've got to rebuild his face. Left arm's gone below the elbow and his leg below the knee. They can get him artificial limbs. They think he can hear, but they're not sure how much his brain works. He's in pain all the time, doc. His face... the way he's all tore up, he can't talk.

"I was talking to a sheriff's deputy that was over there. They're doing what they call 'hamburger cleaning' now – they don't even close the wounds until they're sure he won't get some infection. My boy hurts all the time, Doc. Rita and I want to visit him, contact him somehow, but we can't we call the Philippines to find out how he's doing, and the people at Walter Reed don't know anything."

They sat for a good ten seconds in silence. Pat felt embarrassed about blurting all that out to this young guy he'd just met.

"Shit, I'm sorry, Doc. I must sound like an idiot talking like that."

"No, not at all, it's ok. I've had to talk to a lot of family members whose relatives get injured. My oldest boy is fourteen and the prospect of him going to Vietnam terrifies me."

"Yeah. I thought I'd seen it all in the war, but when your own boy gets..."

After a few more moments of silence, the doctor finished his beer. "Well, I've got to be going, Pat. Thanks for coming with me...care to do it again? Firing that .45 is tricky, like you said."

54

"Yeah, yeah, sure. Just make sure you clean it with the Hoppe's when you get home, Doc. Gimme a holler next time you want to go shooting. You'll get more accurate with practice, but not much, with that weapon."

They both rose and shook hands. Charlie reached for his wallet, but Pat waved him off saying, "Nah, it's on me."

The doctor left, and Pat stood there, contemplating another beer. Checking his watch, he paid and left, then headed home to call Walter Reed with Rita again to see if they had any updates.

18.

Pat was sorting through the boxes on his new desk when District Attorney Daniel Butler strode into the outer office. He was muttering to himself when he picked up the phone messages from the receptionist, dropped a file on one secretary's desk and then stopped in front of Pat's desk.

"Patrick. How's it going so far?"

"Not bad. Got my shooting qualifications taken care of, parking permit and keys to the investigator's car. Right now, I'm organizing the office stuff."

"Good, good. We're busy here, but I'll try to keep breaking you in easy. Cases that should be pieces of cake for an old pro like yourself – insurance frauds, gathering witnesses' statements, background checks, matters of that sort. I'll keep you working a lot with A.D.A. Roth. I believe you and he go back to the pinball investigations under my predecessor Mr. Stone. That will be good, I think the two of you will make a good team. Have you met everyone here in the office?" he said, waving a hand around the room.

"Yes, I've met them. Some I knew from my days in the Buffalo Police."

"Excellent...I was wondering if you might step into my office for a moment."

"Sure," he said, putting a dictionary down on the green metal desk.

Pat closed the door and the DA waved him to a chair as he sat down behind the stacks of paper on his desk.

"Pat," he said. "It's terrible what happened to your son Rory over in Vietnam. I was told that he's very badly hurt and will take a long time to recover. I want you to know that if there's something we can do..."

"I appreciate that," Pat said, eyes lowered.

"I mean that, Pat. I know you just started here, but if you need time off to visit him..."

"Yeah, I might need that. We're not sure how he's doing now, but he's headed for Walter Reed in Washington..."

"Don't they keep you updated?"

"It's the Army, boss. Delayed, incomplete, stiff messages. My wife's – she's a nurse – going crazy trying to find out what's going on, what his condition is, what they're doing for him..."

Dan Butler nodded and knit his brows. "I might be able to help there. Do you know Max Reilly?"

"The congressman? I know of him."

"Let me make a phone call to Max. He and I go back to Troop 163 together. Still play handball with him when he's in town. He should be able to get this straightened out."

Politician, Pat thought. Campaign contributions required.

As he picked up the phone, Butler caught Pat's look. "Don't worry, Max is all right. He always does the right thing by the good people."

19.

After the Army told Pat and Rita when Rory was going to be transferred to Walter Reed, Rita called the evening charge nurse that she knew at the VA Hospital in Buffalo and asked about the Walter Reed doctors, then tried again to get in touch with them. After a week, Rory's attending physician called her back.

"May I speak to Mrs. Rita Brogan?"

"This is she."

"Mrs. Brogan, this is Dr. Pancescu. I was asked to call you by Congressman Reilly. I'll be the attending physician for Private First-Class Rory Brogan."

"Dr. Pancescu, my husband and I are coming down to Washington shortly after our son arrives and would like to meet with you and the other doctors who will be performing the surgeries to review the care plan for our son."

"Well, Mrs. Brogan, we're rather busy here, as you may imagine, and getting all the doctors together at one time would be difficult. Briefly, we'll be restoring his arm and leg to a condition where we can fit him for artificial limbs, and we'll also be scheduling surgeries to restore his face and jaw to the extent we are able. Each surgery, depending on the results, will tell us what the next step is. You are aware that he is currently at the Clark Air Force Base Hospital in the Philippines, and of what his present condition is?"

"Yes, we're aware he's in the Philippines, and that his vitals are stable, his left arm was traumatically amputated just below the elbow, his left leg is also amputated below the knee, his left eye and jaw were damaged. Can he communicate? Can he see out of his right eye?"

"My understanding is his right eye is reactive to light, and we may be able to restore his sight there completely, over time. Because of the significant damage to his head and abdomen, he is being kept on a regimen of painkillers at a level where he is unable to communicate at this time, if he ever will. His left eye, excuse me, but I don't know any other way to put this, but his left eye is destroyed and he will not have vision there again. We feel confident about the prostheses for his leg and arm, but as to the damage to his head and face...we just don't know at this point."

"Doctor...Pancescu," she said, looking at the notes she'd been taking, "I understand that Rory is scheduled to be transferred to Walter Reed next week, arriving at Andrews Air Force Base on Tuesday. My husband and I intend drive down and see him when he gets admitted to Walter Reed. We will be in Washington for a week and will be visiting him daily. We want to meet with you and the other doctors who'll be treating Rory before then and review his plan of care."

"Mrs. Brogan, I understand you're wanting to help your son any way you can, but I don't know if you understand..."

"Dr. Pancescu, I am a graduate of the Mercy Hospital Nursing Program here in Buffalo and worked for a number of years in both the accident room there and in surgery. My husband is a combat veteran of World War II and, currently, a Special Investigator for the Erie County District Attorney. We want to meet with you and the other doctors and review the plan of care for our son when we get to Washington... and I'm sure Congressman Reilly would want the same thing."

"Well... Mrs. Brogan, let me consult with my colleagues, and I'll call you back when we have arranged a time to meet."

"Thank you, doctor. I'll be waiting for your call."

When they'd hung up, Rita sat down, put her hand to her face then looked out the window at the back yard and the garage with the basketball hoop on it. Tearing, she thought of how Pat had taught the boys how to dribble and shoot there, and how the backboard needed a coat of paint.

20.

When Rita came back from church, Pat was watching TV. She came in quietly, hung up her coat and went into the kitchen.

"How'd it go?"

"Pretty good. We said a Rosary and Father Ratajczak was telling us about the students across the street at College A. He said they were trying to get the kids at St. Joe's to come into their storefront."

"Uh huh."

Rita sat down in her chair when the eleven o'clock news came on.

"President Nixon today announced his intention of withdrawing 150,000 American troops from Vietnam over the next year..."

Too late, she thought, it's too late for my Rory.

What the hell are we doing over there? Pat thought. If we're pulling out, what was it all for? Rory...

When they went to bed, he rested his hand on her hip, but she turned away from him.

I didn't do it, he thought, I didn't get him hurt, and lay on his back staring at the ceiling.

21.

Rory felt pain radiating down his left leg and arm like someone was slicing his limbs with serrated knives, cutting in one spot and then another. He was starting to make out the voices now, too. A deeper male voice with a Boston accent was rumbling in his ears, especially when the pain was the worst.

"All right, Nurse Carmody, we'll be closing up on the leg first. Keep an eye on the arm and let me know if the hemorrhaging gets any worse."

"Yes, doctor."

Rory picked his head up and could see dark shadows moving around in front of him.

"I think he may hear us, doctor."

"He just might, nurse, he just might." Rory felt a hand on his right hand. "Son, if you can hear me, pick up your right hand, the one that I'm touching."

Rory lifted that hand.

"Excellent. He's starting to come around. Son, if you can see anything, anything at all, lights, shadows, lift that hand again."

Rory lifted his hand.

"He can hear, he can see something. He understands and reacts to verbal commands. His brain must not have been too permanently damaged. Excellent. Nurse, when was his last dose of morphine?"

"Three hours, twenty minutes ago, doctor."

"Very well. There doesn't seem to be any signs of significant infection. Our friends at the Evac did a good job for this boy. Let's get these wounds closed up, give him his next morphine injection at the four-hour mark as scheduled, and call me back three hours later. As the drug wears off, I want to examine him further for level of consciousness.

As the doctor stitched up the stumps of his arm and his leg, Rory felt like someone was crushing first his foot, then his hand in a vice. Continuous pain ran down those limbs. His head hurt like hell just behind his eyes, and a buzzing noise came and went, roaring around inside his skull.

Please, please, make it stop. Please make the pain stop, he wished, but it kept getting worse until they gave him the next dose of morphine on their schedule. When it kicked in, the buzzing stopped and he heard water lapping against metal. They were in Mr. Wachter's boat up in Canada. Mr. Wachter, Tommy and dad. Mr. Wachter was sitting in the stern and had just shut the motor off.

"Are you ready to try casting, Rory?" Dad asked. He nodded and picked up the fishing pole with the black Zebco reel. "Good boy. Now, hold it out to the side, that's it. When you're ready to cast and you know no one's in the way, push the button down, swing the pole forward until it's pointed right in front of you and then let go of the button."

When the red and white spoon whizzed out and hit the water, dad said, "Nice job, Rory. Good cast. Now, reel it in slowly and let's see if anything bites."

"Can I do it now, dad?" Tommy said.

"We'll let you try off the dock, later, Tommy. You've got to practice there, first, so you don't drop the whole rig in the water by accident."

22.

Tom and Nancy were sitting on the couch watching TV when HR bounced through the door.

"Watching the tube, huh?" he said, leaning forward. They remained silent on the couch. "We could've used more people at the rally. The brothers on the basketball team are getting the racist coach kicked out." Wiping his nose, HR walked over to the TV and began changing the channel.

"Hey, we were watching that," Tom said.

"Gotta catch the news on four. They had a camera crew there."

HR turned and looked at Tom, then Nancy. Nancy pulled her knees up and wrapped her arms around them. He stared at her with blown pupils.

"You know, I don't know if you've got what it takes to be a revolutionary, Nancy. What, are you scared of black people or something? You should've been there tonight with us."

"Hey man, ease up on her," Tom said.

"And where the hell were you? You scared of big black men too?"

"I was working until about an hour ago. We gotta pay the rent, remember?"

"What the fuck, man. We gotta chance to change the world and you're worried about paying some slumlord. Fuck it, man. I'm going out and watch it in the bar. Keep watching Flip Wilson or whatever bullshit's there and see if you can figure the punch lines out."

As the door slammed shut, Nancy put her head on her knees.

23.

The ride down to Washington was peaceful, long and quiet. Pat and Rita enjoyed the views as they rolled through the Pennsylvania hills and Maryland countryside just coming back to life after a snowy winter. Rita knew when his mind was on Rory, as he would speed up and ask her to again calculate the mileage and time to D.C. They got into the motel on New Hampshire Avenue late at night and lay on the bed staring at the textured ceiling until morning, listening to the occasional slamming car door or howling drunk outside.

A quick wash and coffee before dawn, and they drove to Walter Reed, Pat matching the officious MP in military speak for directions and Rita gazing at the blue-robed men hobbling about on crutches and pushed in wheelchairs. They entered the spotless hospital and found Dr. Pancescu waiting for them at the nurses' station. Pat nearly stood at attention when he was introduced to the doctor with major's oak leaves on his collar, and Rita kept looking into the ward as Pancescu explained Rory's condition.

"The good news is, his sight is returning to his right eye, and his hearing is fairly intact. He is still heavily sedated, but is starting to communicate with his right hand – he can write on a chalkboard, and his messages tell us his brain is not damaged as we at first feared. Because the damaged limbs were severed beneath the joints, we believe he will achieve very good use of his leg and arm with the aid of prostheses.

"As I told you over the phone, we don't know how well we can repair the damage to his jaw and face. It will take multiple surgeries, and progress will be measured in small increments, judging the success by his improvement after each surgery."

"Can we see Rory now, doctor?" Rita asked.

"Certainly, but I have to warn you..." he said, as Rita and Pat entered the ward. They walked down the line of amputee patients, the eyes of the injured upon them. Rita went to her son, took his hand and kissed his forehead, stroking the part of the black hair uncovered by bandages. He's so skinny, she thought, observing the skin tautly stretched over the outline of his bones. Rory's good blue eye went wide and grew moist, and his face and battered body began to quiver, shaking the tube inserted into his shattered mouth. Pat went to his left side and held his shoulder.

"It's us, Rory. Mom and Dad."

"We're here, son, can you understand us?"

Rory released his mother's hand and began to wave his around. A nurse brought a small chalk board and placed a piece of chalk in his hand.

"The first thing he wrote was 'do mom and dad know?'" the nurse said. "Then he wrote, 'Tom'. He was just scratching at first, but it's becoming clearer now that his vision's getting better."

Pat looked at the bandaged stumps and the caved in face. They almost destroyed my son. He thought of the kid who screamed, "Pass it to me!" when all the neighborhood kids were shooting hoops in the backyard. Rita held the chalkboard as Rory wrote, Stay with me.

"We'll be here all week, Rory," Rita said. "And we'll keep coming back, as long as this takes," Pat said.

"Do you know who Isada and Gervase are?" the nurse asked. "He keeps writing their names, too."

"Guys in his squad," Pat answered. "We got a letter from his lieutenant – Rory, those guys are all right. Isada got a little shrapnel in the leg and arm, but he's all better and went back on the line. The rest of the guys didn't get a scratch."

Tom, he wrote next.

"He's home, Rory, he's at school. He'll come down and see you next time, when he's on a break."

The rest of the week went swiftly, with Rita carefully watching the treatments, and after the first two days, the nurses let her help with the IVs and taking vital signs. When Rory slept, she sat by the bedside and read magazines. Pat would read the papers to him, avoiding the war news and searching for articles about Buffalo sports.

When the week was up, Pat and Rita sat on either side of Rory until the sun was down and their son went to sleep. Pat held Rita gently around the waist as they walked out, Rita watching the wounded boy over her shoulder until they were out of the ward. She then went to the nurses' station and double checked all the phone numbers she'd gathered so she could call for updates on Rory's condition. The trip back north was also long and silent, with thoughts of surgeries and artificial limbs left unsaid.

At a diner just over the NY State line, they realized the visit was over. Rita looked south out the window.

"I figure we'll be home around 4:00 a.m. I'll just stay up, get a shower and head into work," Pat said.

"Doesn't one of the Sheridans live down in Maryland somewhere?" she asked.

"Yeah, that's right. Cousin Frank's boy settled down there. Lives in... Mount Rainier, I think, is the name of the town. You remember his wife Maureen, she's the girl with the pony tail who took the boys to the beach that time."

"Maybe they've got room for me to stay sometime, when you've got to work."

"Yeah, let's call them, see what we can work out."

24.

Titus Webb was making coffee in the kitchen when the maid came in, cinching up her bathrobe.

"I'm sorry, Mr. Webb, did I oversleep this morning?"

"No, no, Thelma, I just have a great deal to do today and got up extra early," he said as he poured the steaming black liquid into a thick ceramic mug. He walked through the dining room, which he noticed was set for six, and regretted he would miss the wife and children for breakfast. His patent leather shoes slapping on the marble of the foyer's floor, he picked up the gym bag packed the night before and went out the iron-framed door onto the newly-seeded front terrace, which overlooked Delaware Avenue.

The grass will be in perfect condition, he thought, then chuckled to himself. How many times did we tear it up playing football, and mother chasing us to the back of the house to continue our games? "Not proper for the terrace," she would've said.

He took a small sip of the scalding coffee and tossed the gym bag onto the back seat of the Lincoln Continental. Driving down Delaware, he fiddled with the radio dial until he found the news on WEBR.

"Last night, students protesting the ROTC presence on the University of Buffalo campus broke into their offices in Clark Gymnasium and set fire to a third-floor room there. Campus Police responded late as they were tied up outside of Hayes Hall where other students were demonstrating against the war. No suspects were apprehended."

Clever bastards, he thought. Create a distraction to leave your target unguarded. I'm going to drive up there later and see if they've wrecked anything at Baird Hall.

Dressed in white, Titus left the locker room, saluted the attendant, Clarence, with his squash racket and got into the chamber before his partner showed. He bounced one of the two hard rubber balls on the polished wooden floor and swatted it dead center into the foreground wall, just above the tin, then volleyed it back off the left wall, then the right. He continued to wallop the ball, practicing it on the upper and lower parts of the wall, forehand and backhand. When he was breathing hard and sweating freely, he stopped hitting the ball and just trotted side to side on the maple floor, back and forth, sizing up the court.

When a young man entered wearing a Cornell t-shirt, Titus asked, "Good morning, David. Time for three games today?"

"Sure, three games will be great this morning, Mr. Webb." The young man warmed up after Webb stepped back, the older man observing his powerful shots but slower lateral movement.

When he finished, David adjusted his headband and Webb asked, "Ok, label side or not?"

"I'll let you take label, Mr. W.," and Webb spun the racket. It spun, wobbled, and when it landed, read Oliver on the wooden handle.

"Which side do you want, Mr. Webb?"

"I'll take the right to start if you don't mind, David."

David tossed the older man the two rubber balls. He gripped one tightly and bounced the other, thinking, I've got to win this first game, haven't got the stamina for a comeback anymore. He slammed the ball as hard as he could, then moved laterally to the center of the court. David volleyed it off the sidewall and as the ball hit the forward wall, Webb stepped up just in time to get his racket on it before

69

it hit the floor. He slid around his younger opponent intuitively, and his experience won the first match 11-8.

"Need a breather, Mr. W?"

"Can't, David, got a meeting to get to."

They began the second game, but Webb couldn't keep up with the youth's pace and lost, 11-7. In the third game, Webb worked it to 9-9. He carefully placed his lead foot just inside the box before serving, then whacked the ball to slightly above the tin so it would land far back on the court and he slid there. David moved to the spot and Webb hesitated in the blocking position, then moved out of the way. The younger man volleyed it high and Webb couldn't get to it. On the next volley, David fired a thundering shot that bounced off the sidewall directly in front of Webb, and the older man stepped back, but couldn't get the racket in front fast enough.

Both men breathing hard, David asked, "You almost had me there, Mr. W."

"Great game, David," Webb said, waving his racket. "Youth must be served."

They shook hands and Webb hobbled a bit towards the court door.

"You ok, Mr. Webb?" David asked.

"I'm fine," the older man answered, twisting his foot around. "Just getting a touch older."

Toweling off in the locker room, Webb asked his young partner, "I hear Sheraton may be moving you, David."

"There's an assistant manager's job in San Diego, Mr. Webb. Brand new place, right on the water."

"I see, I see. Well, it sounds like a wonderful opportunity, young man," Webb said, trying to conjure someone he could call here in Buffalo to offer the young man a position locally.

"Yeah, I took some time and looked around Southern California quite a bit, Mr. Webb. I like it there. All new highways, beautiful beaches, and no snow."

Double knotting his shoe, Webb said, "Great, that's great, David. But who's going to play squash with me before work now?"

Webb pulled up to the basement entrance of the towering M & T Plaza Building, got out, and tossed the keys to the attendant.

"Thanks, Gerald," he said, reminding himself to send a tip to the garage staff. Gerald touched the keys to his forehead as he climbed in the Continental. Trotting up the Plaza steps to the front entrance, Webb gazed up at the Yamasaki designed green marble that gave way to the white exterior of the high rise that climbed 21 stories into the overcast sky. And made with our own Bethlehem steel, he reflected. V-50 steel that will stand forever.

As he swiftly crossed the foyer, the desk people greeted him. In the elevator, two men in suits nodded, one asking, "Which floor, Mr. Webb?" and pushed the button signaling the twenty-first, where he had scheduled the breakfast meeting with the Bond Club for 8:30. When he entered the dining room, only two others were there, ordering breakfast. Good, Bill Correlli and his lawyer are here, he thought, nodding to the two men who were looking at plans. He poured himself coffee, sat down next to the two men, and ordered poached eggs and toast with some fruit as they waited for the bankers and investment company leaders who made up the club. The movers and shakers downtown, that's who we want to back this, he thought.

"Ready, Bill?" Webb said to the developer.

"You know it. I've been waiting for an opportunity like this all my life. Plans, options, finance estimates, everything. I appreciate you talking to these people first, Titus, you know all of them and you've dealt with them for years."

Webb watched the others file in, most in conservative gray or blue suits, a couple in sport-coats, wide ties and plaid pants. He observed these latter usually had longer hair and wondered why men of business were following their children's fashions.

When they all had their coffee and food ordered, Webb began.

"Gentlemen, it looks like we are all here. Let's start. Mr. Correlli has a magnificent proposal, which, if successful, will bring Buffalo back into the forefront of the nation in both sports and architecture. He is proposing nothing less than the nation's second domed stadium, to be designed by the Steuart, Jones and Burrows firm of Houston Astrodome fame, and they are to be assisted in the design and engineering by Buffalo's own Guyton Thomas company. It will be 100% constructed by local companies.

"If you look at the artists' renderings," he said, as an assistant uncovered two large, full color images on easels, "the Astrodome is on the right, and Buffalo's proposed domed stadium is on the left."

The assembly stared in silence for a few moments before Webb continued. "If you notice," Webb said, now with pointer in one hand and coffee mug in the other, "while the Astrodome rises not quite 250 feet high and the dome is a little over 700 feet in diameter, Buffalo's proposed 'coliseum,' if you will, would rise 300 feet above the bedrock of downtown Buffalo and carry a dome of just over 800 feet in diameter."

A couple of low whistles and impressed nods rose from the table, and one banker said, "That should make Eigen happy and keep the Bills in Buffalo." When the others began to comment, Webb continued. "I think then, gentlemen, one of the first points of discussion for us, as we represent the principal interests that will be investing in this project, is where we might locate this marvelous structure. Mr. Correlli and I have done some preliminary surveying and have found three possible sites in the city I would like to share with you, if you would turn to your right and look at the projector screen."

At this, one young man in a shirt and tie pulled down a large screen and another turned on an overhead projector, upon which he placed a map of the City of Buffalo as the machine hummed to life. Pointing to the screen, Webb indicated three red circles.

"Our preliminary survey has identified three possible locations for this coliseum. The first one is right downtown near the lake. It's a site that's ready to be redeveloped," which got some of the downtown landowners sitting up straight, "a lakeview, and it's near the skyway, the thruway, near the juncture of major city streets, right near War Memorial Auditorium and will bring people downtown again." He paused then moved his pointer northward along the Niagara River.

"The second possible site is here, in Riverside, right on the Niagara. It's along the thruway, easily accessible from the northern and eastern suburbs by the Youngmann Highway and Scajacuada and Kensington Expressways, and what lands are not currently occupied can be assembled without too much difficulty by outright purchases and eminent domain."

He paused again, seeing less enthusiasm in his audience. "The third possible site," Webb said, pointing to a location on Buffalo's East Side, "would be near the Bills' current home at War Memorial Stadium." A quick glance saw eyes lowering and hands signaling for more coffee. "The site could be easily assembled as it would go hand-in-hand with current slum clearance projects and, considering the utilities already available, would have very low site costs. There is plenty of parking once the land is cleared, it is accessible by several bus routes, and it is centrally located in the metropolitan area."

He stopped and looked around the room. "Well, gentlemen, those are the first possibilities. What do you think?"

A haggard looking, darksuited man stubbed out a cigarette and asked, "Have you considered any suburban sites, Titus?"

"As I said, Adam, these are just the first notions our people have come up with. There are, of course, possibilities in the suburbs, but one possible goal we should keep in mind is the revitalization of downtown, particularly the lakefront. There's plenty of land available for redevelopment, we could get federal money from urban renewal sources, the Sabres and Braves will be playing at Memorial Auditorium right nearby, and the State of New York is planning a major expansion of the university system – possibly downtown as well. If all these projects coalesce, it's a marvelous opportunity to bring Buffalo to the forefront of American cities again."

Adam, the representative from Buffalo's biggest bank, looked around and saw the younger eyes upon him. He adjusted his horn-rimmed glassed and spoke up again. "Well, it's a great vision, Titus, but will it work? The city's credit rating is in the cellar. They can't swing a big bond issue for a project this size these days. Then there's the city government. Every Tom, Dick and Harry bureaucrat, union leader and connected contractor's going to get himself and his cronies in on this and gum up the works until they all get their share..."

"Well, those factors will certainly have to be considered, Adam..."

Another banking rep spoke up. "Have any figures on the land assembly been put together on this downtown site, Titus? You can't do it in secret, and the land owners will naturally want to get the most for their property."

A third banker asked, "Has anyone from New York State mentioned any preference for the university's downtown site? I keep hearing Rocky wants all of it way outside the city in Amherst, where he can put lakes and have all kinds of open space."

"Gentlemen, this is all in the preliminary stages," answered Webb. "Any site is going to require some heavy lifting. However, Mr. Correlli here has a marvelous concept that not only keeps the Bills in town but revitalizes downtown and makes Buffalo one of the greatest cities in America again. Our city is known for its architectural marvels, and here we have a chance at building a truly wondrous

74

structure. We owe it to Buffalo, to our legacy, to our children's future to give this dream the greatest consideration."

Cigarettes were stubbed out and coffee drunk. Webb listened to the conversations, and the downtown location wasn't dominant. He and Correlli stood there while the staffers packaged up the demos and the busboys cleaned up.

"What do you think?" Correlli asked him.

His arms crossed, Webb replied, "I think you better look to the Texans for partners and Erie County for bonds, Bill."

Webb left the meeting, drove north, and turned off the radio as he drove up to the university, his mind turning to thoughts of which banks might finance the bonds, which construction firms could handle a project of this size, and, taking heed of the senior banker's warning, he thought of how to get around the single-minded parasites who latched onto projects like this and would bleed them dry with no thought to the consequences.

When he got near the University of Buffalo campus on Main Street, Titus slowed the Lincoln, observing the buildings and wide lawns of the campus for damage from the demonstrations. Bottles and food wrappers littered the area around the bushes and trees in front of the black glass Baird Hall. After parking the car, he paused, hearing music from within — Was that Mahler? and the smell of pot throughout. As he walked around the outside of the music hall, he thought of how he and his family had brought the people from the Philharmonic together with Governor Rockefeller's favorite architects to come up with this most modern of sound gardens. As he kicked away an empty beer bottle, he thought of the Hall's opening – how Lukas Foss had led the orchestra and Andre Previn had shown up for the occasion. Further on, he saw slovenly dressed students sitting on the ground and passing a joint, leaning against an old bank's columns on the lawn, their Ionic majesty now abandoned amongst the overgrowth.

Some way to protest a war. Ill-mannered, spoiled brats are what they are, he thought, reflecting how he postponed Princeton and went into the Army as an enlisted man. He twisted his foot around, thinking about the toes he'd lost from frostbite in the Hurtgen Forest.

25.

When the seat belt lights went out, Mary Ellen Anderson swung her legs out of the aisle, got up out of the seat, and opened the overhead compartment. She caught the salesman in the middle seat looking at her chest as her slender arms reached for her gym bag. No chance, fat boy, she thought as she slung the bag over her shoulder and walked to the exit, tying her long red hair into a ponytail. May need coloring tonight, she thought as she checked the board in the terminal to find her luggage. She liked this new Houston International Airport and chuckled at the model astronaut planting the Texas flag on a simulated moon as she strutted across the polished granite floors to the newsstand.

She grabbed a Wall Street Journal, the Houston Chronicle and the Houston Post and looked over the out-of-town papers. Let's see, Vietnam, Vietnam, student protests, then she noticed the Buffalo Courier Express. "Eigen Considers Moving Bills" the headline read. Hmmm. The old town is really falling apart, she thought, adding the Buffalo paper to the others.

In the cab heading to the office, she unfolded the Buffalo paper and read. "Paul Eigen yesterday discussed the possibility of moving the Buffalo Bills to Seattle if the city does not come up with a plan to replace War Memorial Stadium. 'Seattle has offered to build a new stadium,' he told reporters, 'and a domed stadium at that. It would be bigger than the Astrodome,' he added."

Gathering her papers and the carry-on bag, she put on oversized sunglasses and stepped out of the cab into the bright sunshine. As the driver pulled the Ventura bag out of the trunk, she looked up at the cantilevered white stone shades that protruded from each of the 44 floors and thought, You made it, girl, you really made it. A suit-jacketed man came from behind the desk inside, opened the door and took Mary Ellen's bag.

"Just put it behind your desk, Roy. I won't be long in the office."

"Right, Miss Anderson," he said as she pushed the elevator button for the 23rd floor and thought, Check to see if the Marek contract is signed, find out if Terri's finished with the Peer Company audit and, she chuckled to herself, how many messages did Danny leave for me, thinking of the thirty-year old tennis pro who had been going broke taking her to the opening of every new restaurant in town.

Getting off the elevator, she looked with pride at the name on the dark wood door.

"Suite 2301, Anderson Accounting" it read. Hers. Someday, I'll be the biggest Anderson accounting around, she thought. Not bad for a girl who showed up in Houston fourteen years ago with little more than a business course in bookkeeping and a makeup kit.

She opened the door and walked through the bullpen as the staff looked up and stiffened just a little. "Good morning, good people," she greeted, as Billy slid his behind off Terri's desk and stood up straight.

"The Peer audit is ready on your desk, Miss Anderson," Terri said.

"Excellent, Terri. Can you check on the Marek contract, Billy? Once that's signed, we're off to the races, kids."

"Right away, Miss Anderson," he said, heading back to his desk.

Taking a key out of her pocketbook, Mary Ellen unlocked the heavy door to her office and flicked on the lights, smelling the lemon furniture polish from the huge wooden desk. Just right. No worms are going to get this desk like they did the rest of that office's furniture, reflecting on the railroad magnate's office furniture she had picked up for a song at a bankruptcy auction.

26.

Mary Ellen was looking over the numbers on the Peer audit and was pulling the Texas Instrument calculator out of the top drawer when the intercom buzzed.

"Yes, Christine?" she answered as her fingers began working the keys to check the numbers.

"There is a Mr. Todd on the line from Yarborough and Associates, Miss Anderson, says he's calling for Senator Yarborough."

"Ok, I'll take it, Christine, thank you." Hitting the blinking line, she said, "Mary Ellen Anderson."

A stentorian voice on the other end said, "Miss Anderson, this is Randolph Todd, Vice President of Yarborough and Associates." He paused a moment, then continued. "Senator Yarborough would be pleased if you could make yourself available next Tuesday at one o'clock in the Senator's offices."

"Hmmm, let me see... Mr. Todd, is it?" She held the phone next to the latest copy of Accountancy Journal on her desk and riffed through it for several seconds. "Well, Mr. Todd, we did have a meeting with one of our clients set up for then, but his issues have been resolved. Yes, I believe we can arrange to meet you then. Now, just where does Mr. Yarborough want to meet?"

"Oh, Miss Anderson, you have a sense of humor, I see. Why, the Senator is looking forward to meeting you in his office on the sixth floor of the Astrodome, of course."

"I'll see Mr. Yarborough then, Mr. Todd."

After hanging up, she drummed her nails on the desk for a few seconds, then buzzed her secretary.

"Christine, enter an appointment on the schedule for one o'clock next Tuesday with Yarborough and Associates. Billy Cannon will accompany me."

"Yes, Miss Anderson."

"Oh, and Christine. Tell Billy to wear his best suit."

"Yes, Miss Anderson."

Putting the Peer audit in front of her again, Mary Ellen returned to checking the numbers.

When Tuesday arrived, Mary Ellen's red hair was pulled into a high ponytail, and she wore an electric blue dress that came three inches below her knees when she sat. Her matching shoes added another inch to her five-ten frame, and she carried no purse as she swept through the outer office.

"Ready, Billy?" she said, assuring herself there were no coffee stains on his shirt.

"You look very nice, Miss Anderson," Terri said from the next desk.

"Thank you, Terri. Is the cab waiting, Billy?"

"Yes, it's downstairs, Miss Anderson," Billy replied, grabbing his briefcase.

In the cab, she asked, "Got Yarborough's history down, Billy?"

"Yes, Ma'am. Born 1925, graduate of the McCombs School of Business at the top of his class, also has an engineering degree from Texas A&M. Known for ramrodding the expansion of the Houston Ship Channel further into the bayou, later developing an industrial park next to it. Served two terms as State Senator and the power behind the planning and building of the Astrodome. Known to drive his people hard, himself harder, sleeping only four to five hours at night. Has a ranch along the Pedernales near the Johnsons, goes deer hunting with him from time to time.

"Wife, Doreen, an Austin debutant. Three children, all teenagers. Two boys, both football players, and a daughter, interested in music."

"Very good, Billy. Now," she said as the driver opened the cab door, "let's see what the great showman has in mind."

Todd met them at the entrance. "Miss Anderson," he smiled, "come right this way," and led them into the elevator.

"The Senator is looking forward to meeting you," he said as Billy took in the green velvet carpet on the car walls. When they got out on the 6th Floor, they were met by a young assistant named Chip, and both aides flanked the guests on their way down the hall to the Senator's office. Once there, each man grabbed a handle and pulled open the teak doors.

Across twenty feet of blue carpet from them sat Yarborough, behind a gold inlaid Louis XIV desk, talking on a French phone. He waved them in, crushed out a Marlboro, hung up and came around the desk in his shirtsleeves.

"Right on time," Yarborough said. "I like that. Miss Anderson, it is a pleasure to meet you," he said, taking her hand between both his. "And this is?" he said turning slightly to Billy.

"William Cannon, sir," Billy said.

Todd jumped in. "Mr. Cannon is Miss Anderson's assistant, Senator. Graduate of the University of Texas, like yourself."

"Very good, very good. Well, shall we all be seated?" He gestured to the zebra skinned chairs on coasters before his desk. Returning to his raised chair, he said, "I hear great things about Anderson Accounting, Miss, very great things," lighting up a Marlboro.

"I see where your company was brought in by the State of Texas, did audits on several firms who had contracts to build roads here in Harris County.

"We did," she said.

81

"Saved the taxpayers roughly two hundred thousand dollars, I hear."

"$210,400."

"Yes. I also hear that you audited some offshore oil rig contractors for my friend Jimmy Connelly at Lone Star Oil. Saved him a fair amount of money."

"They were overcharging him just over thirty thousand dollars."

"Those offshore boys can be some pretty rough customers, Miss."

"My firm gets paid to do a thorough job, Mr. Yarborough."

"So I understand, so I understand, Miss. Well. The reason I invited you here today for our little chat is that I am considering, that is, Yarborough and Associates, are considering, a partnership with a development firm in New York State for a very large project. We are considering your company as an auditor to verify their bona fides as it were."

Mary Ellen shifted and tugged her dress slightly further over her knee. "Mr. Yarborough, we have familiarity with New York accounting practices, and have the personnel to handle the task. May I ask where this development firm is located?"

"They're based in Buffalo and its suburbs, Miss Anderson," Yarborough said, his eyes never leaving hers. Lighting one Marlboro with another, he continued. "If we were to select you for this project, what would your initial steps be?"

"Well, to begin, we would want to see their tax returns for the last five years, check their profitability and see if there were any irregularities there. We would contact the Better Business Bureau there and see if there are any complaints, outstanding or in the past. We would contact firms this developer does business with and check to see if their payments are on time and current. We would check bankruptcy records and see if they or any subsidiaries had declared bankruptcy at any time. We would ask for references and check these thoroughly."

"Hmm, I see. As you may be aware, there may be some, shall we say, connections to organized crime by companies up there. Do you believe you could root out any such connections?"

"Such connections are quite possible, but we have methods to discover such irregularities which members of the Anderson firm have learned through extensive training with the IRS. May I ask what the project you are considering is?"

"Yarborough and Associates, Miss Anderson," he said, standing up and leaning forward on his desk, "is considering building the world's second domed stadium, along with an outside development including an amusement park, world class golf course, enclosed shopping mall and residential development, the like of which you have never seen."

27.

Mary Ellen looked at the assignment list she had drawn up and buzzed her secretary.

"Christine. Would you have Billy and Terri come to my office please?"

"Right away, Miss Anderson."

Mary Ellen tented her fingers as the two came in. They might as well be holding hands, she thought.

"Well, Billy, Terri, I see both of you are all caught up on your current work assignments. And very good work it is, I must say."

The two smiled, their eyes angling towards each other.

"So, how would the both of you like to take a trip?"

They nodded.

"Good. We've been hired by Senator Yarborough. He is considering a partnership with a developer in New York to build a new stadium up there, and he wants us to examine them."

"Manhattan?" Billy asked.

"No, in Buffalo, Billy."

The two youths' faces fell.

"This is going to be a very important contract for us, you two. Yarborough and Associates is quite possibly the biggest developer in the State of Texas. They and the developer in Buffalo, a Mr. William Correlli, are thinking of building another domed stadium there, plus a large commercial and residential development surrounding it. Senator Yarborough wants to know the Buffalo developer's financial condition, and if he has any connections to organized crime. The two of you, having an IRS background, and, being my best employees, are ideal for this project.

"Don't look so glum, Billy. It won't be snowing up there. In fact, it will be quite nice this time of year," she said, reflecting. "Now, here's a short list of tasks to perform. I'll be getting more information to you about the development firm later today, and they've pledged complete cooperation. I'm also making arrangements for a local firm to assist you with the local resources – banks, the IRS, local BBB office, etc. Now what do you think? Can the two of you handle this?"

"I'm certain we can," Billy said.

"Won't you be coming, Miss Anderson?" Terri asked.

"No, I have other work here." She paused, then continued, "Very well then. I'll have Christine make arrangements for your plane tickets, hotel rooms and a rental car."

28.

The night duty nurse had helped Rory out of his bed, into a wheelchair and rolled him over to a window just as she was getting off. Rory nodded his thanks and noticed a big guy in hospital whites coming on the ward.

The big guy had a blonde crew cut and Popeye forearms. He looked around, then, pointing his clipboard at Rory, said. "Is this one Brogan?"

"That's him," the night nurse said as she headed for the exit.

"Private Brogan," the big guy said, "I am Specialist 6th Class McKenna, and for the next several weeks I am your physical therapist. My job is to get what's left of your left arm and leg into shape so we can fit them with the prostheses that are going to get you out of here. Do you follow, soldier?"

Rory blinked a watery blue eye.

"Pick up your good arm if you understand me, Brogan."

Rory raised his right hand in a fist and nodded.

"Outstanding. Now let's get your ass out of that wheelchair and down the hall to the p.t. room," and with that, he wrapped a big arm around Rory's waist and helped him up, putting Rory's shortened arm behind his neck. McKenna walked a moaning Rory down the hallway, where a legless Corporal on short "stubbie" wooden legs smiled and said in a Bugs Bunny voice, "You'll be sorreee."

The PT room was filled with moaning, crying and determined men who were being twisted, cajoled, ordered and encouraged to use whatever was left of their limbs on mats, in chairs, on tables and parallel bars. McKenna sat Rory in a chair, and for the next half hour manipulated Rory's shoulder, arm and leg at every angle. With his damaged jaw, Rory moaned like a dying dog at first, then simply closed his eye and nodded silently as the unused nerves and muscles started painfully to come back to life.

"Ok, that's enough for today," McKenna said as Rory was about to pass out from the unaccustomed exertion. The big Spec 6 then plucked him up and walked him back to the ward, the crippled Corporal giving him a thumbs up and Rory nodding as he went past.

As he arranged the pillows around and under Rory on his bunk, McKenna said, "Day one of your new life, soldier. The harder you work with me on this detail, the quicker you'll be agile, mobile and hostile again."

McKenna then picked up his clipboard, and, looking around the room, said, "Next?"

29.

Just after eight a.m., a crew-cut Chip pulled up in front of the Charter House Hotel in a rented Ford, and the senator was in the back seat before the front desk clerk could say good morning. Passing back a pack of Marlboros, Chip said, "Downtown first, Senator?"

"Yassir," Yarborough answered, lighting up and tossing the match out the window. "Time to see in person just what we're getting into around here."

As they drove down Delaware Avenue, Yarborough noted the mansions along the former millionaires' row being renovated into offices and apartments. Circling Niagara Square, he noted the 32-story art deco City Hall with the bronze statues of two former mayors, Fillmore and Cleveland, looking down upon them.

"Very well done," he commented. Heading up Court Street, he admired the M & T Plaza Building and Lafayette Square. Gesturing with his cigarette towards a tall building that was a series of rectangular prisms, he said, "You know architecture, Chip, what's that building on the left?"

"I believe that's the Rand Building, Senator. Not as tall, but considered the model for the Empire State Building in New York City. Finished just before the Depression."

"Like a number of things around here," the developer said.

Going down Main Street in the business district by Lake Erie, they slowly approached the potential downtown site for the stadium. Yarborough looked at his watch.

"Should be more people coming in for work here downtown, about now, Chip."

"Pretty sparse, Senator."

"Right you are, my boy, right you are."

At the foot of Main Street, they pulled over, and Yarborough got out, zipping up his jacket. Chip followed. Yarborough looked up at the Skyway overhead.

"Hmmm, some highway access, but it'll block the view and it's too low." Looking to the left, he saw Memorial Auditorium and to the right, the crumbling D.L. & W. Railroad Station. In front, he smelled the Buffalo River and observed the tumble-down warehouses along rotting piers.

"They were right, boy, your architect boys were right. It'll never work. Not enough room, too many obstacles to move. It'll take decades to make this right again, if ever." He flung his smoke into the street and returned to the car.

"Let's head up Main Street and take a gander at the next proposed site."

"You mean the one on the river, or the one inland, Senator?"

"Skip the one on the river. Too crowded there to assemble what we need. Too expensive and using eminent domain would take forever."

Chip got the door for the senator and drove up Main Street.

"What a shame, young man, what a shame," Yarborough said, waving a hand at the closed stores and porno theaters. "This was once a great city with a thriving downtown. Happening all over America, boy, just terrible. We've got to think big, son, very big, to overcome this decay."

Turning right at North Street, Chip made sure the doors were locked.

"Good God, son, the riots took a toll here," the senator noted, observing burned out wooden houses along the route. "What do they call this section?"

"We're on the East Side, Senator, and the area to our right is called the Fruit Belt, after the names of the streets, Orange, Lemon, Peach and so forth."

Turning left on Jefferson, Yarborough saw the empty commercial street and the Buffalo Bills' current home.

"Hmmph. I do believe the Coliseum in Rome is in better condition. No sir, we can't fix this, not even with Texas money. We'd go broke trying. No one will show up here. No need to stop, Mr. Chip, no need at all. I must say, you've done most excellent research, sir, most excellent. Now, let's head on up to the wide-open spaces you talk about out in... Lancaster, I believe it's called?"

30.

Mary Ellen Anderson came into the office and saw Billy and Terri's desks empty. Christine saw her stop and said, "Terri's down in the coffee shop and Billy's in the bathroom, Miss Anderson. They got in from the airport and are hoping to take the rest of the day off like you said they could."

"Thank you, Christine," she said, pulling her glasses out as she walked. Sitting down in her office, she separated the reports. Let's see, I.R.S. Returns for five years, good. Better Business Bureau Reports, good. Financial report, good. Hmm, and here's the real estate reports and government survey.

A knock came on the door, and a breathless and unshaven Billy entered.

"Are all the reports ok, Miss Anderson?"

Taking the files, Mary Ellen looked over her glasses and smiled.

"They are, Billy, good job. But, when we go to see Senator Yarborough, make sure you wear a shirt that covers up the love bites."

Billy reached for his open collar, nodded and left quickly.

The intercom buzzed.

"Miss Anderson, Senator Yarborough on line 1."

"Mary Ellen Anderson."

"Well, hello, Miss Mary Ellen. And how are you this fine day? Say, how are those reports coming along?"

"They're finished, Senator, and a week early. I'd just like to take a final look at them to make sure they're in apple pie order before I deliver them to you in person."

"Why, Miss Mary Ellen, you never cease to surprise me with your efficiency. That truly is tremendous. I can't wait for you to deliver those reports to me in person. Do you have any plans for lunch tomorrow?"

"I can make myself available for lunch, Senator, but perhaps I should come by your office tomorrow at, say, 10:30, so we could go over these reports without any distractions."

Mary Ellen spent the rest of the day going over the files for Yarborough. Lastly, she went over the summary of the local political situation in Buffalo. Very good, she thought, they went to the library, checked the newspaper indexes and dug up clippings on all the principal politicians. Going way back, too, back to when I lived there in the fifties.

Among the clippings was one about the former mayor of Buffalo. "Mayor Jezerowski, campaign manager Owczarczak called before grand jury looking into pinball payoffs," one read. Yeah, those guys. Their mobster friends would've killed me if I hadn't disappeared.

With Billy handing her the files, Mary Ellen explained all their findings about Yarborough's potential partners in Buffalo. She passed the files to Chip, who handed them to Todd, who placed them on the desk next to Yarborough, who kept his eyes on Mary Ellen through a cloud of tobacco smoke. The Senator was relieved to hear about good finances, bills paid up in full and on time, no outrageous complaints against the firm, no serious criminal records and most importantly, no mafia connections with Correlli and company. He gave an affirmative nod to Chip when she reported that the prices of real estate in Lancaster were the cheapest of the potential sites they were considering.

Lastly, Mary Ellen passed over a ten-page report on local government in Western New York and a file full of newspaper clippings. "You didn't ask for this, Senator, but as an added bonus, Anderson and

Company has done an analysis of the political situation in Buffalo and Erie County. We have done some background checks on the people you'll be dealing with on the municipal, county and state level, and I think you'll find some interesting reading there, particularly in the newspaper clippings we've included that go back some years."

"Well, Miss Mary Ellen, I do thank you for this additional information, and we will be sure to examine it carefully. As you know, I do have some little experience in the field of government, as do my associates."

"Senator Yarborough, your experience in government will be invaluable in your work up there in Buffalo, and if I may be frank, I think you will find dealing with the local politicians there almost as challenging as dealing with any companies involved with organized crime."

31.

It was Rory's eighth day working with both the prostheses on the parallel bars, coordinating gripping the bar and walking.

"Damn good," McKenna said. "Your first day was rough, but you've got it down now, Brogan. Your balance has come along just fine, and that's the hard part. I think you're ready to try it without the parallel bars now. You're not tired, are you?" he said.

Rory shook his head, even though his breathing was labored, his leg hurt and the stump itched like hell under the sock that cushioned the limb from the prosthesis. The weeks of lying in bed and no solid food had drained the energy and about twenty pounds out of him.

"Alright then soldier, here's what I want you to do. I want you to move your feet just like you've been doing, but when you go beyond the bars, just hold your arms out to the side at about forty-five degrees – that will help you keep your balance. Got it?"

Rory nodded. He stepped gingerly forward on the artificial leg, followed with the good one and slowly lifted his hands out to the side. He stopped, found himself steadily upright without the bars and smiled.

"Alright there, soldier," McKenna said. "Go ahead and take a few more steps forward, see how that mustang rides."

Rory took one, then two, then a third step, wobbled, regained his balance and took a fourth.

"Outstanding, Brogan, outstanding. You'll be meeting your folks at the door on your feet next time they come to visit. Ready to try one more thing today?"

Sweating profusely, Rory nodded again.

"Ok. I want you to try turning right. First, take a step with the prosthesis forward then move your right forward on an angle – you know, a flanking move. Then, swing the left around and let it land just a little ahead of the right and you've made your first right turn. Got it?"

Rory nodded, thought for a second, then moved his left, then planted his right on an angle and swung his left over. His torso went forward, then back, then came back to straight and he was still standing.

"Terrific, Brogan, good job. You'll be getting discharge papers from here before..."

When he stopped, Rory looked up and saw himself in front of a full-length mirror. While McKenna talked, he took it all in, the skinny guy, half his face covered in bandages, cheekbones jutting out, a claw for a hand and a wooden post with a plastic foot for a leg. He found himself sitting on the floor suddenly and McKenna was helping him up.

"Whoa, there, soldier. That was a lot for one day. Good job. Orderly, here, help Private Brogan back to his room. Momentary lack of concentration, there, Brogan. Don't worry, you'll get it. Now, go rest up and we'll have you out here again tomorrow."

The orderly got him back to the ward, and he swung both legs up onto the bed and carefully unhitched his artificial leg. Still breathing hard, he rolled the sock off the stump and when he felt the fresh air cooling the area, he leaned back on the pillow.

As he got his breath back, he picked up the chalkboard and started writing. When he finished, he waved it to get the attention of the guy in the bunk next to him who was reading Sports Illustrated. Paul Gordon reached over and grasped the chalkboard with his left hook.

Started walking without the parallel bars today

"Great Rory, you'll be outta here in no time, now, brother."

Rory looked down and said nothing. Then wrote.

Lots more surgery for my face

"Hey man, you started going without the training wheels today, that's a big step."

Rory nodded, then looked down at the board. Gordon watched him, then asked, "Ok, what's wrong now?"

Rory scribbled one word.

Chicks

"Huh?"

No woman wants a guy with half a face 1 leg + claw for a hand

"Ahh, shit, man. They're going to fix your face up ok. You'll be fine out there. Ask Slick Rick over there," Gordon said, indicating a man with one leg and an eye patch hobbling towards them on a crutch. "He's been away on weekends. You did ok, right, Rick?"

"Yeah, I did ok. Only it wasn't the artificial leg and bad eye that scared some of them off, it was the G.I. Soon as they see the short hair, they figure you for a soldier and bail out. My advice is stick to babes working in stores. Going to the mat for Uncle Sam ain't popular with the college girls, so don't waste your time."

Rory thought about that, and thought about Tommy at U.B. "The Berkeley of the East," they were calling it on the news. Shit, he thought, I hope he's not getting caught up in that bullshit. He remembered when he was on the safety patrol at St. Joes in eighth grade. Tommy would be coming down the driveway at school with the other kids, grin at him and run ahead out of line. Rory would catch him and put him back, both of them laughing. Kid stuff, he thought. Tommy wouldn't get involved with those protestor assholes, he's too smart for that.

32.

"The chair recognizes Mr. Jezerowski," and Joseph Jezerowski, representative of the 5th District of the Erie County Legislature, placed his half glasses on the desk before him and slowly stood up, looking around the chamber to see who was paying attention. His double-breasted blue suit freshly pressed, gray hair smartly parted on the side and handkerchief neatly tucked into coat pocket, "Jazz" Jezerowski was a contrast to most of the other legislators who were reduced to shirtsleeves at this point in the evening.

"I realize this session has been lengthy, gentlemen," he said, "so I will be brief. The Finance and Management Committee has added an amendment to proposed Local Law Number 16, this amendment stating that the requirements for bidding on the roof maintenance contracts for county buildings include the provision that all bidders be bonded to the amount of $500,000. This is just a technical change, Mr. Chairman, and, if you so rule, will not require an additional public hearing. This minor change, however, will assure the taxpayers of not having to pay for shoddy work on any size structure within the county inventory."

"And who are the sponsors of this amendment?" the chairman asked.

"Mr. Chair, this amendment is sponsored by myself," Jazz said, then turning to his left and gesturing with an open hand, "Majority Leader Mr. Ludlow and," placing a hand on the shoulder of the man seated to his right, "First District representative Mr. Fort."

The chairman, making notes, did not look up. "Mr. Ludlow, Mr. Fort, do you acknowledge sponsoring this Amendment?"

Both answered, "Yes," and Jazz took his hand off Fort's shoulder.

"Mr. Clerk, was this Amendment presented to you at least three business days previous to this presentation?"

"It was," the clerk answered.

"And has the Amended bill been distributed to each member of the Legislature, Mr. Clerk?"

"It has," the clerk acknowledged.

"Very well." The chair looked up after glancing at the amendment and began speaking very rapidly. "I see no reason to schedule any further public hearings for this amendment, as it is just a technical change as Mr. Jezerowski states, and the chair so rules. Is there any objection to this body concerning this Amendment to proposed Local Law number 16?" He and Jazz looked around the chamber. Several members were writing, others shoving papers in briefcases, and at least one was nodding off.

"Seeing none, the Amendment is accepted as written. Now, if there are no further amendments, discussions or objections to proposed local Law No. 16, is there a call for a vote on the measure?"

Jazz nodded to Ludlow. "I wish to call for a vote on the measure at this time," Ludlow said.

"Do we have a second?" the chair said.

Jazz intoned, "Seconded."

"Very well," the chairman said. "Since there has been a call for a vote on the measure by Mr. Ludlow and it has been seconded by Mr. Jezerowski, we will take a vote on the measure. All those in favor of the proposed Local Law No. 16 answer by saying 'aye'."

A number of voices answered, "Aye."

"All those against answer 'nay'," was met with silence, and the regulations for bidding on county roof contracts were passed on to the Clerk of the Legislature to be certified and sent to the County Executive for his signature, along with other bills passed that session.

The chair asked for any further business and noticed several members pulling on sport coats and looking at their watches. When the meeting was adjourned, Jazz made a point to ride the elevator down with Ludlow and Fort.

"Well, gentlemen," Jazz said, "Mr. Hayes should be happy with the minor adjustment we made to the roofing bid requirements."

"I was glad to sponsor the Amendment, but what's the difference?" Fort asked.

"Al, of all the potential bidders for the county roof contract, Hayes' company is the only one with a $500,000 bond," Ludlow said.

"Yes, that happy coincidence is correct," Jazz said, "and I'm sure Mr. Hayes will remember the sponsors of that Amendment when he considers making donations at election time. Now, how about some supper at Mr. Bala's Marina? The view of the ice moving down the river should be very heartening, showing us that summer cannot be far off."

When they sat down to dinner and had ordered drinks, Jazz informed his younger colleagues about the sometimes staid, and sometimes colorful, backgrounds of their fellow members of the legislature. "Get to know your fellow legislators well. Know their concerns. Find out who their friends are. Discover who has wronged them in the past and keep these facts in the back of your mind."

Jazz hoped the two younger county legislators were paying attention to his advice. They were both in their early thirties, he figured, and in Jazz's experience, youth was impatient. He had been amongst the first elected to the newly established County Legislature and had helped establish the ways and means of its operations. The Board of Supervisors that the Legislature replaced had been invariably tribal, parochial and severely divided between the city and the suburbs.

With the new County Legislature and Executive, there were opportunities, and, he thought, if these young men could grasp the folkways of lawmaking and avoid some of the crudities that had ruined more than one career in politics, they could prosper together.

After his term as mayor of Buffalo, Jazz had returned to his law practice and watched as the clouds of controversy that hovered over his administration dissipated. When the courts had insisted on proportional representation for local legislative bodies, New York State decided to redesign the county government in Erie County, and the Republican governor sought fellow Republicans, a minority in Western New York, to establish the new workings. Jazz had been one of the handful of loyalists picked to draw the district lines, which gave the G.O.P. rather more representation in the new County Legislature than perhaps their numbers warranted. He also designed one particular district to encompass his life-long neighborhood on the East Side of Buffalo, where his constituents would post red and white "JAZZ!" campaign posters on their homes and businesses. However, although he still maintained his law office and the apartment above it for his residence of record on Broadway, and he still visited the clubhouses and church festivals to speak of past glories in that declining neighborhood, he and his wife spent most of their time at their rancher in the countryside east of the city. "When the kids were grown, we didn't need the big house on Woltz anymore," he explained.

Jazz worried about the two young men. Even now, finishing their quiet dinner in the marina's restaurant overlooking the river, he could tell they wanted to be up and gone, Ludlow's foot tapping the floor continuously throughout the meal.

"There are going to be a number of complex issues before us in the Legislature with this domed stadium project, gentlemen. There will be the selection of a site. Designers – architects, engineers, construction firms – will have to be chosen. The financing will be huge

100

– picking the firms to sell the bonds, deciding the amount of the issue, insurance, the list goes on and on, and we in the Legislature will be making those decisions. Any number of people and firms will be bidding on these matters, and they will be competing very fervently to be picked. This may be the biggest issue before the Legislature in our careers, men. It is an opportunity not to be trifled with, to be sure." Jazz paused, then concluded, "Well, I've rambled on long enough, and there are families awaiting us at home."

Fort reached for his wallet. Jazz held up his hand. "No, no, this one's on me. You've listened to me talk throughout dinner, it's the least I could do."

Fort stood up and straightened his dark suit coat over his linebacker's torso. "Thanks, Jazz. I'll get the next one," he said. Ludlow also stood up, buttoning his plaid sports coat and slicking back his thinning dark hair. "Great dinner, Jazz. Will see you at the next meeting two Thursdays from now."

Out in the parking lot, Jazz observed the two young men get in their cars and drive away, Fort in his older station wagon, and Ludlow in a new Ford Torino. On the back of the Torino's bumper were two stickers. One in red, white and blue read "Ludlow for Legislator Now!" and the other "No More Snow, Football in the Dome!" Impatience, Jazz thought. I'll have to keep an eye on that young man.

33.

Al Fort went over to the bench and listened to the players' comments as they came into the locker room, their cleats clacking loudly on the concrete floor.

"I'm beat, man. Those last wind sprints did me in."

"It's the hills, they get me every time."

When they had settled down, Fort put one foot up on the bench and spoke.

"Last practice before the season starts, boys. You know what we're up against – last year's champs were mostly juniors, and they've only gotten better. You practiced hard, in all kinds of weather – you guys didn't skip practice, and that attitude will make you winners. This last week I had you finish up practice with wind sprints up the hill in the park. There's two reasons for that – I don't want your energy to fade in the last innings, especially if a game goes into extra innings, and two, to get you extra quickness for fielding and stealing bases – that can make all the difference in a tight game. Tomorrow, when you get out there, you'll be ready. You're the best team I've worked with in years, men. Don't leave anything behind. Play as hard as you can all the time tomorrow. You've shown me you've got the skills – hitting, pitching and fielding, and you've got the character to beat any team in the league, and tomorrow you'll show everyone. Now, get your hands in here." Blue-sleeved arms reached into the crowded circle.

"Ready! One, two, three, VICTORY!"

Cheers and whistles went up as the players moved back to their spots and began undressing. A lanky youth with a sweatshirt covered with frozen mud came up to Fort.

"Hey coach, you gotta minute?"

"Sure, Frankie. C'mon in the office."

Once they were alone, the youth nodded, hesitated and then said, "Coach, I was talking to the guys, and we were wondering if you could lift Mitch's suspension for this opening game. He's a senior, and he feels bad about it and I know he hasn't touched any pot since he got caught that time..."

"Frankie, you're a good team captain and loyal to your men. It took guts to come up to me and stand up for Mitch. I admire that. But remember what I said about character? Huh? I laid down the rules when we started to practice. Mitch knew them and broke them. And not just once, either. If I let him back for this game, all the guys who did follow the rules will look like saps and what I said about showing character will mean nothing. I'm sorry, Frank, but I'm sticking to my guns on this one, and Mitch watches the game from the stands. Hopefully, he'll learn from this and be a better man down the line because of it."

The boy nodded his head and said, "Ok, coach."

"Alright, then. Go home, get a good meal and rest up that big right arm. How does it feel?"

The boy rotated his shoulder. "Good, coach, I'll be ready."

"Put a heating pad on it if it's sore. That'll help. But no matter what, you and the rest of the guys'll be ready."

As Frankie left the coach's office, Fort thought, I'll never forget what AD Ray told all the coaches when I was a senior playing first base here. "We're building character here first, then winning athletes. Qualities that will define these young men for the rest of their lives. Do it right and they'll be champions at whatever they take up, and of good character for the rest of their lives."

34.

When the foreman pointed to his watch, Tom shut down the forklift, undid the bandana around his head and wiped his face as he walked to the breakroom. The other guys all went for coffee, but Tom fished out some change from his jeans and got a 7-Up. Sitting down at the table, he said, "I don't know how you guys drink coffee all day long like that."

"Caffeine, kid, caffeine," gray haired Nick said. "Do it for as many years as I have and you'll need every bit of cranking power you can get to work through the day."

Tom nodded and picked up the front section of that morning's Courier-Express. Just under the fold he read, "Calley My Lai Trial to Be Delayed. Both sides request postponement to prepare further"

"Huh, that's a mess," Nick said, looking over Tom's shoulder.

"It's bullshit, if you ask me," Lee said. "Any one of those people could've been planting mines. That's how most of those GIs were getting hurt around there."

"But shooting unarmed women and kids? That's insane!" Nick retorted.

Tom thought of his wounded brother in the hospital in Washington, and then of the pictures of the dead black pajamaed Viet Cong on TV, and the bodies of the women and children from the massacre at My Lai.

"Little kids, man. They just shot everyone there. Said they raped some women, too, then killed them. You can't justify that, man!" Tom said.

Everyone started shouting his opinion, and it kept up until break time was over. All the warehousemen went back to work, angry and silent.

The whole war is dead wrong, Tom thought. The whole system isn't working. Maybe HR is right. Maybe the whole system is rotten... Rory... How could Rory take part in something like this war?

35.

Rex Yarborough stood up before the please remain seated light was extinguished, tugged on the tail of his black sharkskin suit coat, bounced on his toes, cracked his knuckles and said, "Showtime, folks, time to show these Yankees how a big production is run."

The rest of the staff, all dressed in gray or khaki, unbuckled their seat belts and followed the former senator to the forward hatch of the plane. A capped stewardess gently laid her hand on the door's lock to prevent the impatient passengers opening it before the air stairs were in place.

When the hatch swung open, the senator looked sternly over the heads of the thirty or so people there to greet him, walked swiftly down the steps and grasped Bill Correlli's outstretched hand in both of his.

"Hello, partner!" he boomed, "It is a pleasure to finally visit your great city." Turning slightly to his left and nodding, "My wife Doreen," who reached forward and smiled as Chip whispered names from his right.

"Ah, the honorable Mr. Burgos. The man who leads his county to greatness. A pleasure, sir, a very great pleasure to meet you." Before anyone could guide him, the senator strode through the assembled reporters and politicians to the array of microphones, waited for the "on" lights of the television cameras to light and began speaking as the crowd reassembled around him.

"Today, good people of Buffalo and Erie County, marks a new beginning in your long and distinguished history. Today, Yarborough and Associates brings the world-famous design team of Steuart, Jones and Burrows from Houston and joins with," he said, slamming his hands together in front of himself, " Mr. Correlli's firm and their designers, the renowned Guyton Thomas firm, and your great civic leaders in building a sports and entertainment complex the like of which you've never seen. We will not only bring you a domed stadium for your football team, but a major league baseball franchise, a world class golf course, an amusement park that will make Mr. Walt Disney jealous, shopping venues it will take hours to simply walk through... in-of-doors I might add... and all surrounded by parks and houses designed by these great architects. The future has arrived for Western New York, my friends, and it's going to be built in Lancaster!" With that, he turned and led the crowd through the airport. Even the weariest travelers turned to watch the short man with the long stride get out ahead of the politicians and businessmen to the waiting limousine.

Rolling down the Kensington Expressway, Yarborough silently observed the abandoned stores on the nearby streets covered with graffiti, the darkened wooden houses with the peeling paint and the empty lots while County Executive Burgos assured him of the Legislature's enthusiasm for the project. As they detoured through Delaware Park on the mayor's directions, the senator spoke.

"Ahh, some of Mr. Olmsted's finest work," he said, interrupting the mayor's reciting the names of the Bills' draft choices. As they went around Gates Circle with the fountain's water jet lit in red, white and blue for the occasion, he said, "Wonderful work, that." When they pulled up in front of the white pillared Park Lane Restaurant, "Formerly the Porter Norton Mansion, I believe, gentlemen," he commented to his staff, and to the mayor, "Isn't that correct, sir?" as he strode into the octagonal entry hall.

"Yes, yes, I believe it is," the mayor followed, then introduced him to the portly owner in a red tuxedo jacket, who bowed and shook his hand.

"Welcome to Buffalo, Senator Yarborough," he said, with more than a trace of his native Greece. He nodded to the white coated maître d', who led them to the Veranda Room, where a table for twenty was prepared.

As water glasses were filled and drink orders taken, Yarborough raised a finger to Chip, who produced a fresh pack of Marlboros. Yarborough pulled a cut-glass ashtray front and center, and, after lighting up, kept the pack in his left hand, turning it over end-to-end while he listened to the politicians talk.

Webb and Yarborough bracketed Correlli at the table.

"You're in the big time now, Bill," Webb said. "The man from Texas has got the financing and experience to make this dream come true."

"Titus, I can't thank you enough for setting this up with Yarborough and the rest of it," Correlli said. "You even came up with the name of the company for this development – Yarcor Enterprises."

"This area's been good to my family, Bill. I want to see it prosper again. We just had to find the right people with the vision to see it happen. It's too bad the local financial community wouldn't get on board."

Salads were served, followed by venison, lamb and beef ("It had better be perfect!" the owner warned the chef, "Dis man is from big cattle country!"). The legislators jockeyed for position to hear the great builder's words. As port was being poured and a new ashtray replaced the filled one before him, the Texan leaned towards Correlli and told him, "Billy, there are two keys to making this Yarcor development a success. One, you've got to keep the stadium filled. It's absolutely necessary to get a Major League Baseball franchise in there, and when the football and baseball teams aren't in town, get boxing, concerts, rodeos, circuses, conventions, what have you, in there. I've got a staff working night and day to make sure there's tickets being sold for the dome each and every day – and tours! Why, they're calling the Astrodome the 8th Wonder of the World! Sell it as such, boy, sell it, and you'll get tourists in there to gawk at everything from the Astroturf to the air conditioners."

"The second key, my friend, is the surrounding development. The amusement park, the golf course, the housing developments and the shopping mall. They've all got to be up and running at the same time for this to work. One part falls out and we'll both get too close to the dollar knife, son."

Correlli nodded and wiped his brow. Ludlow looked at Fort and gave him a thumbs up. After dinner, as they walked to their cars on elm shaded Chapin Parkway, Ludlow turned to Fort and said, "This is going to work out just fine, buddy."

"What do you mean?" Fort answered. "This development has a long way to go, and a lot can go wrong. And who knows if this will go over with the public? A lot of my constituents keep telling me $50 million's too much money to spend on a stadium."

Ludlow stopped and turned to him. "I mean, my friend, that these guys," he said, jerking his thumb towards the limousine gliding by, "are going to be spending a lot of dough to get this together, and our re-election campaigns can be the beneficiaries of some of it. They're going to need our votes to get it through."

Fort looked down, his hands in his pockets. "Uh huh," he said, and pulled out the keys to the station wagon with the worn seats.

36.

Al Fort was sitting at the kitchen table paying bills when his daughter rushed to answer the phone.

"Hi!... Oh... Dad, it's Mr. Ludlow." Fort looked up as she stretched the cord over to where he sat.

"Not Jackie, huh?" he smiled as he took the receiver. "Hello, Gus. What's up?"

"Did you get the invite yet?"

"What invite?"

"From the developers. The Texans want to bring us down to Houston, show us what they can do."

"Wow, that'll be a trip to remember."

"Sure will. And that's where we can make the proposition to them."

Fort looked around to see who might be listening. "I dunno, Gus. I know some of the other guys have done it with developers, but it just doesn't seem right."

"Hey, they want to convince us this is a good deal for Erie County, I say, convince me. They got more money than God, let 'em spend it. They get what they want, and we get re-elected."

"Yeah, but you've been talking a lot more than just some regular campaign contributions."

"Damn right I am. Look, when you wanted to get your job with the city, you knew it was going to cost you contributions to the party to get it, right?"

"Yeah, but that's what I had to do."

"And they're still collecting on that, aren't they? What is it, these days?"

"Uh, well..."

"Time for somebody else to pay you back for that, my friend. Somebody with plenty of cash that will never miss it. Nobody gets hurt here, Al, it's not like we're stealing it, it's just a bonus, and a once in a lifetime opportunity, my friend."

"Yeah, lemme think about it, Gus," he said, staring at the orthodontist's bill on top of the stack of invoices, stamped overdue.

"Yeah, think about it, Al, and be looking out for the invite to Houston. Wait until we get a look at the Astrodome. Imagine that in Buffalo. Everybody wins on this deal."

The moment he hung up, the phone rang again.

"Honey, it's me," his wife said. "I'm over at bingo and the car won't start."

"Damn it. Ok, lemme go call Orslitz. We'll be by in a little bit to get it jump started." Second time for that, he thought. I'm getting sick and tired of that damned old car breaking down.

37.

"You're going to get a broken neck, Al," Ludlow said.

"What?" Fort returned.

"The way you're ogling everything here. You'll twist your neck until it breaks."

"And this, gentlemen, is the foyer to the Presidential Suite," the Astrodome tour guide said. "The statue here is of Demosthenes, the great Greek statesman. The curving stairway, designed by Prentiss and Hughes, leads to the upstairs bedroom, which is modeled after the Lincoln Bedroom in the White House."

When the tour of the Astrodome hotel was completed, the businessmen and politicians from Buffalo were treated to lunch in the New Orleans Kitchen on the sixth level. Ludlow made a point to see that he and Fort were seated with Seth Davies from the Buffalo architectural firm Guyton Thomas and the principals of Steuart, Jones and Burrows from Texas. Jazz nodded at Chip and slid into the chair next to Yarborough.

As everyone but himself sat down, the senator made a sweeping gesture with his right hand at the sights beyond the glass front of the restaurant where the Lucite dome glittered in the Texas sunlight over the air conditioned 60,000 seats.

"Well, gentlemen, what do you think of our Astrodome?"

"Amazing, simply amazing," Seth Davies, the lead architect from Guyton Thomas, said, eyeglasses shaking loose from his reddened face.

Yarborough smiled and, tapping Buffalo's current mayor on the shoulder to his right, said, "The décor in the New Orleans Room here was designed by Toulee of Paris. I have found that there is no point to settling for the second rate, and that's why the Astrodome complex has become the 8th Wonder of the World." Leaning away from the current mayor of Buffalo and towards Jazz on his left, Yarborough said in a lower tone, "Don't you agree, mayor?"

"I certainly do, Senator. Everything first-class and," Jazz said, "leave nothing to chance," to which Yarborough nodded, smiling.

As they took away the dishes from the main course, Jazz and Yarborough overheard Ludlow talking about how his support as majority leader was needed for the passage of any bill in the County Legislature.

Yarborough tapped the ash off his cigarette, tilted his head towards Ludlow, then turned back towards Jazz and said in a low voice, "A very confident man, your Mr. Ludlow, mayor. Very confident. Let us hope he is not reckless in his enthusiasm."

"Youth, Senator, youth. He has the optimism of youth."

Throughout lunch, Yarborough kept pointing out the grand features of the Astrodome while Jazz and the others listened. When waiters appeared from all points carrying dessert plates, he stood up and spoke up for the entire room to hear.

"And this piece-de-resistance, gentlemen, is a New Orleans specialty – praline monkey bread pudding, designed exclusively for you by Chef Guadagna himself," at which Yarborough extended his arm palm-up towards the white hatted chef who appeared and bowed.

Yarborough settled back into his seat, and everyone picked up their forks in anticipation as the dessert was put before them.

"I love this," Yarborough said, putting his fork into the doughy sweet.

Seeing Steuart rise from the table, Jazz also quietly excused himself and headed for the men's room. Once there, he admired the marble vanities and ceramic tile floors, and his glance about the room showed him and Steuart to be alone. "Even the Gent's Room is first class, Mr. Steuart."

Picking up a linen towel, Steuart said, "No detail is too small to be overlooked for a project like this, Mr. Jezerowski."

"I can see that," Jazz said, "It doesn't pay to leave anything to chance."

"I quite agree," Steuart said, wiping his hands.

"In that vein, I know that my support would be unwavering for the current project if I could be certain that the location of the coliseum was in the ideal spot."

"I understand, Mr. Mayor, I understand you completely." Lowering his voice, he went on. "The man you should speak to is a most capable fellow. He is a local real estate agent by the name of Hanlon. He lives in what you good people call South Buffalo, I believe."

So, Johnny Hanlon's this outfit's straw buyer, Jazz thought. The two men looked each other in the eye, nodded, and returned to dessert.

"Wait 'til you see what we can do for your coliseum, gentlemen," Jones said at the other end of the table. "And I have to say," he added, clamping his hand on Davies's shoulder, "this man's firm has made inestimable contributions to the task. Why, he had the soil samples analyzed, the region's water table and the utilities all mapped out and informed us about a great many things about building on your Niagara Frontier as soon as we asked. Very prompt and extremely detailed. This is going to be a great partnership for this tremendous project."

"Maybe, gentlemen, myself and Mr. Fort could help explain things about the political situation to you, as well," Ludlow said.

"Well, that'd be just fine, young man, just fine. Always like to get an understanding of local ways when doing business, now, don't we, Burrows?"

"We surely do, Mr. Jones, we surely do."

"That being the case, let me buy you guys a drink at the bar after lunch," Ludlow said, his eyes moving from one principal to another. They got up, and Ludlow grinned as he dropped his napkin and winked at Fort.

Ludlow placed himself at the end, with the three architectural principals lined up next to him, Davies just beyond and Fort posted next to him. He dropped a fifty on the bar and signaled the white-coated barman for a round with his index finger. He took a sip of Galliano, and the others stood quietly drinking until the barman moved away. Davies, poking his glasses back up his nose, said, "I always drink Drambuie after a great meal."

"Here's to us, gentlemen, and to the building of a great stadium," Ludlow toasted. They all raised their glasses.

"I figure this project will take five to six years to finish, men. That means numerous votes in the Legislature over at least two election cycles. Several campaigns to make sure the votes go your way, especially for Mr. Fort and myself. We'll need financial help to make sure we can be there in the legislature for you guys, right to the finish. The papers are saying the vote is close now, but two solid votes going right down the line on this should help you sleep soundly at night, whatever suite you're in."

While Jones and Burrows looked down, Steuart looked Ludlow in the eye and said, "How much support do you think would be adequate, Mr. Ludlow?"

"Well, I figure the bill for planning and engineering stands at $1.6 million, and the county's planning on selling $50 million in bonds, so $100,000 doesn't seem too much to us, does it, Al?"

115

They all turned and looked at Fort, who nodded. Davies signaled for another Drambuie.

Waiting until the bartender was gone, Steuart said, "My understanding, sir, is that less than half that amount is customary in your part of the country."

"Normally, yes. But this is an extraordinary project, as y'all have been telling us."

"Perhaps then, we could contribute $50,000 through outside channels, as they say, and maximize the campaign contributions through public means, Mr. Ludlow. Would that suit you sir?"

"I think that's an adequate compromise, Mr. Steuart. What do think, Al?"

Fort pulled his tie loose and nodded.

"Well, it's agreed then," Steuart said. "Mr. Davies here will make the necessary arrangements," he added, looking at the blinking architect.

38.

Jazz left his office on Broadway and smelled smoke – burning paint and old wood smoke. Hearing sirens, he looked up the street and spotted the flashing red lights of the fire trucks as they pulled up to a two-story commercial building.

I'll be damned, he thought. That looks like it might be Ocky's old place on fire. Jazz got in his car and drove the few blocks down, leaving his Oldsmobile double-parked behind a chief's car. As soon as an aerial ladder reached the roof, black-coated firemen scrambled up it with power saws and axes and began cutting holes. Orange flames and black smoke emitted from the upper floor windows as other fire-fighters dragged heavy hose lines through the front door into the restaurant.

Jazz stayed across the street to keep the smoke out of his clothes.

Huh. I wonder what Ocky would think now, Jazz thought. He always stashed money in the floors. I hope he got it all when he moved out.

Watching the firemen work, Jazz thought about how Ocky's wife had run the place while he was away. When Jazz picked him up at the release center at Wallkill, his first words were, "I'm going to sell the place, Jazz, and get the hell out of Buffalo."

"I'll get it sold for you, pal," Jazz said. "You just take it easy and I'll take care of everything."

Jazz went to the Small Business Administration and found a loan program for minorities. Then he went to Councilman Edwards, who found him Maurice with an idea for a soul food place and started lining up other pols to get it through. Frankowski was tough, but Jazz convinced him that encouraging minority business was better than no business. Maurice was grateful. So grateful, in fact, that he paid for his son Chet Jezerowski's last year in school.

"Think it was an accident?" the voice said at Jazz's elbow.

Jazz turned slowly. "Well, if it isn't Mr. Bray of the Fourth Estate. Working the fire beat, are we?" he said, remembering that behind the cherubic face was a mind like a steel trap.

"Of course. Wasn't this Ocky Owczarczak's place before he left town, Mayor?"

"It certainly was, Mr. Bray, it certainly was. And I was proud to assist Maurice in getting the loan to buy it. He's one of the up-and-coming minority businessmen in the neighborhood now. This is tragic, truly tragic."

"No opinions on the cause of the fire? Do you catch a whiff of gasoline like I do, Mr. Mayor?"

"I'm certain that the fire department will determine the cause soon enough."

Bray nodded and smiled, then went over to the white helmeted chief giving orders.

39.

Jazz was in his law office on Broadway on a quiet Saturday morning, sitting at the big mahogany desk he'd had in his office in City Hall when he was mayor. Checking the clock given to him years before by the Polish Falcons, he judged his wife's cousin Ted Engler would be just sitting down to do paperwork in his own office and dialed the housing contractor's number.

"Top Flite Construction. Ted."

"Cousin Theodore, Jazz here. No rest for the weary, eh?"

"Force of long habit, Jazz. Gotta get the details taken care of if you want to get ahead in this world." Ted was always glad to hear from his cousin's well-connected husband.

"Diligence, cuz, diligence. It's what keeps our heads above water these days. Speaking of which, I think I may have found some opportunities for us both that I'd like to discuss with you over lunch. That is, if you can break away around noon today."

"Sure Jazz, always looking for good places to put some houses, even if the market is slow these days."

"Building the houses may not even be necessary in this instance," Jazz said as he flipped through the Yellow Pages until he came to the H's and found the listing for Hanlon Commercial Real Estate. Writing down the number, he finished his call with Engler and made a long-distance call to Nevada.

"Con's House of Cards, Ocky speaking."

"Cornelius, my old friend, how's the sunshine out west?"

"Bright, Jazz, very bright. Everybody's getting a good tan lately."

"Excellent, Ocky, excellent. I wish I could get some of that sunshine back east here. It has been a bit dreary lately, but things could brighten up with a few rays of your excellent Nevada sun."

"How many rays were you thinking, Jazz?"

"Oh, about twenty rays of sunshine would really put us in a great mood, Ocky."

"Not a problem, Jazz. When are you and the Missus coming out here?"

"Well, this domed stadium deal is just heating up here, Ock. I'd like to leave that as my legacy to Erie County. When all that's said and done, I might even retire from politics. Between you and me, Ocky, now that the kids are up and gone, we might even think about retiring altogether and relocating out west with you, my old friend."

40.

Seth Davies climbed out of the Pontiac and hung on to the door until he was sure of his footing in the parking lot. Stephanie looked at him over the hood.

"Watch how much you drink tonight," she said.

He nodded and put away his glasses as they walked up the steps and through the doors that read "Buffalo Launch Club." The heat inside caused his face to flush as Stephanie grabbed his arm and waved to a couple across the foyer.

"Look, it's Jim and Dot! Hello, dear. We haven't seen you since we took the boat out of the water last year."

Seth took her coat and went to check it in the coatroom when Landice Cooper came out, bending over to adjust her shoe.

"Landice, hello," he said, glancing at her exposed bosom in the low-cut dress and remembering a time years ago.

"Oh, hi, Seth," she said, brushing a blonde lock back into her coiffure. "You here for the installment of officers?"

"Most certainly..."

"Good. I'll sit with you then. Charley and I are through, if you haven't heard, and I came by myself," she said with just the slightest slur.

"Uh, fine, Landice. Let me put our coats away, and I'll take you over to Stephanie."

When they met with Stephanie at the entrance to the dining room, Stephanie's eyes went wide.

"Landice," she said.

"Stephanie," Landice answered, embracing her. "I'm going stag tonight, dear, and Seth said it was ok to sit with you." Stephanie's glance at Seth said that it was not all right, but she marched over to the table and sat down. Stephanie placed herself between the two, sliding her own chair closer to Seth.

"There we are, kids," Landice said, pulling up a strap to her dress. She waved to a waiter. "Let's have a cocktail before dinner, shall we?"

Nobody at their table heard much of what the speakers said, with Stephanie glaring at Seth every time his eyes settled on Landice's boobs. When Landice waved to order brandies after dinner, Stephanie gently put her hand on Seth's and said, "Not for us, dear, Seth has to drive us back to Tonawanda."

He nodded, his mind on the sweaty encounter outside years ago.

The ride back across Grand Island was silent. After they crossed the bridge, Seth turned on the radio and began spinning the dial through the stations.

"Ought to get the weather report for tomorrow."

"I know about you and her, from before," Stephanie said, and Seth kept changing the channels. Getting out of the car in the driveway, she said, "You better stay away from that bitch," and slammed the car door.

41.

Rory sat on the bed and picked up the tray table with the hook arm and settled it across his thighs. He reached into the drawer in the table next to his bed and pulled out the writing tablet and a pen, then wiped his good eye so it would focus better. He exhaled and started writing.

> *Tom,*
> *When are you coming down to visit? Mom and dad have been here, but you're always in school or something. You got some girl stashed in that apartment of yours in Allentown?*

He stopped, remembering. He didn't come to my graduation from Basic Training at Ft. Dix, either.

> *I've got a new arm and a leg, and they're working on my face. I was almost as ugly as you are for a while there, but when I get back, I'll be able to drive. The money's in the bank, and when the Army cuts me loose, I'm going to buy a car. It'll be used, but we'll be able to get around. Won't be back until fall or winter most likely, so I'll miss the beach this year. Getting a tan wouldn't match my new limbs anyway.*

He always was a little squeamish about blood and guts, maybe that's why he hasn't been down.

How's things going at school? I read about all the trouble on the UB campus. I saw a picture of those punks waving a NVA flag at a demonstration. They must be out of their minds to fall for that bullshit. Anyway, keep your grades up. Uncle Sam's got a billet waiting for you at Ft. Dix if you don't!

Send me a letter, you bum. Catch a bus and come down. Now that I'm getting mobile, we can go hang out in D.C.

-Rory

Rory remembered when he got his driver's license. No more practicing driving with dad, he was on his own, and couldn't think of enough reasons to get behind the wheel. Trips to the store for mom, put gas in the car for dad, anything, and Tommy always wanted to go with him. His younger brother, sitting next to him, buckled in the front seat, smiling. Mom worried, watching them go with her arms crossed, dad telling her they'll be fine. I'll be able to drive again with the prosthesis. I'll just have to be careful because of just having one eye now. He touched the bandages over the place where his eye would be. I guess things will never be the same again, he thought as he folded the letter up and put it in the envelope.

42.

Kevin stuck his elbow out the pickup's window, the sun feeling good on his arm and face.

"Where we headed first, palsy?" his partner Jack asked, looking over the clipboard list of vending clients and pouring black coffee down.

"West side today. Figure we'd go to the Last Call, then head over to Record Theater and pick up some of the new 45's."

"Hey, as long as we're on the west side..." and Kevin smiled as Jack said, "Let's have some laughs and pick up Sammy."

Rolling slowly down a leafy street of two story wooden houses, they pulled up in front of a gray house badly in need of new paint. Parking out front, they walked up the creaking steps and pounded on the door. They knew that the bell hadn't worked for years and Sammy had no intention of fixing it, much less paying someone to fix it.

The door swung open and a bowed man in striped pajamas bellowed, "All right! All right, you sons-a-bitches, get in here while I get dressed. Better still, get the hell out and get me some coffee. Ask the Spanish broad at the store on the corner, she knows how I like it."

Shaking their heads and laughing, the two young men did as they were bidden.

"You want coffee for Sammy?" the girl behind the counter said. "Ok, take it to him, here. Keep that crazy old man outta here today. He always talk sex to me."

When they returned, Sammy was waiting on the porch, spiky gray hair angled back, rumpled brown suit, white shirt, stained black and gold striped tie, no shave.

"It better be hot, you bastards, or I'll spank that bitch like she needs it! All right, let's go," Sammy said, jumping in the front seat of the pickup. "Where we headed first?"

"The Last Call on Ferry. We've gotta cash out the juke and the cigarette machine there," Jackie said.

"Great! Testa, Scaduto and those guys'll be in there," Sammy said, muttering "Let's see here…" and fishing a golfer's pencil out of a suit coat pocket.

Pulling up in front of the one story yellow brick bar, Sammy hopped out of the pickup, dropped his coffee cup in the gutter and went inside, greeted by the men who had spotted him through the bar's picture window.

"Whattya need, boys, whattya need?" he said, pulling a small white pad out of the other coat pocket. Greetings exchanged, they started.

"What's the line on the Yankees game?"

"Oakland is minus one-thirty," Sammy said.

"Hah!" one bettor said. "The morning paper had 'em at one-sixty-five."

It went on like that while Jack and Kevin changed records on the jukebox, refilled the cigarette machine, and laughed at Sammy's act.

"Gimme a VO with plain water on the side, Carmine, and stugatz here is payin'," Sammy said, indicating a bespectacled man with a snap brim hat who shook his head while his friends laughed.

When they got back in the truck, Sammy said, "That damned Riccio, he'll never learn. Finally paid up for last week and takes a sucker bet on the Cardinals today. That one," he said, putting a note sheet in an inner pocket, "I'll book on the side."

They made several similar stops, Sammy knowing people everywhere, taking bets and cadging drinks. Around noon he announced, "Ok, boys, it's lunchtime. My treat. Let's go to the Queen's Plate."

Soon the pickup truck was in the parking lot of a restaurant near the Peace Bridge to Canada, a quiet place with white tablecloths. Just inside the front door, Sammy nodded to the owner, Louie, and looked over the business crowd at the bar.

"Go ahead, boys, there's lunch," Sammy said, indicating a side table with a large complimentary tureen of split pea soup, crackers and bread. The two vendors chuckled, exchanged greetings with the owner, and went to get bowls of soup and watch the show while Sammy sidled next to a brunette in a tight red Birkin dress at the bar.

On the other side of the brunette sat a tall thin man with wavy white hair drinking scotch. He adjusted his glasses and watched with interest as Sammy went to work on the much younger woman, starting with a drawn-out hello and calling for drinks for both of them. The bartender complied and the woman smiled, took the tiniest of sips and kept her eyes down while Sammy speculated on her height and weight.

"I'm amazing that way. I can tell a girl's sizes just from the way she carries herself, and you, my dear, do it with style," Sammy said.

"I've got to get back to work," she said, still smiling.

"Here's your check, Nicole," the bartender announced, sliding the check to her.

"Of course, Nicole. I should have known," Sammy said as she paid and retreated out of the bar.

Sammy pulled a pack of Tareytons out of a suit coat pocket and lit up. "She'll be back," he said. "I got her name this time," he said to the scotch drinker, "I'll find out what's in those 36C cups next time."

The scotch drinker lifted a finger and the bartender refilled the rocks glass with J & B.

"Not heading back to the office, huh?" Sammy commented.

"We just finished lunch with a client, and one of the partners is taking him to the airport. He's headed back to Houston with plans for the new stadium."

"Uh huh. So, you're a builder? Lots of construction guys come in here and make deals. You know Fatta?"

"Well, I've heard the name, of course. But no, I'm an architect. With Guyton Thomas in the Tishman Building. Seth Davies," he said, extending his hand.

"Sam Messina," Sammy said, taking it.

"You ready, Sammy?" Kevin said, waiting by the door with Jack.

"Yeah, I'm ready," Sammy replied, "as soon as you get my check, Kevin."

"Your check? Why would I get your check?"

"Hey! I bought the lunch, didn't I? Pay the man, you cheapskate."

Laughing and arguing, the two vendors and Sammy left. "Who was that guy?" Seth asked the bartender.

"Sammy M," the bartender answered. "He's the owner's cousin. Comes in regular, but usually around dinner time."

"Hmm, interesting. What's he do?"

"A little of this, a little of that," the bartender said, removing Sammy's empty glass and wiping down the bar.

Two more scotches and Seth figured the partners would be on their way back from the airport, so he returned to the office to check the results on the soil samples his assistant had collected and think about the money the stadium deal would bring.

43.

Seth showed up at the Queen's Plate regularly for about two weeks, watching the women and the locals, including Sammy. Quietly, Sammy would nod at one or the other, then approach, hear a few quiet words and return to his place at the bar. One Friday night Sammy was standing next to him and Seth heard, "Fifty on the Mets? Done." Sammy turned and saw a glassy-eyed Seth staring at him.

"Something I can do for you, pal?"

Seth focused his eyes and leaned forward. He raised a finger and said, "I think I have some work for you."

"What are you talking about?"

"Jus' a simple delivery or two. Easy," he said, waving a hand before him.

"I don't do dope, you drunk."

"Nah, nah, nah. Jus' cash. Gotta be delivered to some...guys in office."

"This gotta do with the big construction you were talkin' about?"

Seth leaned back quickly. "You remember that?"

"It works just fine," Sammy said, tapping his head with his forefinger.

"Good. Job's gotta be done on the qt, know what I mean?"

"Yeah, I know, but are you gonna remember tomorrow?"

Seth threw his chin up and frowned.

Sammy looked right back at him. "Alright. If you do, you buy the coffee at Nick's Amherst tomorrow at 9:00."

"I'm in my office at 9:00."

"Tell them you've got a meeting with a client, dummy. Hey, Nicole! Let's look at you!"

44.

Seth Davies leaned forward in the shower, his hands on the faucets, the water pouring over his head for a good five minutes. When he finally emerged from the bathroom showered, shaved and thinking clearly, he walked into their bedroom to find his wife gripping the clothes he'd dumped on the floor the previous night just below her chin.

"You were with her again last night, weren't you?"

"What? Don't be ridiculous, Stephanie, I was with the Seneca clients having dinner."

"There's, there's, oh God, it's all over your shorts!"

"We ate at Chef's, spilled some clam sauce."

"You liar!" she shouted, throwing the clothes at him. "You were with that whore from the club again! Ohhh!" She stomped past him, and he heard her Chrysler squeal out of the driveway as he squeezed Visine into his eyes until it ran down his cheeks.

He looked through his pockets until he found the bar nap. "Nick's – Amherst," it read. He looked it up in the phone book. Yeah, ok, it's in Buffalo, in Black Rock, not the Town of Amherst. Half an hour later, Sammy was staring at him when he came through the door.

"You made it," he said, signaling for another coffee. Seth looked around and saw only the waitress and a man with bushy hair standing behind the register reading the morning paper.

"Don't worry, nobody's going to remember you," Sammy said.

Davies waited until the waitress had brought the coffee and left. He cleared his throat and said, "I understand you do a number of odd jobs."

"Get to the point, Mr. Architect."

"Can you deliver some money for me?"

Sammy's eyes lit up. "To who?"

"Two public figures."

"Football players? Politicians? Who?"

Davies whispered, "County Legislators."

"Which ones?"

"Fort and Ludlow."

"I get two-fifty apiece. I'll tell you where and when, when you give me the money."

"You see..."

"I couldn't give a shit. Just get the money...and don't say nothing to that drunk broad you hang out with, either, dummy."

The man at the register suddenly crushed the newspaper and shredded it, shouting, "What the hell's the matter with those assholes! First, it's fifty million for a football stadium! Now, it's seventy million! Who's gonna pay for this bullshit! My goddamn taxes!"

Davies jolted upright at the commotion, and Sammy was halfway to the door, shaking his head, laughing. Pissant doesn't have the slightest idea what he's doing, Sammy thought.

45.

Seth Davies looked around the suburban Tonawanda home he had designed himself, saw the two paintings of Seine bridges they'd bought on vacation in Paris and shuddered. It's over, he thought. Over and done. He picked up the suitcases and, going down the hallway, spied the plaque. "Presented to Seth Davies," it read. "On behalf of the New York State AIA Best Commercial Design Award, 1958." He put down the suitcases, opened one up and placed the plaque between his tweed jacket and a mohair sweater. Closing the case, he took a quick glance out the front window and rushed to get the suitcases in the car. Got to be long gone before she comes back. Wheeling the Pontiac onto the street, he headed back towards the city and a room at the Hotel Graystone. I can hang the plaque up there. I'm going to be living there for quite a while, he thought, taking a sip from his flask.

46.

When Sammy suggested meeting at the Central Train Terminal, Seth Davies paused while Sammy waited for his answer. "Well?" the little man said, staring at him.

"Yes, certainly," the architect said, remembering the rising approach to the soaring art deco building on a Memorial Drive choked with cabs and honking sedans. Inside, the clacking of the changing arrival boards matched the clicking of heels on the terrazzo tiled floors as the light streamed in through Roman arches in the concourse.

"Hey! Meet me on the Curtiss Street side, 10:30 sharp tomorrow morning, and don't be late, you lush."

Davies was lost in thought about trains, and when he looked up, Sammy was gone, the bill unpaid. He tossed three dollars on the table and drove back to the hotel, resisting the urge to drive out to the old railroad station, cold, dark and haunted by more than ghosts this time of night.

When Davies pulled up in front of the terminal at the former Van Dyke Cab stand, there wasn't a car in sight. He checked his watch. 10:05. Plenty of time to look around. He hesitated, worried for a moment about illegal parking, then shook his head and went inside the creaking brass doors and looked around. To his right were the marble and brass grilled ticket booths, abandoned. To his left was a put-up wooden booth, painted institutional green and a sign reading "Train Tickets." Ahead of him stretched the tile floor, puddles of muddy water and trash scattered about it. Pigeons fluttered overhead, flying around nests built in shattered windows at the top of the arches, through which streams of multi-colored light illuminated the dust floating throughout the interior of the concourse. He turned around and left, heading out to where rusting iron posts held up the roofs of the outdoor platforms.

"You cocksucker! You son of a bitch! Whaddya you doin' screwing around in the station?" Sammy shouted, coming out from behind a post. He approached with the tail of his brown raincoat flapping, hunched over and his gray hair spiked up.

"Somebody coulda seen you, you dumb son of a bitch! You got the money?"

"There's nobody around, Sam," Davies replied, stepping through the weeds and withdrawing the brown paper package from under his coat.

"Over here," Sammy signaled, indicating an old baggage cart as he snatched the envelope. Davies looked around, hands in his pockets, while Sammy counted the hundreds and fifties on the rotting wooden cart.

"Our engineers planned the demolition of the old ice house and Pullman service building a few years ago – over there," he said, pointing with a shaking hand.

"Yeah, well, that guy over there's helping in the demolition now," Sammy said, nodding towards a bug-eyed junkie hauling a clanking laundry bag filled with copper pipe along the terminal wall. "It's all here, you bastard. Now get the hell out of here before someone spots us."

Sammy hurried across the weed-choked tracks to where his polished red Buick waited on Hilton Street and drove off.

Suddenly mindful that other junkies might be about, Davies went back to the front of the terminal and left without looking back.

135

47.

Sammy pulled his Buick around the back of Becker's Restaurant, then drove back out onto Bailey. Only two cars in the lot, he thought. Good. Nice and quiet. Checking his watch, he saw he was five minutes early. Just right. Parking on Chauncey, he walked past the office building on the corner and through the back door of Becker's just as Fort came through the front door. A brief nod, and he touched the exposed corner of the manila envelope under his coat. He sat down at the third table and slipped the envelope under the chair's cushion. Just as the yawning waitress came through the swinging door from the kitchen, Sammy was headed back out the rear door.

"Umm, I guess I'll sit here," Fort said, moving rapidly to the table just vacated.

"Sure," the hair-netted woman said, shrugging, "any place you like," noticing the well-dressed man putting his hands on the cushion seat. "Coffee?"

"Uhh, yeah. Coffee. Ok."

The wife must not let him eat out much, she thought, holding out a menu.

"Uhh, no, just coffee today, thanks."

Must be up to something, she thought. Maybe going to meet a girlfriend here.

Fort thought about the money under the seat cushion. It'll get us all caught up on the orthodontist's bills and the new furnace, he thought. The next payment and we'll have a new car.

The waitress brought the coffee and noticed Fort's hands clenched on the table. Girlfriend, she thought.

Fort picked up the cup with both hands and took a sip. Shit, I forgot the cream. He put it down.

The waitress went back into the open kitchen and said to the cook, "The doctor told us my mom has got to start treatment for her congestive heart failure now or she ...."

"Jeese, Chloe, that's bad. You gotta get that taken care of. My Aunt Wanda had the same thing. Her legs swelled up like water balloons."

"Yeah, but where we gonna get the money? She's not old enough for Medicare and insurance won't pay for all of it."

"How much you need, Chloe? I'll front you what I can. You been here a long time. You can pay me back when you can."

Chloe wiped her nose. "Thanks, Ralph. I'll start working doubles to pay you back. I've done it before."

Fort put the coffee down and stood up. I can't do this, he thought. He dropped a dollar on the table and left.

As Sammy drove back past Becker's, he noticed the license plate in the lot that read Erie County No. 18 and shook his head. Oh well, they never saw me, he thought, and patted his coat pocket. Two-fifty each for the delivery as agreed, and an extra C-note for carrying charges, he chuckled. Who the hell they gonna complain to? and he laughed out loud as he headed off down William. Maybe a day at the track, or maybe ride around with the boys – just the thing for a good score like today's, he thought.

48.

"What? You can't do it?" Seth cupped his hand around the receiver and spun in his chair to see if anyone was listening.

"I just can't do it," Fort told him.

"Where... where's the money?"

"I guess still under the cushion, in the restaurant."

"You've got to. You agreed. You told me. You can't go back on your word now."

"I can't. I just can't," Fort said, and hung up the pay phone.

Davies looked at his watch. Damn. It's only 10:00 a.m. No telling where Sammy might be. I've got to find him, tell him to get the money. His hands shook. He took another look around, then went over to the wooden flat file cabinet, opened the lowest drawer and reached to the back for the flask. He took a swig, took a deep breath, smoothed down his tie and went out into the hallway, carefully measuring his steps past the other offices and into the reception area. With index and middle finger, he tapped on the secretary's desk.

"Miss Odien, I have to meet a client," he said quietly, and slipped out the office door. She shook her head.

Davies hurried into the Queen's Plate as they unlocked the front door. The bartender spotted the architect in the mirror as he emptied a roll of quarters into the register. He turned and looking over the top of his glasses, said, "What can I do you for, this early in the day?"

"Sammy been in?"

"You're the first one through the door."

"Do you know where he is?"

"He sometimes hits The Broderick Park Inn this time."

"Ok. Good. Phone?"

The bartender indicated the pay phone in the hallway exit. Davies went there, fumbling in his pocket for change. He pulled up the phone book and dialed.

"Broderick Park."

"Uh, good afternoon. Is Sammy Messina there?"

"Who wants to know?"

"Huh? My name is Seth. I'm an associate."

The bartender repeated, "Seth?" looking at Sammy at the bar. Sammy nodded and took the phone.

"What?"

"You've got to go back and pick up the money. Fort...Fort didn't, I mean, he backed out. Oh, Lord. You've simply got to go back and get it."

"You're off your rocker," Sammy said, and hung up. "He ever calls again, you never heard of me, Paulie," to which the bartender nodded.

Louie and the bartender watched Davies spilling change in the hallway as he retreated into the parking lot.

"Whaddya figure?" Louie said.

"Better than a fifth, maybe close to two a day," the bartender replied.

"He used to be one of the biggest architects going."

"Hope he's got his crypt designed."

49.

Fort tried to call Ludlow at his job at the carpet showroom, but he wasn't there. He wasn't at home, and Fort finally got through to him at his legislative office.

"I gotta talk to you."

"Ok, so talk to me."

"I can't, you know."

"Ok," he said, looking at his watch. "It's a little early for lunch, but I can meet you at Early Times."

"Yeah, it's important. See you."

The mustachioed bartender was flipping a pack of Parliaments to Ludlow when Fort came in. "Oh look, we almost got a quorum," the bartender said.

"We'll be grabbing a table, Mike," Ludlow said as Fort gritted his teeth.

Fort looked around, clenched his fists on the table, and exhaled.

"I couldn't do it, Gus."

"Whaddya mean?"

"I couldn't take the money."

Ludlow stared at Fort for a long moment, then said, "Where's the money now?"

"In the restaurant I guess, under the seat cushion."

"Uh, look, Al, we've already figured this out. We covered ourselves by mentioning an approach to the DA's office. They said to call them back if it went any further. Nobody knows about the actual deal. We can't back out now."

Fort dropped his head and shook it. "I can't do it. I just can't."

Ludlow sat back in his chair. "Alright, Al, I'll take care of it. Don't worry." Then, leaning forward, he whispered, "Which table were you at, and which side of it?"

50.

Davies' hands shook as he turned into Becker's parking lot. He took a deep breath as he opened the car door and straightened up as he walked into the restaurant. Slowly, he rotated his head. It has to be that table, he thought, looking at the table Fort had left ninety minutes before. As the waitress approached, he pointed and sat himself where he figured the money was.

Holding out a menu, she asked, "Coffee?"

He took the menu and managed a smile. "Yes, certainly." When she left, he reached under the cushions and found nothing. Checking to see if anyone was watching, he felt under it again, and then slid around the table and searched under the other side. Finding nothing, he was frozen in thought as the waitress approached with the coffee.

"Like this side better?" she asked.

"Um, yes, yes I do."

What'll it be today? The roast beef looks real good."

"Just coffee, thank you."

Double crossed, he thought. Damned Fort lied. Or maybe Sammy. I never should have trusted him. Who, damn it, who? I'll get them. I'll get them both.

51.

Sammy Messina was sitting on the pavement next to the truck at closing time, wondering how he got there. He heard the two young guys, Kevin and Jack, laughing in the truck. Finally, Kevin came around and started to help him up.

"Who kicked me?" Sammy asked.

Kevin busted out in laughter again as he pulled him up.

"Did Jack kick me?"

Gasping for breath, Kevin got out, "Nobody kicked you, you old drunk, you fell out of the truck when you opened the door."

One hand on the hood, Sammy got his feet underneath himself and started laughing as well. Spotting his Buick, he shuffled his feet across the lot and waved to the still chuckling Kevin and Jack as they drove away. He paused by the driver's door to light a cigarette, remembering that was where they started earlier today, at cousin Louie's joint right behind him, and shook his head. Too much VO.

He waved his hand as the boys drove off. Doesn't matter, he thought. Big score today. Got my pay and skimmed those fools for more. The only thing I didn't score was Nicole. Yet.

52.

The next night, Seth tried calling Ludlow at home at 5:00, 6:00 and 7:00, his anxiety level increasing as the whiskey level in the J & B bottle went down. The ice in the bucket on the dresser was just about gone when Ludlow finally picked up the phone just after 8:00.

"We have to meet," Seth said.

"Ok, where?" Ludlow replied.

"Jack's Cellar. It'll be quiet there tonight."

"I'll be there in twenty minutes."

Davies walked through the empty streets of downtown and descended into the tavern. The bespectacled owner nodded and poured scotch. Davies took a big slurp and looked around. The only other customers were two guys at the other end of the bar, watching the TV.

"Did you hear that?" the one guy said. "Imlach caught 'em trying to fix the NHL draft."

The owner, wiping a glass, spun around. "What? What happened?" he said.

"The first-round pick was decided by a roll on a roulette wheel," the other guy said. "Campbell called out Pittsburgh won it, but they didn't, and Imlach caught 'em at it."

"So, the Sabres get Perrault. Imlach's gonna make a great coach," the first guy said. When Ludlow came in, Seth blurted out, "The money wasn't there. Did you get it?"

"No, I didn't," Ludlow whispered.

"Are you guys lying to me? How do I know Fort didn't snatch it? Or you?"

"Keep your voice down, for Christ's sake. Fort told me it was there. He just got cold feet, is all. What about your pal? The guy you sent to deliver it?"

"I'm looking for him. He moves around a lot."

"Look, Davies. You better take care of this yourself from now on. We'll set it up between you and me, nobody else. And you still owe us that first ten grand, wherever it is. We got a deal, and I'm gonna keep our end of it. You and the money men gotta come up with the cash. We vote the other way, and your coliseum doesn't happen."

"What about Fort? What's he going to do now? Will he go to the DA or something?"

"Don't worry about Fort. He's scared. I already talked to him. He'll come through on our side, you just come through with the cash. The biggest vote's not for a while, so there's plenty of time."

Davies finished his scotch and shook his head. Ludlow tapped his index finger on the bar. "Let me know when you come up with more money." Ludlow turned away, went out the door and back up onto the street.

I can't trust any of these guys, Davies thought. He walked back to the hotel, worrying until he got back to his room where Landice was watching TV.

"Where are we going for dinner tonight? And don't say the Beef Baron, I'm sick of that place."

53.

Rita got off the Trailways bus at the station on New York Avenue and coughed diesel smoke as she waited for the driver to open the baggage compartments.

"Rita! Rita Brogan!" she heard from behind her. Turning around, Rita saw a woman with a blonde ponytail waving at her. Maureen Sheridan, Rita thought. We haven't seen them since they moved down here. She looks great.

The two women embraced, smiling.

"I'm so glad you could put me up, Maureen. I hope I'm not putting you out."

"Noooo, we're glad to have you. Wait until you see our house. Tons of room. Here, let me take that," she said, grabbing Rita's suitcase. "The car's just over here," she said, walking swiftly past the vagrants congregating in the station. "Not the nicest neighborhood in DC," she said, putting the suitcase in the Impala's trunk.

"So," Maureen asked. "How's Rory doing? The last we heard, he was walking on his artificial leg and could use his new arm."

Maureen doesn't beat around the bush, Rita thought. "He's much better. He's walking on the prosthesis, he can do just about everything with the arm, and they've started with the plastic surgery on his face."

"Do you want to go see him now? Can we get in there?" Maureen asked.

Rita checked her watch. 10:30 a.m. Visiting hours just started half an hour ago. "Is it a problem for you? Do you have someplace else to be?"

"Noooo. Let's ride over there now, Rita. I know how you must want to see your boy."

"Yes, if it's OK, Maureen."

"Of course it is. Frank's very big on helping the boys coming home from Vietnam. He was in the Marines, you know, oh, before this war got started, but he says those protestors are so bad, the nasty things they say about the boys coming back..."

Rita looked down and silently nodded, wondering what Tommy was doing.

"Well...how's Pat doing? I guess he couldn't come down this time with his new job with the DA's office."

"He's ok. He came down the first time we visited. It really bothers him about Rory. I guess it brings back bad memories from his war, too. He'll come down again later on."

"And Tommy? He was always such a handsome boy, and so serious..."

"Oh, he's in school at UB and working at A.M. & A's. He's got an apartment with some friends now and likes that...I wished he could have come down with me, but he can't miss school."

Rita thought about how Tom looked away when she brought up coming down to visit Rory. He was always saying he couldn't take off from work or school. The two boys used to be so close, with Rory showing him the things he learned in basketball practice and driving him places. Tommy hardly ever came by the house anymore or talked with them on the phone. And the arguments he would have with Pat about school and Vietnam, it was horrible.

Maureen's face lit up as they pulled up to the gate and were directed by the creased and polished MP to the parking lot. She had to pick up her pace as Rita led her to the ward where Rory was and was breathless as Rita signed them in.

"Mrs. Brogan?" a white-coated doctor said, holding a clipboard. "I'm Dr. Conway, one of the doctors working with Private Brogan. He was operated on less than a week ago and the other doctors are examining him now to check the results."

"How did it go, doctor?" Rita asked. Maureen stepped back and remained silent.

"Well, the initial surgeries to his face to restore the structure seem to have gone well. His maxilla and mandible bones were very badly damaged and a lot of the lost bone had to be replaced with plates and held together with screws, but we believe those parts will work again. The reconstruction of his orbit, that is the bone surrounding the eye, will take longer, quite possibly several more surgeries. Oh, by the way, the sight in his right eye is almost completely restored, and his hearing, while imperfect, is very much improved."

Rita looked past the doctor as an orderly walked in with a blue-robed Rory.

"As I was saying, we hope to be able to start the skin grafts on his face after..." the doctor said.

"Rory!" Rita said and rushed to him. She put her arms around her son and he hesitated, then put both the real and the artificial arm around his mother. He put the good side of his face against her cheek. She stepped back and looked.

"You're walking again! Still so skinny."

He walked over to his bed and picked up the chalkboard. He touched the bandaged side of his face and wrote: *Jaw fixed. Dental work later. Artificial eye later. Put on 10 lbs.*

"Oh, Rory, that's wonderful! Oh, you remember cousin Maureen," she said.

He nodded and put out his good hand. Maureen took it in both hers.

"I'm glad you're getting better. Maybe you can come stay with us in Mt. Rainier?" Maureen said.

Rory rubbed away the chalk with his sleeve and wrote: How's Dad and Tom?

"Your dad's fine, Rory. He wishes he could come down, but he's got work."

Rory nodded.

"And Tommy's back in school…"

Rory stopped, then wrote, *Why didn't Tom come down this summer?*

Rita looked at her son and said, "Well, he was working full time this summer at the warehouse. We don't see him as much, now that he's got his own place. Sometimes he and dad argue…about where he's living… and the war."

54.

Seth Davies sat at the bar by himself in Manny's Supper Club, staring into his scotch. The bartender noted that he was ordering doubles tonight and hadn't taken his glasses off like he normally did. Davies muttered his order for the second, and just lifted a finger for the third. Siefert contemplated tactics.

"I heard Mr. Guyton was going to stop in tonight, Mr. Davies."

"Huh? Phil Guyton? Coming here?"

"That's my understanding, He might be coming with Mr. Thomas, too."

"I'll take my tab, Sief," he said, tossing back the whisky. "I gotta go."

As his glass was coming down, Siefert slid the check under it.

Braced by the fresh air, Seth Davies wasn't ready to go home. When he got inside Jack's Cellar on Swan, he squeezed in between two husky guys watching the news on TV and ordered another double J&B.

"You think they'll ever build this dome stadium?" the first big guy said, jutting his chin towards the TV.

"How? Where's the money going to come from? Did they bring back some from the moon?" the second guy said.

"Texas," Davies slurred.

"Texas?" the first guy said.

"Yeah, Texas. The boys with the big money are doing it from Texas, and they're buyin' legislators to make sure," Davies said. The two big men looked at each other over Davies's head.

"They say the vote's going to be close," the first big man said quietly.

"Got two, three votes in the bag," Davies said, taking a big slurp. "That's all it'll take to make sure it swings right."

"Never can tell, it might take a lot…"

"They wanted a hundred gran'," Davies got out, adjusting his glasses. "Got 'em down to fifty. My company and the Texans split the cost, so we get the plans and engineer."

The second big man signaled the bartender, pointing at Davies's scotch.

"Yeah, that's good. Thanks," Davies said raising the whisky glass to toast him. "But that SOB Sammy, or maybe Fort, snatched some of it. Gotta get it back."

"Sammy, doesn't he work at the axle plant on Delevan?" the second big man said.

"Naw, little bookie guy Sammy. Everybody knows him. Broderick Park, the Queen's Plate…" Davies said, waving his free hand.

"Oh, that Sammy. Sure, everybody knows him," Marty Meegan said, who decided he'd delay a little longer before heading over to the Aud to watch the Sabres practice.

55.

When Davies shut off the alarm clock, Landice was still snoring. He laid back down, then heard something slide under the door. Curious, he got up and found an unsealed envelope. Opening it, it was an invoice from the hotel for $220.00, marked past due.

Damn, first Stephanie serves me with divorce papers, now this, he thought, perspiration breaking out on his brow. There's almost nothing in the bank account and the bills for the Tonawanda house are rolling in, too. He looked at the clock and hurried into the shower. While he was shaving, he realized he hadn't picked up the laundry or stopped by the cleaners and would have to wear something off the pile in the corner to work. He brushed his teeth thoroughly and rinsed out his whiskey glass, poured some mint Scope in it and gargled for twenty seconds.

He knotted his tie in the mirror, and, tossing the hotel bill in a dresser drawer, went down the steps at the end of the hall and out the back way, avoiding the front desk. When he got into work, he hurried by Phil Guyton's office, hung his suit coat up and turned back his shirt cuffs. Looking over his desk, he found two memos. The first one was marked urgent and read: "Need results of concrete sample tests for N. Falls job." Ok, call McLaughlin, he'll have them done by now. The second one made him freeze. "Gus called, wants update on project." I'll have to ask Phil for another check, and see if Steuart, Jones, and Burrows had come through with their share. As he walked out into the hallway, he saw one of the young draftsmen backing out of Phil's office and a blueprint flying out at him.

"Goddammit, Rusnak, I told you put it in 1:50, not 1:100. How the hell is anybody supposed to read this crap!"

No good, I'll have to ask Art for the check, he thought. He walked down the hallway where Art Thomas was sipping coffee and looking out the window. He rapped on the doorframe.

"Good morning, Art. How are you today?"

"Oh, c'mon in, Seth. I was just contemplating getting season tickets for the Sabres for the company. The papers say they look good in practice. That'll make clients happy, don't you think?"

"Sure, sure, if we can resist using all of them ourselves. Say, I got a memo from, uh, our friend at County Hall. He's looking for an update."

"Ah, shit, you know how to ruin a guy's day, Seth. All right, I'll get you a check." Going to his desk, Art sat down and pulled out the business checkbook with the side vouchers.

"I'll tell you Seth, I've been in this business thirty-five years, and for the last twenty years it's been going downhill," he said. "The bigger the job, the more we've got to pay out to get the work. And if you don't pay out, forget it. When I started in this town, there was more work than you could shake a stick at, and we were getting calls from Rochester, Syracuse, up in Canada. Now look at it. We have to pay out to make sure we can keep working."

"Er, have we gotten anything from Steuart, Jones and Burrows for their next, umm, share deposit?"

"Damn it. That, too. All right, I'll get that for you, too. Make sure you keep this confidential, Seth. Be careful. We need this job, but we don't need trouble."

"Certainly, certainly, Art, I'll take care of it," Davies said, holding onto the doorframe. Returning to his office, he called Ludlow.

"I'm having lunch with some constituents at the Cloisters at 12:30, ok?" Ludlow said. "It looks like rain today, so wear a raincoat. I'll be wearing my checked raincoat – you can't miss it."

"Fine, fine, Gus, I'll make sure to keep dry," Davies said.

Davies left the office, cashed the two checks and was at the bar of the Cloisters at 12:15. When Ludlow and his friends arrived, they put their coats in the cloakroom, and, as they were escorted to their table in the atrium of the restaurant, Ludlow nodded at Seth. Davies finished his drink, dropped a five on the bar and went to get his coat. In the small room, he pulled two envelopes out of his coat pocket, both with $5,000 dollars in hundreds. His hands trembling, he found Ludlow's sporty raincoat and stuffed one of the envelopes in an inside pocket. He held the other envelope in his hand, hesitated, then shoved it back in his own pocket. When he walked out of the cloakroom, he saw Ludlow watching him while his constituents took in the cascading faux waterfall on the atrium's glass. Davies gave him a nod and hurried out to the street.

56.

Seth Davies had come back from lunch and was looking at a report on the utility lines from the site in Lancaster when the phone buzzed. It might be Landice, he thought, snatching up the receiver.

"Seth Davies here," he answered pleasantly.

"Mr. Davies, this is Jay Rooney from the County Attorney's office. I understand you're one of the lead architects with Guyton Thomas and will be the principal contact with the Steuart, Jones, and Burrows firm of Texas on the plans for the proposed stadium here in Lancaster. Is that true?"

"Uh, did you say County Attorney's Office, Mr., Mr...."

"Rooney, Jay Rooney, sir. Yes, I'm with the County Attorney's Office, and I was wondering if we could get together to discuss the county's payments and taxes concerning your out-of-state partners with the stadium project."

"Well, you'd probably want to talk to our comptroller about those matters, Mr. Rooney. I'm not familiar with the financial arrangements."

"Hmmm. We understood, well... it doesn't matter. We'd like to get together with you and the comptroller and discuss the financials, so we can arrange payments to your firm, the Steuart, Jones, and Burrows firm of Texas and make sure the taxes are properly taken care of. You can bring the firm's attorney if you like."

"Attorney? I don't think... Mr. Rooney, I'm going to have to get back to you on this. I'll have to talk to the principals before we can arrange any meetings with your office. Let me have your number, and

I'll be back in touch with you as soon as we've had a chance to discuss the matter here."

Seth's hand shook as he wrote down the county attorney's number. They're suspicious. They know something. Maybe Fort talked to them. I've got to do something. I've got to talk to somebody about this. Maybe that sneaky bastard Sammy got caught at something... He pulled out his wallet and took out a business card. There it is, Geoffrey Sturges, Attorney at Law. He was the one Art said I should call about handling the divorce. Said he'd represented everyone big in town at one time or another. He'll have to fix this. I just can't take it anymore...

57.

The district attorney took his glasses off and rubbed his eyes. Immediately before him were three files, the first marked "Fort/Ludlow," the second "Seth Davies/Attorney Geoff Sturges" and the third was a legal pad with notes, entitled, "Tip from B.P.D. Lt. Meegan."

His intercom buzzed.

"Yes?"

"Mr. Roth and Mr. Brogan are here, sir."

"Thank you, Mary Agnes, send them in."

The door opened, and the D.A. waved the Assistant District Attorney and the Investigator to chairs. He folded his hands, paused, and observed his men. Roth, the Ivy league lawyer in the well-tailored blue suit and dark hair just touching his ears. Brogan, tall, his curly black hair more than half gray, dark blue eyes, old style brown sport coat with narrow lapels, black tie and khaki pants with a sharp crease. No doubt about which one's the cop, he thought.

Butler picked up the morning paper and shook his head. Actual Cost of Domed Stadium May Go Higher than $70 Million, the headlines read.

"Jon, Pat. Did you see the Courier's headlines today?" he said, tossing the front page across the desk.

"Yeah," Pat responded. "First shovel's not in the ground, and they're twenty million plus short already."

"And that's not the only problem with this stadium deal, gentlemen. I'm hearing rumbles that someone may be attempting to criminally influence the occupants of the 4th Floor," he said, referring to the County Legislature's offices.

Pat nodded silently, remembering a case from two decades previous where he'd dealt with politicians. The prospect of dealing with the politically powerful was not appealing.

"Jon Roth, I have here the file," the DA said, holding up the first document, "of an interview with County Legislators Fort and Ludlow. It says that they claim that 'a planner of the stadium development' offered to contribute $10,000 to each of their re-election campaign funds, 'hinting' that he wanted them to vote to approve the contract with their firm for designing a domed stadium in Erie County."

Roth nodded.

"Further, it says that Fort and Ludlow told this 'agent of the developer' that was above the allowable campaign limits, but they wanted to report it, according to Ludlow's words, 'just in case.' It also states that they wanted to know if they could accept airline tickets and free hotel rooms down in Texas from the developers of the proposed domed stadium. And you told them, no. Then what?"

Roth nodded. "Since there was not a criminal investigation underway, I asked the County Attorney's Office, not someone from our office, to write a letter asking the proposed stadium's local architects, Guyton Thomas, to call his office and set up an interview at a time and place of his convenience to discuss taxes, bonding, etc. I planned on attending the meeting, and, along with the routine questions the County Attorney's office would ask about contracts that the Guyton Thomas firm had with their Texan partners, I planned to ask if they had had any contact with the members of the County Legislature and see where that led.

"The County Attorney's office duly wrote and sent the letter, but there was no response. They followed up with phone calls to the firm, but that also met with no arrangements for a meeting. When one of

the lawyers in the County Attorney's Office called the lead architect, a Mr. Seth Davies, directly, he thought Mr. Davies to be possibly
intoxicated and unlikely to be helpful, and that's where the matter
stands at the present time."

The DA nodded. "Ok," he said. "I have here," he said, holding
up the second file, "a letter from Geoffrey Sturges, Attorney at Law,
requesting an interview with the District Attorney's Office with him
and his client, Seth Davies, architect with the Guyton Thomas firm
here in Buffalo.

"This office knows Sturges well. He's represented bank embez-
zlers, bluebloods who seduced babysitters, mob bosses. He's very
smooth, extremely thorough, and just the lawyer I'd go to if I was
swirling down the toilet.

"Now, to add to this, I have a report from you, Pat," he said,
now picking up the legal pad, "about information from a Lieutenant
Meegan of the Buffalo Police who says Mr. Davies has been boasting,
while in his cups, that he has two County Legislators in his pocket
for votes on the proposed domed stadium deal, and he implicated his
Texas partners in this conspiracy as well."

"That's what Meegan told me," Pat said, "and I've known Meegs
for twenty years. He's good. He got the architect talking at the bar
and this guy Davies told him the where, the whos and how much,"
Pat said.

"All right, gentlemen, it seems we have a corruption investigation
to handle here. I know I said I was going to break you in easy, Patrick,
but I want you on this now. You two both have experience in these
matters and are the best men to handle it.

"Start with the architect. Meet with him and Sturges. It'll probably be in Sturges' office on the 16th Floor over in the Rand Building,
so be prepared. What you find out will decide where you take it from
there. Get a formal statement from Lt. Meegan, Pat. And whatever

you do, stay away from Fort and Ludlow, for now. We don't know where this may lead, and we don't want these guys going to ground.

"The press is all over this stadium issue. The News and The Courier were at each other's throats over where to locate this stadium. The city could lose our NFL franchise, for Christ's sake. Keep me informed about what you're doing. You'll have to step very carefully on this one, there's a minefield out there that could blow us all up..."

Pat winced, and the DA remembered Pat's son.

58.

Jazz watched the two young legislators throughout the meeting. They hadn't met him for drinks lately, and they didn't come in together like they usually did, Ludlow jollying everyone he met and Fort smiling at his side. While the Chairman guided the legislature through the several parliamentary procedures, he noticed the two friends not exchanging a word. A vote for approving the increased bond issue for the stadium passed easily, Yarborough's man Chip rushing out to phone Houston with the good news. When the session was over, Jazz waited behind one of the chamber's Calacatta marble columns as the other legislators left the chamber. He watched as Ludlow stood by Fort's desk.

"You ok?" Ludlow said in a low voice.

Fort looked up from where he was stuffing papers in his briefcase. "Yeah, yeah, I'm fine."

"I've got your share, pal. When do you want to collect?"

"I can't, Gus. Like I said, I can't do it."

"Think about it, Al. We're covered all the way around as long as we keep quiet. Nobody's going to say a word to wreck this thing and the money's rolling in."

Fort closed his briefcase and kept his eyes down.

"I'll hang onto your shares until you're ready, partner. You're still with us on this thing, right?"

Fort nodded silently, thinking about the phone calls and letters he'd been getting, almost all of them complaining about subsidizing millionaire team owners. I just wish Gus would forget he ever invited me into this scam.

Jazz watched as Ludlow walked away and thought he'd better wait a while before telling them about the locations in Lancaster that Hanlon was planning on buying up.

59.

Pat and Jon walked slowly as they crossed Lafayette Square, accompanied by Patti Mazur, the DA's most experienced court reporter, who said her feet hurt. Roth carried a brief case, and Pat had Patti's Datawriter in its carrying box.

As the elevator came to the top floor, Jon said, "Remember, don't scare this guy. We want this architect talking." Brogan nodded. Patti, in double knit gray, stared at the floor in silence.

A young blonde woman in glasses and a tight business suit greeted them at the suite entrance and guided them to a wooden paneled conference room. They sat in polished, dark wooden chairs. Patti set up the stenographic machine on a table to the side.

Ten seconds later, Attorney Sturges entered, looking at his watch. "Thank you for coming, gentlemen." He shook hands with the D.A.'s men and said, "My client will be in momentarily." Sturges, a tall man with a long face, stood smiling with his fingertips just touching his desk.

A knock on the door, and another woman in a business suit followed Seth Davies into the room. She guided him to a chair on Sturges' left and handed him a ceramic cup filled with steaming coffee.

"All right, gentlemen, this is Seth Davies, architect with the Guyton Thomas firm of this city. He has reason to believe there is some significant malfeasance occurring in the legislative process here in Erie County and is here to report it as a good citizen."

Davies nodded, holding the coffee with both hands.

"However, before Mr. Davies makes any statements, there are two items that I must mention. One, at no time will Mr. Davies be interviewed without myself present, and two, the district attorney has already granted Mr. Davies transactional immunity for any criminal actions he may testify to."

Roth began, "Myself and Special Investigator Brogan are aware of these conditions and will adhere to them. If, however, we discover that your client has lied to us, Mr. Davies will be liable for a charge of perjury," and nodded towards Patti tapping away.

"I have explained that to Mr. Davies, and he understands the consequences," Sturges said. "Shall we begin, gentlemen?"

Roth cleared his throat and said, "Mr. Davies, in your own words, tell us what transpired between yourself, the members of the Steuart, Jones, and Burrows firm and the Erie County Legislators concerning their votes and any other attempts to influence governmental officials concerning the dome stadium measure."

Sturges nodded to Davies, and Pat wondered where the strings he used to hold Davies were. An hour later, and after two bathroom breaks for the architect, Davies had told the story of the arrangements made in Houston with the architects and of the failed passing of first $10,000 in Becker's.

"So, you don't know what happened to the money?" Pat asked. Davies shook his head. Patti looked up.

"Please answer verbally, Mr. Davies," Sturges said.

"No, I don't know. It was gone." Davies answered.

"On what other occasions did you give, or attempt to give, money to Misters Ludlow and Fort for the purposes of bribing them?" Roth asked.

Davies looked at Sturges, who nodded.

"On July 25th, I went to the Old Road Post Inn on Main Street for lunch. Before I went inside I met Mr. Ludlow in the parking lot and gave him a manila envelope with $5,000 in one-hundred-dollar bills."

"Where did this money come from?" Roth asked.

"I'd just cashed a check across the street at the Marine Midland Bank."

"Who was this check from?"

"Steuart, Jones and Burrows."

"Did you use Mr. Messina as a go-between anymore?" Pat asked.

"No, no." Davies said, shaking his head. "I didn't trust him anymore," his voice trailing off.

"Did you pay anyone else, or have anyone else deliver bribe money?"

"No," Davies answered. "After that first time it was all between myself and Mr. Ludlow."

When the times, dates and amounts were all established, Davies was starting to sweat and shake. Sturges ended the interview, and on the way down in the elevator, Pat said to Roth, "This is dynamite, but this guy Davies is shaky as hell. We're going to need someone to watch him."

"Right. We've got to find any other witnesses that saw what happened in Becker's, and we've got to see what we can get out of this Messina character as well. I wonder how Butler will want to play the Texans and the architects here in Buffalo?"

"I can handle Messina and the people at Becker's, counselor. And I'll talk to the sheriff about getting someone to mind the architect to make sure he doesn't kill himself before he testifies. The sheriff and I go back a long way. He'll have someone for the job."

60.

Lou Constantino was looking at a framed picture of himself and Brogan from the Buffalo Evening News that read "Gambling Squad Cops Raid Pearl Street Bar" when the desk buzzer sounded.

"Sheriff, District Attorney's Special Investigator Brogan is here," the receptionist said, and Lou heard Pat in the background mutter, "Please, just Pat Brogan..."

Lou rose and came around the desk and both men smiled when Pat entered. The two gripped each other's hand firmly.

"Good to see you, old friend," Lou said.

"It sure is, Lou. It sure is."

Lou waved him to a chair, then sat down, turning the News photo towards Pat.

" Jeez, we almost got killed in that joint," Pat said.

"The good old days, Pat. They were wild, weren't they?"

"Sure were, Lou. That case," Pat said, nodding towards the photo, "led back to politicians then, just like now."

"It's a big case you've got now, Pat. A real big one. The DA tells me there's no one he'd rather have it, either. I know I wouldn't."

"Thanks, Lou. Always good to know there's someone to back me up, especially if it's you, partner."

"How can I help?"

"I need a babysitter for a witness, Lou. Someone who can handle a serious alky."

The sheriff nodded, then smiled again. "I've got just the man for you. My cousin Vince. He's a sergeant at the jail. He can handle the worst of 'em. I tried to get him out on the road, but when they gave him straight day work at the jail, he wanted to stay put. Let me get in touch with him, we'll meet up and get you what you need. How does that sound?"

"Just right, Sheriff. Just what we need."

"What else can I do for you, Pat?"

"Ahh, nothing much, but I did see an operation out in Alden that the County covers you might want to know about."

"Oh, what's that?" Lou said picking up a pencil and moving a pad in front of himself.

"A place called Kinay's out on Wescott Road has got quite a shop going there. We stop in there for pizza once in a while, coming back from Wende, and every time we do, there's a guy making book, all seasons. Keeps quiet when we're in there, but I see people stuffing the paper in their pockets."

Lou shook his head and put the pencil down. "This isn't 1950 anymore, Pat. Bookmaking's small potatoes, and I haven't got the manpower. When was this, in the evening? Saturdays? I'll tell Augustinelli to have patrol start to get in there regular, make some noise.

"Drugs and patrol, Pat. That's where all my resources go these days. The old timers thought I was crazy when I started the Narcotics Squad after I got elected, but it's the busiest crew I've got. Dope is the mob's biggest moneymaker, and they'll kill anyone at the drop of a hat that tries to get in on it. All the kids are smoking pot—in the city, all over the suburbs, and even the teachers at UB are having pot parties, taking LSD, even getting into cocaine."

Lou shook his head. "They think they're 'liberated' doing this. The teachers. Professors and everything. Inviting the kids into their houses, everybody's getting high. It's all over the campuses and the administrators do nothing. It's all out of control, Pat. There's no respect for the law these days. I've got three guys working the UB campus now for the DA — watching the teachers, the radicals and all the dope they're passing around."

At the mention of pot, Pat's eyes had zoned out, thinking about the times Tommy had come home reeking of it. "Just had a couple beers, dad," he would giggle when he was in high school, and now, over in Allentown, God knows what he's doing, he thought.

"Hey, partner," Lou called him back into the room, "You ok? You zoned out on me. Like in the old days when you first came on the Gambling Squad," he said, playfully punching Pat's shoulder.

"Yeah, those days. Crazy," Pat said, refocusing.

"They were crazy, all right. We did some damn good work back then. You, me, the D & D boys and the rest of them. Remember what Wachter used to say, 'We're crushing 'em out there, men.'"

They both smiled at the memory, then Lou said, "Hell, Patrick, you've never been out on my boat yet. You and Rita will have to come out with Bitzer and me while the weather's still nice. We keep it over at Brobeil Marine on the East River."

"Still a swabbie after all these years?" Pat chuckled. "I woulda thought you had enough seafaring after standing those freezing watches in the North Atlantic during the war."

"This," Lou said, walking with Pat to the door, "is different. Watching the sun go down over the Lake on the 'Hungarian Rhapsody' is a whole different ball game than waiting for a torpedo on the USS Janssen."

"All right, boss. I'll give you a holler soon. Rita'd like that a lot. Give my regards to the Bitzer and your kids for us," and he left smiling.

61.

"Corroboration, men, that's what we need," Butler said, leaning forward, his palms on top of two stacks of files, papers and law books with page markers stuck in them. Brogan and Roth watched as the district attorney knitted his brow, stared at the smaller stack on his left and carefully jiggled a file out from near the top.

"This is my urgent stack," he chuckled as he handed the file to Roth. "Now that we've got the Grand Jury to indict these developers on Davies' testimony, you're going to Houston, Jon. You're going to meet Steuart, Jones and Burrows, and you're going to offer them immunity from prosecution if they come clean and agree to testify about the bribery. If not, tell them there will be extraditions, filings with architectural and engineering licensing boards and a tremendous amount of negative publicity for them, all of which is very expensive and bad for business. Don't take any of that corn pone malarkey from them. If they hesitate, mention to them that they will be transported here, separated and housed in the general population of the Erie County Holding Center until they can make bail, which may take some time – they'll come around quick enough.

"And you, Patrick," he said, handing two files to Brogan, "while Jon is in the Lone Star State, are going to interview the waitress who Davies says was working when his bag man was supposed to pass on ten grand to Fort. See what she knows. More importantly, you're going to confront the principals at Guyton Thomas and see if they want to cooperate, too. We've made an appointment with them for a Mr. Brogan from Erie County. Davies fed them some story about taxes and bonding, so they agreed to the meeting but don't know what it's really about yet. Now, you have the sergeant from the sheriff's office going with you. Get Davies out of there first, then you go talk to Guyton and Thomas. Not a good idea to have those people in the same place when you tell them they might be going to jail. Ok, any questions, gentlemen?"

They both shook their heads, took the files and left.

62.

The banquet room of Ilio DiPaolo's was filled with short-haired men talking in groups. A painted caricature hung from the ceiling reading, "Farewell Captain Tedesco," showing a man with an over-sized tam-o-shanter swinging a golf club.

"If you know where one of these guys worked, you know where they all worked," Lou said, tipping his drink at a couple of the small groups. "Over there, Pat," he said, "are the murder dicks. See, there's Tedesco, still got the same flat top, it's just turned gray, is all."

"Yeah, and young Leo Dunleavy's head of Homicide now," Pat said, indicating a crew-cutted man in a tan sports coat.

Lou regarded Pat. "He was young Leo when he was a rookie working with us twenty years ago, Pat. Now, he's running one of the best homicide outfits in the country."

"Gentlemen," a serious voice said from behind. Pat and Lou turned to see a tall, slender man with gray eyes in a dark suit stand with his hands clasped behind his back.

"Inspector Wachter!" Pat said.

"Boss! Great to see you," Lou said, grasping the older man's hand.

"Well," the retired policeman said. "How are my two best investi-gators doing?" he said, eagerly shaking hands with them both.

"Just great, boss. Up to my eyes in work. Getting it done the way you taught me," Lou said.

"And you, Patrick. I understand you're assisting our district attorney in some rather sensitive matters these days."

In a low voice, Pat said, "Politicians, again, Inspector. A bunch of vultures."

Both younger men leaned forward to hear Wachter.

"The DA, Butler, is a good man, you can trust him. Keep him informed of what you're doing and he'll stand by you. And remember," he added, raising an index finger, "make your friendly witnesses as comfortable as possible. Let them have their lawyers present. Do the interviews where they're most at ease. Handle them nice and easy and you'll get what you need out of them if you're patient."

"How about the big shots?" Pat asked.

"These guys aren't hop heads or stick-up men. People with money fear two things: jail and going broke. If you convince them they're going to do time, or if it's going to be so expensive that they'll go broke trying to stay out of jail, they'll come around."

A red-faced motorcycle policeman banged a spoon against a water glass.

"Well, gentlemen," Wachter said, "let's sit down and hear some war stories about Captain Tedesco, shall we?"

63.

Pat waited about a minute when Chloe was seated in the bullpen, then opened an inner office door, smiled and gently said, "Miss Chloe Ostrander?"

She smiled back and said, "Yes, that's me," and rose.

Pat held the door and directed her to the seat in front of his desk. Sitting down, he said, "Any trouble finding this office, Miss Ostrander?"

"No, none at all. I had a cousin who used to work in the County Clerk's Office on the first floor. I knew where this was."

"Great. Would you like some coffee or water?" he said, indicating a water pitcher covered with condensation and a coffee pot on a hot plate. The smell of fresh coffee filled the room.

"No, thank you. I already had breakfast at home."

"All right then. I was wondering if I might ask you some questions about people who may have come into your restaurant June 15th. Your boss tells me you worked Thursday, June 15th, for breakfast and lunch. Is that right?"

"Yes, I did. I've started working some dinner shifts, too."

"Do you recall what happened at work that day? How was business that morning? Was it slow?"

"Yeah, pretty slow, a few guys came in, ordered coffee and left almost right away. They all sat at the same table, ordered coffee, then zoomed out. One guy moved to the other side, then left before the coffee came. Weird."

173

"Miss Ostrander, this was a while ago. How do you remember what happened that day?"

"That was the day after I found out about my mom's congestive heart failure. My boss said he would help me with the bills, and I'd start working doubles to pay him back. Besides, like I said, those guys were acting weird."

"Do you think you might recognize these men if I showed you their pictures?"

"I think so. They all had suit coats and ties. Business men, you know?"

"Ahh, that's good. Let me show you some pictures, and let's see if you recognize any of the men who sat at that table. If you can, then maybe you could describe what they were wearing for me."

Pat took twelve photographs from an envelope and slowly spread them in two lines on his desk before Chloe. She leaned forward, looking over the pictures.

"Him," she said, pointing at a carefully trimmed campaign picture of Fort. "He was real jittery. I figured he was fooling around, meeting a girlfriend. He came in first."

"He had a wedding band on?"

"Yup. And he wasn't acting like anyone meeting his wife, either."

"Anyone else?"

"Mmmm, him," she said, putting her index finger on an image of Ludlow. "He was in and out of there real fast."

"Any of these other gentlemen sit in your station that Thursday morning?"

"Him," she said, indicating Davies. "Can't miss those silver locks. Nice suit, but he smelled like booze. And it was at ten-thirty in the morning, too."

"I see. Please take another careful look, Miss Ostrander, and let me know if you recognize anyone else who came into Becker's that morning," he said, resisting the urge to shove Sammy and a couple of other architects' and Legislators' pictures a little forward.

"Nooo, I think that's it. But I think that guy top right plays for the Bills. He comes in sometimes, but not that day..."

Corroboration, Pat thought. Got 'em.

64.

Vince Constantino hadn't worn his pinstripe suit for a while, and it was tight on his big shoulders and legs. When a bleary-eyed Davies came out of the elevator, Constantino said, "Here's our guy."

"That's him," Pat said. "Mr. Davies, go with Sgt. Constantino. Do what he tells you."

The two policemen nodded to each other as Davies adjusted his glasses.

"I'll take your car keys, Mr. Davies," Vince said. Pat watched as they left the building, then he got on the elevator to head up to the Guyton Thomas offices. Once there, briefcase in hand, he was directed to the conference room, where Phil Guyton and Art Thomas were waiting.

"I dunno where Seth is," Thomas said. "He was just in his office a minute ago…"

Pat entered the room, shut the door and turned to the architects.

Holding up his badge, Brogan said, "Mr. Guyton, Mr. Thomas, I'm Special Investigator Brogan of the District Attorney's Office. I'm here to tell you that you have been indicted by the Grand Jury of Erie County for conspiracy and for bribing members of the Erie County Legislature."

"What the fuck? What did that son of a bitch…" Guyton said, looking out the conference room window towards Davies's office.

Thomas clapped his hands on top of his head and shook it.

"Gentlemen," Pat said, "we have a great deal of testimony, under oath before the Grand Jury, concerning your firm's bribing Erie

County Legislators. We also have documentation. The district attorney is prepared to offer transactional immunity to the both of you, as he has for others, for your testimony against Misters Fort and Ludlow. If you decide not to accept this offer…" he ended, dropping two pairs of handcuffs on the table.

Brogan let that sink in, then added, "Your associates in Texas have also agreed to testify for the prosecution," hoping that was true, as they didn't have confirmation from Roth yet.

"That drunken asshole!" Guyton shouted, picking up a chair and throwing it across the room.

"Phil, take it easy!" Thomas yelled, grabbing his partner. "It's over," he said, "the whole damn thing's over," his voice trailing off.

"Damn it all! Damn it all!" Guyton swore. "This could've… Shit," he said. He stopped, thought for a while, then, looking at Thomas said, "You're right, Art. I guess we have no choice. All right, Mr. Investigator, what the hell happens next?"

Pat continued in a low voice, "You will come into the DA's office. There, we will take your testimony, and if we find it to be truthful, you'll be offered transactional immunity from prosecution in this matter. If not, the penalty for perjury can be up to seven years in a place like Attica. With a substantial fine." While he spoke, Guyton thought about cleaning out Davies' office and transferring his work to someone else in the firm. Thomas thought about changing the firm's name when it was all over, maybe having to merge with another group of architects.

65.

Rita turned around on the bridge and looked at the men sitting in the stern of the boat. "I can't hear a word they're saying with this engine roaring."

"Vhat difference does it make?" Bitzer said. "All they talk about is job. They talk about old job and laugh. Then, they talk about new jobs that bothers them and get another drink. Bah!" she said, with a wave of her hand. "I have a good idea. You run the boat, Rita."

"I never have…"

"Come, it's easy, just like the car, only with waves and no stop lights. Look at where you want to go and keep boat on course." She stepped away and nodded Rita over. "Now, see the radio towers on land, there?"

"Yes."

"Aim towards it and turn wheel to keep on straight."

Another boat sped past them, sending waves into the hull.

"Whoa," Rita said, "it's bouncing all over."

"Ok, just turn wheel a little left. Now, aim further left, not too much, good. See, just like life. Waves hit, you adjust, keep on course. Simple."

Rita nodded. She hoped they would see more of the Constantinos. Bitzer always made her feel better.

"Hey, stay on course there, woman!" Lou shouted from the stern, and Pat laughed, handing him another beer. Pat looked at the two women at the wheel. Bitzer always seemed so confident, and Rita was down so much these days.

"Ok, more to the left, Rita, aim for that island with the old house on it, there. Don't let them distract you. You ok?"

"Yes, I'm ok. When I saw the flag on the other boat over there, it made me think of Rory..."

Bitzer put her arm around Rita's waist and squeezed gently. "You are a good mother. You are doing all you can for your boy. Verje a kommunistak!"

"What?"

"Damn the communists. When the Russians came in November of '56, their tanks smash everything. I remember running through the alleys with my cousins to get away from them. When they destroyed the building up where we were hiding, Sebestyen... Sebestyen... we found him covered in bricks. Kristof and I dug him out. We carried him to where the freedom fighters were... they could do nothing."

"Hey! You're going to run aground on Motor Island!"

Both women laughed, and Bitzer took the wheel. Rita got quiet, thinking about Tommy and the radical students.

"How's Rita doing, Pat?" Lou asked.

"She's doing ok. Gotten really involved at church lately."

In a Lee Marvin voice, Lou said, "Pardner, it's been my experience that there ain't nothin' more ruthless and treacherous than a genuine good woman."

They both laughed.

"We've got some good women there, Patrick," Lou said, and Pat looked at them, remembering Rita back when, the strutting nurse at Mercy Hospital with her chestnut hair in a Victory roll, and the slender Hungarian woman next to her now smiling and friendly to his worried wife.

"We sure do, Lou, we sure do."

Lou paused, then smiled. "Say, do you remember the two girls we got lashed up with during the pinball investigation? Do you know whatever happened to them?"

Pat looked forward, then at Lou.

"Don't worry, they can't hear us over the engine unless we shout," Lou said, smiling.

Pat shook his head, thinking of the redhead's long sculpted legs, took a sip of beer and said, "The Miami police got a lead on Helen – she'd changed her name and had been working in a bank down there for a while – but disappeared again, no one knows where. When the investigation was over, everyone stopped looking."

"Yeah, she was something to look at, and smart, too. If we'd gotten her to testify, I'll bet we could've gotten that damned Jezerowski, even after his pal Ocky clammed up and took the fall for him. Mmmm, and that blonde," Lou said. "Betty. She had the most amazing figure. Any idea where she is? I remember she left town after the trials were over, too."

"Went down to New York, got some acting jobs doing cigarette commercials, stuff like that. Heard she married some TV producer down there."

"Wow," Lou said, shaking his head. "Good thing Wachter liked us and those girls didn't say anything. He made the whole thing go away or our goose would've been cooked."

Pat held out his beer for a toast. "Here's to Inspector Wachter. Best boss ever."

Lou tapped his beer against Pat's. "Here, here, partner, here, here."

Pat thought about those two girls. How he and Lou had met them in the place on Clinton Street and taken them dancing at Frank's over on East Ferry. How Helen's leg was against him in the cab... and how Wachter exploded when he found out they were seeing state's witnesses. That was a close one, he thought. Could've blown the whole case and lost our jobs, too. Get her out of your head, stupid. She's long gone and you've got a wonderful wife who needs you more than ever with Rory hurt and Tommy out there feeling his oats.

66.

Bill Correlli changed into his work shoes when he got to the job site in Amherst, waved to the guys on the job and started walking the job with the foreman, Tim. He saw the lines were straight, the footers looked to be the right size and the concrete joints were ok.

"I figure we'll be done with the foundations by Thursday, and they can start laying the pipes Friday or the next week," Tim said.

"Good, good, Timmy. We can start moving the guys over to the Millersport job next week." Tim nodded and smiled, glad that he and his crew were working for a company that was getting steady work.

"Ok, Tim, keep up the good work," Correlli said, then shook his hand and headed for his car. Tim nodded, surprised at the boss' cursory inspection. Correlli drove off without changing his shoes, which got him evil looks from the receptionist when he walked through the office. Checking his messages, there was nothing from Yarborough or his people.

"Shit," he said, noticing his muddy tracks. "Sorry, Cindy," he shouted to the receptionist as he took off the boots. Dialing Titus Webb's number, he picked up the morning paper with the story of the Seattle Pilots going bankrupt and their current availability.

"Hello, Titus Webb here."

"Titus, Bill Correlli. Have you seen the news?"

"I did, Bill. I think there's an opportunity for Buffalo and your project there."

"Would you be interested?"

"Well, Bill, I'll tell you. As an investor, I might, but not as a lead or sole owner. From what I've learned, there are several entanglements with the team's bankruptcy, not the least of which are existing contracts with the State of Washington and rather daunting debts created by the owners. Now, that being said, I'm more than willing to sound out some people about putting together a group to bring the team to Buffalo."

"I can't thank you enough, Titus, for this, and for all the help you've been giving me."

"It's an opportunity for Buffalo, Bill, and I'm glad to be a part of it. Have you spoken to the senator about this yet?"

"He's next on my list of people to call, Titus, right after I get off the phone with you."

When they'd hung up, Correlli took a deep breath and thought, Going to make this work, got to make this work, as he dialed the Houston number.

67.

Brogan got off the elevator on the sixth floor of Erie County Hall and saw the red-headed girl turning the corner towards him. Not as tall. Green eyes, not blue. Damn, I'm thinking about her again. He entered the DA's office, was waved into Butler's private office and sat down, file on his lap. The DA, walking around his desk in a gray Hong Kong suit, was on the phone. "No! Absolutely not. Return the check, that would be a conflict of interest. Goodbye." The DA sat heavily in his chair. He took his glasses off, proceeded to wipe them with a handkerchief, held them up to the light, shook his head and put them back on. "Elections. You just can't be too careful about the money people offer." He looked over the stacks of files at his Investigator.

"What have you got for me, Pat?"

"First and foremost, depositions from Guyton and Thomas. Also, more corroboration of the drunk's story about the hand-off in Becker's Restaurant. The waitress positively identified Davies, Ludlow and Fort as being in Becker's. She didn't see Messina, but he was there, I'm sure, doing the drop for the architect."

"Can you prove it? Do you know much about this Messina?"

"He's a small-time bookie and he'll steal anything that isn't nailed down. I came across him a couple of times. He goes all the way back to Prohibition, a teenager running whiskey around town for Tutulomundo." Pat held up the file. "I've got it all right here."

"So, what's the plan?"

"There's a bunch of unpaid tickets on his new Buick. I had the car towed, then told him he had to come in and talk to me before we'd release it."

"Good," the DA said nodding.

"He was sitting outside my office for about an hour. Then I had a deputy take him down to one of the rooms off of the tunnel." Checking his watch, Pat said, "He's been down there for about twenty minutes now, and the deputy's right outside. When I'm finished here, I'll go talk to him."

"Very good. Just be careful, there's going to be a lot of publicity when the papers get wind of this, and we've got to nail these guys nice and clean. Keep the deputy with you."

Pat stood up and slapped the file against his leg. "Right. Ok, let me get down there and see how much this bagman knows."

Pat rode the elevator to the basement of the County Building and exited through the brass doors into a dimly lit tunnel with damp cement walls and an earthy smell. Heading to his left, he saw two gray uniformed sheriff's deputies escorting a prisoner clanking down the tunnel in shackles. He nodded to the deputies and walked to a steel door watched by a third deputy, hands folded before him. Pat motioned him to the side and whispered, "How is he?"

The young deputy smiled and whispered back, "He's been bitching about seeing you, where the hell were you. Said he had appointments to keep."

"Good. Anything else?"

"Yeah, he also was bitching about his car."

"Ok. Here's the plan. You go inside and just stand there. If he stands up and starts talking, sit him down. Then I'll come in after another minute or two and start talking to him. Don't say anything, just sit him down if he jumps up."

"Gotcha," he said. The deputy opened the steel door, entered, then closed it firmly. From inside, Pat could hear Sammy saying, "Where the hell is this guy, this Brogan, anyway? I got places to be."

Pat waited another two minutes, then entered the room, file in hand. Sammy was sitting in the only chair, and a single light bulb hung from the ceiling. The tan paint on the concrete walls was flaked and the white ceiling was streaked black with mold.

"You Brogan? What the hell is this? Where's my car?" Sammy blurted out, bouncing up off the folding chair. The deputy clapped a big hand on Sammy's shoulder and sat him down. Pat walked slowly in front of Sammy and the two stared at each other for a several seconds.

"Still writing for Russo, Sammy?" Pat said evenly.

"What? What's this about? I came down here on my own time to pay my fines and get my car," Sammy answered.

"The Last Call, the Queen's Plate, Broderick Park, a couple of other places where you been taking bets, Sammy. They could have license trouble because of you."

"What!? You're crazy, I don't even know you."

"When you ripped off Yellow Cab, how'd you get away with that? T's boys might've broke your legs or worse over that scam, Sammy."

"What the hell are you talkin' about? That was ten years ago..."

"Turning all your bets in to Russo? He might not think you're funny anymore if you're booking some bets on the side, Sammy," Pat said.

"You're a crazy man," Sammy said, pulling his coat pockets inside out. "See, not even a pencil!"

Pat chuckled. "You're a weasel, Sammy, but nobody ever said you were stupid. You wouldn't bring your slips into a police station. We've known about you for years," he said, slapping the file loudly against his leg. "Everybody in town knows what you're up to. But if Broderick's or The Last Call get slammed with a suspension or fine from the State Liquor Authority? Even your cousin Louie's going to get pissed off if he gets his liquor license suspended. And if word got back to Russo that you were holding out on him..."

"Look, I just came here to get my car, I'll pay the fines for the tickets, I've got cash, see," Sammy said, pulling a thick roll of bills from his pants pocket.

"Deputy Vallone, did you see that?"

"Yes, I did," the young deputy said, smiling.

"I think this bookie's trying to bribe us."

"You got it all wrong!" Sammy shouted.

"I want to know about Becker's, Sammy," Pat said. "Becker's, on William. I want know about you and the architect."

"Huh?" Sammy said.

"You've been being a bag man for the architect, Davies, Sammy. Becker's. The train station. I want you to tell me about it."

"I don't know what you're saying. I'm getting old. I go all over town, see lots of people. I can't keep things straight anymore. My family's probably worried about me right now."

"If you don't tell me, Sammy, Russo might be very unhappy with you. Adornetto at the Last Call? He doesn't like paying fines, and he's got a temper. Paulie at Broderick's will be looking for you, too. You're too old to run, Sammy, you've got nowhere to go."

"I don't know anything about that. I'm half off my head sometimes. I say a lot of things. Ever since the war. I'm a disabled veteran..."

"What did you say?" Pat said in a rising tone.

"I'm a disabled veteran..."

Pat threw the file at the wall, reached down, grabbed Sammy by the lapels and threw him against the block wall. Vallone, momentarily stunned, stood still until Pat dragged Sammy across the room and started slamming him like a rag doll against the wall, screaming, "You son of a bitch! You got kicked out of the Army in '43 for

186

stealing, you no-good rat bastard. You never saw combat! You never got wounded!"

Vallone leaped across the room and grabbed Pat in a bear hug and pulled him back. Sammy slumped to the floor, covering his head with his arms.

"Boss stop it! We can't..."

"He's fuckin' insane! Get him off me! Help!" Sammy screamed.

"I'll kill the little bastard!" Pat shouted, struggling to get loose. "It's all in the prick's file! He got a dishonorable discharge, the no-good SOB!"

Vallone wrestled Pat out into the tunnel and kicked the steel door shut. Pat kept trying to get loose. "I'm gonna kill the bastard! I'm going to kill him!" Pat yelled.

Vallone looked up and down the corridor, no one was there. "You gotta calm down, boss! We can't do this!" he said, realizing it wasn't an act.

After about ten seconds, Pat stopped struggling.

"You ok now?" Vallone asked, relaxing his grip.

"Ahh, fuck him," Pat said. "Just fuck him, the little son of a bitch."

"Get yourself straightened out," Vallone said. "Go upstairs. I'll take care of things down here."

Breathing heavily, Pat nodded, looked at Vallone, and nodded again.

"You'll be ok. It'll be ok," Vallone said. "Just go upstairs." Pat turned and headed down the tunnel, back into County Hall.

68.

When deputy Vallone had gotten Sammy out of the tunnel, he dragged him out to his red Buick.

"Hey, that Brogan guy roughed me up. I'm gonna call my lawyer," Sammy said.

Vallone's eyes narrowed as he handed him the keys. "You ain't seen roughed up yet, you little pissant. Now get outta here."

"What about the fines?"

"They're gone. Now, get the hell outta here," the deputy said, stepping forward.

Sammy jumped in the car, chuckling. A block later, he started to think. When he got home, he took fifteen hundred dollars and divided it into three piles. He put the money in envelopes and tucked them in his coat pockets. Then he went to the Queen's Plate, Broderick's and the Last Call. He gave the owners each an envelope.

Paulie, at Broderick's, said, "What's this for?"

"Because you let me do business. And in case there's some expenses, down the line."

Paulie nodded and took the money.

Then Sammy went to the kid down the street from him and bought an ounce of grass and a tinfoil of coke, then called Nicole at her house out in Hamburg.

"I gotta present for you baby."

"Oh, what is it?"

"Something you come into the city to get."

"Oh, yeah!"

"But I might have to stay at your house for a while, later on."

"How come?"

"I need a vacation."

"Well, you'll have to help with expenses if you're going to stay here."

"Sure, baby. Uncle Sammy'll help pay the bills."

69.

Jazz got off the elevator and smiled for the cameras as he entered the legislative chamber. "You look like a punter at the track, Bill," Jazz said as he walked past the developer, tapping him on the shoulder.

"I guess I do at that, Jazz," Correlli said, the folded paper with the list of legislators in his hand. He looked at it again. Red mark next to a name meant definitely yes, black mark definitely no. Blue mark meant maybe, with a red or black dot indicating which way the legislator was leaning. He counted the red marks again. Damn, it's close. He looked over the blue marks with the red dots and checked the names. Got to talk to them as they come in the chamber...

The chairman loved meetings like this. He wore his best three-piece suit, got his haircut, and gargled so he would sound his best for the TV. All the legislators were present for the big vote, the press was there in force, the visitors' seats were filled and people were standing up in the back of the room. He gaveled the meeting to order, had the reading of the minutes of the previous meeting waived, worked through the old business and then saw the TV cameras come to life when committee chairman Jezerowski brought up the bill to award the contract to build the nation's second dome stadium to the Yarcor Corporation.

"As this is expected to be a particularly critical vote, Mr. Chairman, I would ask that the legislature be polled," Jazz said.

"I think that is a most reasonable proposition, Mr. Jezerowski. Mr. Clerk, you will poll the legislature for the vote on Local Law 36, awarding the contract to make the Yarcor Corporation the general contractor for the construction of the domed stadium."

The room fell silent as the clerk called the roll, and all eyes were on the board illuminating the votes.

"The first six votes will tell the tale," Bray from the Courier Express said.

"If they don't sweep all six, the boys from Texas will have egg on their faces," Mix, the Evening News reporter, said, looking at his notes where he'd written leads for both possibilities. "Texans stifled as contract voted down." He liked that one.

"I can't believe they'd shut it down at this point," whispered the area's biggest concrete contractor, hoping the dinners he'd bought for the men from Texas would pay off. "The county already spent over a million for the plans."

"Mr. Jezerowski," the clerk said.

"The Representative for the Fifth Legislative District votes aye," Jazz said.

"Mr. Ludlow," the Clerk said.

"Aye," Ludlow said. Jazz nodded.

"Mr. Hirsch?"

"Aye."

"Mr. McNamara."

"Aye."

"Mr. Fort?"

"Nay," Fort said, looking down at his desk.

"That's it," Bray said.

"The other southtown districts won't support it. It's done for," Mix said.

"Oh shee-it," Chip whispered, wondering if he should wait until the vote was complete to call Yarborough. Ludlow stared at Fort, who remained looking down.

As the chamber disgorged the crowd, Chip slid into Ludlow's office and made the call to Houston.

"Well?" Yarborough said, lighting up a Marlboro.

"They voted it down, Mr. Yarborough," Chip said.

"Get the hell out of there, boy. Looks like the redhead was right. You can't depend on those damn politicians up there."

70.

Alex realized it was over when Bill Monte said, "Make sure all the machinery is cleaned up good, boys. The money we get from the sale of the drop hammers is going to pay for your severance checks." Today, on the final day of the Stadler-Murphy Tool Company, Alex Missel rolled the barrel of hydraulic oil onto the tail lift of the truck with the South Carolina plates. When the southern businessmen had come through the plant to look over the machinery last month, the rumor spread they were going to keep the tool works open because the nearby Chevy plant still needed them. Never should've bought into that one, he thought.

Taking off his work gloves, Alex walked into the break room, where Tyrone Johnson was packing up the plates and cups into boxes.

"You want any of this stuff, man? It's all goin' to the Goodwill if you don't."

Alex reached into the cabinet and pulled out a green and white coffee cup that read Seneca Indians, Class of 1966. He'd brought that in a week after he started work here four years ago. He took a paper towel off the roll over the sink and tucked it inside the cup and put it in the box in front of his locker. He watched Tyrone empty out the rest of the cabinet, the plain cups, the mismatched silverware that the guys had brought in, even the chipped ceramic plates. Gerry Andreason sat at the big wooden table in the center of the room reading the sports page. The headlines read *Bills Drop Final Pre-Season Game.*

"Damn Bills lost again – twenty-seven to nothing," he said, tossing down the sports section. "The regular season is going to be a disaster."

"Yeah, the defense couldn't hold 'em. Bobby James was hurt and got burned twice," Tyrone said.

"Yeah, but the offense has looked good sometimes," Alex put in. "They got Simpson, two good receivers with Moses and Briscoe, and it looks like this new guy Shaw can throw the ball, too."

"No blocking," Gerry said. "Even O.J. Simpson can't run when there's nobody opening up holes."

"Offense can't be that good," Tyrone said, "no points last night. Not even a field goal."

"They'll get better, you watch. Enyart's ok for short gains, and he'll be a great blocking back for Simpson. He might even be the next Cookie Gilchrist," Alex said, remembering when he and his dad had watched the Bills in the championship years of '64 and '65.

"Never happen," Gerry said, and Tyrone shook his head.

"You ready?" Tyrone asked, picking up the box of kitchenware.

"Yeah," Gerry said. "Lemme get this junk out of here and go home. The Bills lose, and I got no job after today. Hey, Tyrone, you taking this table?"

"Yeah, man, it's solid. It'll fit right nice in my mom's kitchen. Just have to sand it down, slap a few coats of varnish on it."

Most of the other workers had already left, headed off to the bar on the last day of the Stadler-Murphy Tool Company. "I'll give you a hand with the table, Ty," Alex said, trying to delay the inevitable. When it was loaded, they stood there, hands in their pockets.

"What're you gonna do, man?" Alex asked.

"Leave town," Ty answered. "Move in with a cousin in Dallas, Texas. He says there's plenty of jobs out there, and no fuckin' snow!" he laughed. "You?"

"Not sure. Still got the part time job at Touma Brothers warehouse, loading, unloading candy and other stuff for vendors. Might turn into full time."

They shook hands, and Ty drove east out Ferry Street to his house off Michigan. Alex went downtown, then out Clinton to his "upper" flat in Kaisertown. When he got home, Agnes was wiping her face with a washcloth.

"How ya feel?" he said, putting his hand on her stomach.

She nodded, eyes closed. "Ok. The doctor said the baby might come any time now. How'd it go?"

Alex shrugged. "Ennh. It's over. Gotta go see Big Mike at the warehouse, see if I can pick up some hours."

"Is the medical insurance gonna last until the baby's born?"

"Yeah, six months free, then we gotta pick up the whole cost or lose it."

"Boy, I hope Touma comes through with something full time soon, otherwise we're gonna hafta get into the money we been saving towards the house."

"Something'll come up, you'll see. I'll check at Touma this after, then head over to the Forge and see if they've looked at my application. They can always use me."

71.

Mary Ellen heard the sonorous voice of Randolph Todd as if he were in the room with her.

"Miss Anderson," he drawled out. Hmmm, I'm no longer Miss Mary Ellen, she thought.

"Mr. Todd, what can I do for you?"

"Well, Miss Anderson, I'm sure you have heard that Yarborough and Associates has suffered some reverses in our efforts to build the coliseum and related development up in New York State. Our firm does not take such rejection lightly, especially after investing so much time and money in the effort. We have therefore engaged the law firm of Lafonara, Peck and Lauria to represent us up there to recover our expenses and what we believe our firm is due. The government people in Erie County seem to be reluctant to admit they have erred and need to be made to see their failure to do what is honorable in this instance."

"And what can I do for you?" she said, thinking, I'm not the damned jury!

"Our lawyer in this matter, Mr. Lauria, would like to depose you as part of his preparation of our case."

"Up there?"

"Yes, ma'am. A brief visit of a day or two should be sufficient. Yarborough and Associates would, of course, pay all your expenses and reimburse you for your time."

Five minutes later, Mary Ellen was telling Christine to get her plane reservations to Buffalo and a hotel room outside the city, near the airport. Damn, I hoped this job was over and done with. Now I've got to fly back to that damned city. It's been twenty years. Who'd know me back there now? The bad guys are dead or out of sight, the vendor's association is closed down, the politicians...some of the politicians like Jezerowski are still around. I warned Yarborough about them. Those characters have got nine lives. That cop who was crazy about me. Brogan. Oh hell, he's probably married with kids and retired, too. I better check and make sure when I get there, though.

72.

Alex woke up to the baby's crying and, cradling her with one arm, got a bottle out of the refrigerator and proceeded to warm it up in a pan of water on the stove. Agnes had gone out to her cleaning job. Alex held the baby with one arm and tucked the bottom of the warm bottle under his chin while he turned on the radio.

"There, Sarah, we can dance to the music while you drink your milk," he said, gently bouncing the smiling baby. 9:30, he thought, the mail should be in, and they trotted down the steps, hearing Mrs. Linneman's vacuum cleaner hum in the lower flat as he went to the common hallway and scooped up the mail.

Hmmm, Linneman, Linneman, Linneman, he thought as he flipped through the envelopes. Here, that's for us, ahh, Niagara Mohawk. Shit, we'll have to put that electric bill off for a couple of weeks until next money comes in. What's this? Erie County, Official Business.

Placing the empty bottle and other mail in his bathrobe pocket, Alex put Sarah over his shoulder and bounced up the stairs, getting a contented belch about halfway up. Works every time, he thought, tearing open the official envelope with his teeth.

"Official Summons," it read. "You are hereby summoned to the Supreme Court of the State of New York to serve as a petit juror on..."

Shit. This is bound to screw up whatever work I can line up. What the hell do they want me for this for? Dammitall! We'll have to get a babysitter.

73.

Jurors, Jerry Hallinan figured, were like produce. Pick them when they're ripe. Retired, good. They have patience. Women, most of the time, they have sympathy. Watch for anger signs, though – watch their expressions when they look at the client. The unemployed, great, they're bored, he thought. So, when he checked his profile on Alex Missel that read "Machinist/tool and die man, out of work, says wife is working," Jerry figured Alex wouldn't squawk about getting out of the house for a few days, so he saved his last challenge for the Black bus driver from Masten Park. That guy probably thinks all politicians are crooks in the first place, and he lives right by the stadium – a bitter Bills fan who sees this as a chance to hammer a couple of white politicians.

The jury picked, and, opening statements made, Roth began the State's case by calling Seth Davies. He glanced back at Sgt. Constantino, who had led the architect into the courtroom. Constantino nodded. Roth continued to watch as Davies took the stand, then approached the witness box with a small smile after Davies was sworn.

In an even voice, Roth asked, "Please state your name for the record."

"Seth Adam Davies."

"What is your home address, Mr. Davies?"

"1032 Sinclair Drive, Town of Tonawanda."

"Mr. Davies, are you employed by the Guyton Thomas Company, architects and engineers, as an architect?"

Adjusting the microphone, Davies answered, "Yes. Yes I am." Hallinan scribbled notes.

"Did you also win the AIA of New York State Award for Best Commercial Design in 1958?"

"Yes, I did," Davies said, nodding.

Hallinan's foot began tapping on the floor. "Butter wouldn't melt in his mouth," he whispered to his assistant and clenched his fists.

"Mr. Davies, in your capacity as an architect with Guyton Thomas, have you had dealings with the defendants, Misters Ludlow and Fort?"

"Yes, I have."

"Would you describe for the court your dealings with Misters Ludlow and Fort?"

"I delivered bribes to them so they would vote to approve contracts with Guyton Thomas and Steuart, Jones and Burrows to design and engineer, and the Yarcor Corporation to construct, the dome stadium in Lancaster, Erie County."

Davies went back against his seat when Hallinan jumped up.

"Your Honor, I object! The prosecution..."

The judge waved his gavel in Hallinan's direction. "Relax, Mr. Hallinan, you'll get your chance."

When Hallinan sat back down, Roth resumed questioning Davies for the next hour and a half, getting him to describe the meetings in Houston with the developers, cashing the checks and passing the money to Ludlow. Ludlow doodled on a legal pad while Fort bit his nails and stared at the defendant's table. When Roth finished his questioning, Davies pulled out a handkerchief and wiped his reddened face.

Jerry Hallinan pushed his chair back, loudly scraping it against the floor. The judge closed his eyes and shook his head.

"Mr. Hallinan, please. Ladies and gentlemen, it's now 11:30. We'll adjourn for lunch, and then, Mr. Hallinan, you can cross examine the witness."

Constantino allowed Davies two drinks at lunch and watched him carefully as he went past the bar on the way to the men's room. When they returned to the courtroom, Hallinan was rotating his neck and flexing his shoulders.

As the judge entered the court, the court deputy called out, "All rise. The Honorable Ross Oberpfalz presiding."

After the judge had settled in and everyone had resumed their seats, the judge said, "Now, Mr. Hallinan, now, you may cross examine the witness," holding his gavel at the ready.

Hallinan, bending forward at the waist rolled around the defendants table, then stood up straight just in front of the witness box and looked Davies right in the eyes, his hands gripping the rail between them like he intended to rip it out.

"Mr. Davies, you testified that you reside at 1032 Sinclair Drive in the Town of Tonawanda, did you not?"

"Yes," Davies gasped, clearing his throat.

"Isn't it a fact, though, that you currently reside at the Hotel Graystone on Johnson Park in Buffalo with a woman not married to you?"

Davies nodded.

"Your Honor! Please direct the witness to answer the question!" Hallinan said.

"Answer the question, Mr. Davies," the judge said evenly.

"Yes," Davies answered in a voice just above a whisper.

"Speak up, Mr. Davies," the judge ordered.

"Yes," Davies said again, clearing his throat.

"And isn't it true that you haven't shown up for work at Guyton Thomas for over a month?" Hallinan asked loudly.

"I, I've been, uh..."

"Do you still work for Guyton Thomas, or was that a lie too?" Hallinan thundered. "So, Mr. Davies. You have a house in Tonawanda with a mortgage to pay, a wife to support – you are still married to Stephanie Davies, are you not?"

"Your Honor!" Roth shouted.

The judge winced. "Enough of the theatrics, gentlemen. Everyone in Western New York can hear you, and it's giving me a headache. Mr. Hallinan, where are you going with this?"

"The money, Your Honor. The money. Mr. Davies has a lot of extraordinary expenses, and I think the jury wants to know how he's paying for all of it."

"Very well, Mr. Hallinan, but keep it civil. And beneath 100 decibels."

"Yes, Your Honor." Swinging around towards the freely sweating Davies, he asked, "Just how are you paying for all this, Mr. Davies? The mistress, the hotel, the mortgage, the eating out every day in restaurants – all that when you're not working?"

Wiping his brow with his coat sleeve, Davies stammered, "It's been hard. I've had to go into my savings…"

Hallinan looked over at the jury and said, "I don't believe any of these hard-working people would believe that, Mr. Davies. I think you cooked up this whole scheme to support your sordid life and are trying to throw the blame onto my clients."

Roth was on his feet, yelling, "Your Honor! Defense counsel…"

The judge was rubbing his forehead as he said, "Counsel will meet with me in my chambers immediately if not sooner. This show-boating's going to stop or some attorney's going to be spending the night on a city mattress."

As Hallinan walked towards the judge's chamber, he checked the jury's reactions out of the corner of his eye. I might have to spend a night in jail, but they'll know he's a lying sleaze when I'm through with him, he thought.

Alex Missel waited to see what the judge would do, and, five minutes later, the judge and both attorneys returned from chambers. He saw a quieter Hallinan slide around in front of Davies like a wrestler looking for an opening and he saw Davies squirm and stutter. What got Alex's blood boiling was Ludlow's little smile, doodling away, and Fort's nervous fidgeting. These bastards are guilty as hell, he thought, and Mr. Doodles there thinks he's going to get away with it.

"Mr. Davies, you testified that you gave Mr. Ludlow $5,000 in the parking lot of the Old Road Post Inn on Main Street. What day did you do that?"

"Uhh, it was in July."

"What day in July, Mr. Davies?"

"I'm not sure, it was towards the end of the month."

"So, you say, you gave $5,000, in cash, to Mr. Ludlow in a restaurant parking lot, but you can't remember what day it was? How many days do you go around with $5,000 in your possession, Mr. Davies? I'm sure if these good people," he said, gesturing to the jury, "had $5,000 dollars at one time, they'd certainly remember what day it was!"

Hallinan let that sink in and caught a juror nodding in agreement, then asked, "Did you always give the money you claim you gave to bribe these two men to Mr. Ludlow?"

"Uhh, well, personally, that's who I gave the money to."

Hallinan turned his head on a slight angle. "Personally, Mr. Davies," he said quietly. "What do you mean by that, personally?"

"Uh, I mean that I personally gave the money to Mr. Ludlow."

"Nobody else?"

"Well, I tried to get some to Mr. Fort through another person."

"What person is this, Mr. Davies?"

"Sammy Messina. He was supposed to deliver $10,000 to Mr. Fort."

"Well, did he?"

"I don't know. The money disappeared."

"So, this mysterious Mr. Messina, whom the government hasn't produced yet," Hallinan said, glancing over at Roth, "supposedly gave $10,000 to Mr. Fort, but you weren't there to see it, and the money's nowhere to be found. What else disappears when you get into the scotch, Mr. Davies?"

"Your Honor, I object!" Roth yelled.

"Enough, Mr. Hallinan!" the judge said, slamming the gavel. "I warned you for the last time! Mr. Hallinan, I find that you are in contempt of this court! Deputy, you will take lead attorney for the defense into custody on a charge of contempt of court." As the deputy led a handcuffed Hallinan away and his assistant stood up to continue, Roth sat down, wondering how Brogan was doing with his latest gambit to find Sammy.

Pat Brogan went with Terry McCann from the Liquor Board to serve the three subpoenas. When they got to their last stop, the Queen's Plate, everyone at the bar looked at them. McCann was young, and this was his first job out of college. Louie held the subpoena and slapped it in his palm. Looking over his glasses at the young man, he said, "Gambling? Nobody's taking bets in my place." He turned around to the bar. "Anybody passing out football cards, anything like that, to you guys?" They all shook their heads and turned back to their drinks.

"Nonetheless," McCann said, "You are required to appear before the Liquor Board at the time and date stated."

"Ok, kid, don't worry, I'll be there," Louie said, smiling at Brogan.

Back in the car, McCann asked, "What is the point of this again?"

"To piss the bar owners off," Brogan said. "If they're mad enough, they'll find Sammy for us."

"Huh. None of these guys seemed real mad to me," McCann said.

74.

The trial lasted five days. After Hallinan had worked over Davies in his cross-examination, Roth called the waitress, Steuart, Jones and Burroughs and corroborated the architect's story. When it was the defense's turn to call witnesses, Hallinan started with the waitress.

"Miss Ostrander, you work at Becker's Restaurant Monday through Saturday, do you not?"

Sitting up straight in her best dress, she answered, "Yes, I do."

"And how many hours a week do you work there?"

"Well, I used to work 48, but now it's closer to sixty. I've got bills to pay. See, my mother is sick..."

"Miss Ostrander, that's a lot of hours. With all that work, can you keep track of when customers come and go?"

"Sure. When you've been doing this job as long as I have, you get to know people. Some of them you can set your clock by."

"So, you're sure that you saw my client, Mr. Fort, in the restaurant on June 13th of this year, and Mr. Davies there as well."

"Oh yes, I saw them both there that day, like I told Mr. Brogan in the District Attorney's Office."

"But, Miss Ostrander, did you see them there at the same time in the restaurant?"

"No, your client came in and left, and that Mr. Davies came in later."

"So, you never saw them together, and you never saw Mr. Fort pick up anything from the restaurant?"

"No, no I didn't."

"And you never saw my other client, Mister Ludlow, at all that day in the restaurant?"

"No, I didn't."

"And you never saw this man," showing her a picture of Sammy Messina, "at all that day in the restaurant?"

"No, never saw him."

"Thank you, Miss Ostrander, that will be all. Your witness, Mr. Roth."

"Thank you," Roth said rising. "Just a few questions, Miss Ostrander," he said, shuffling some papers on the table. "Did you take a break that day when Mr. Fort and Mr. Davies came into Becker's Restaurant?"

"Sure, Kathy takes whatever tables I have, then when I come back, I spell her so she can have lunch."

"Do you leave the restaurant on your break?"

"I did that day, I had to get to the pharmacy for my mother, see..."

"I see. So, Mr. Ludlow and the man in the picture identified as Mr. Messina may have come into Becker's and you wouldn't have known it? Is that right?"

"I object! Mr. Roth is calling for speculation..." Hallinan's assistant said.

"That's all I have for this witness, Your Honor." Roth said, and sat down.

The following day, when Hallinan had served his day in jail, he called Davies to the stand. Seth only had one scotch in the morning and one with lunch under Vince's supervision. By the time he was through testifying, he was dreaming of the green J & B bottle, and, as he stepped out of the witness box, Hallinan said with a smile, "I'd like to reserve the right to recall this witness, your honor," which got Davies stumbling towards the exit.

Hallinan never recalled Davies, but it kept the man shaking in the courthouse until both sides rested their case. As soon as the jury settled in to make its decision, everyone started speculating about the missing $10,000.

"Hey!" Alex Missel said. "We got a job to do here. Those two grafters out there are laughing at us, figuring that defense lawyer's got us softened up with all his yelling at the architect."

"He had the shakes by the time they were done with him," the restaurant manager said.

"Yeah, but that doesn't mean he was lying," the surveyor said, wishing they could get some beer in the jury room.

"Whoa!" the jury foreman, an accountant, said. "Let's get a vote here on all the charges first, to see where we stand."

Ten of the twelve thought the two were guilty of conspiracy, but they were evenly split on the bribery charges.

"If they were bribed, why'd Fort vote against the contract?" the union business agent asked.

"Because they're a pair of double-crossing politician rats," the garbage collector said, and he and Alex led the charge to convince the rest of the legislators' guilt.

After having the statute on conspiracy read again, and realizing that talking about taking bribes was enough, and that no money had to change hands for the law's conditions to be met, the jury was agreed Ludlow and Fort were both guilty of conspiracy.

Soon, everyone was agreed that Ludlow was guilty of bribery, and Alex and the garbage collector worked on convincing the beautician of Fort's guilt on that count.

"That Fort, I don't know. Did you see his wife sitting there?" she said.

"He was at the restaurant to pick up $10,000 cash!" Alex yelled.

"And he looks so sad," she added.

"You'd look sad too if you were staring at three to five in Attica," the garbage collector said.

After deliberating in the afternoon and the following morning, the jury came out with the verdict at 2:00 P.M. on a Friday afternoon.

"Have you reached a verdict?" the judged asked, thinking, Another verdict just before the weekend, never fails.

"We have, Your Honor," the accountant said.

"And how do you find on the charges?"

"We find Mr. Alfred Fort and Mr. August Ludlow guilty of conspiracy in the third degree."

Fort hung his head and muttered, "I didn't do anything wrong. I didn't do anything."

"We find Mr. August Ludlow guilty of bribe receiving in the third degree.

"We find Mr. Alfred Fort not guilty of any bribery charges."

Hallinan jumped up, saying "Your Honor, I make a motion that the guilty verdicts be set aside..." but was drowned out by the crowd of reporters pushing their way out of the courtroom and spectators jumping up and yelling.

"Mr. Hallinan, I will entertain any and all motions you may have on Monday. The defendants will be allowed to remain free on bail until such motions are resolved and sentencing is pronounced. The jury is dismissed, and I thank you for your service."

Turning off the microphone, the judge was heard to mutter, "Time to get the hell out of here."

Alex Missel watched the occupants of the defendants table as the courtroom cleared.

"I've got six motions ready and that doesn't include the appeal," Hallinan said to Ludlow, who nodded and snapped his pencil in two. Fort shook his head and wept.

You bastards are going to jail, Alex thought. I hope the judge throws the book at you. I'm out of work and my savings got ate up listening to your bullshit for the past week, you thieves. Now, I'm going home to my wife and baby and see if there's any work out there.

75.

Jazz sat behind the desk in his office and just listened to the phone ring. As soon as one caller gave up, another would start. The secretary at County Hall told him he had a stack of messages with the "Please return call" and "Urgent" boxes checked. The wife was telling him at home, "Will you please call these people? The phone won't stop ringing! It's cousin Ted and a bunch of other people! They're driving me nuts! What's this all about anyway?"

In front of him was the morning Courier. The headlines read *Legislature Dooms Dome* by Robert Bray. That, my dear, is what it's all about. On top of the newspaper was a notepad with some figures on how much the taxes would be for the properties in Lancaster they'd bought for the next two, five and ten years. With no stadium, no development, nobody might buy those plots for a decade the way things are going around here.

76.

Tom and Nancy walked across the lawn to the Student Union where Professor Fred was leading a protest rally. Nancy kicked the leaves and said, "I love fall. Do you, Tom?" He nodded and smiled as they entered the building. HR waved from across the room, and they worked their way over to him.

"This is great!" HR said. "The movement has picked up the same momentum it had when school ended last spring! The people will be heard, you watch!"

The crowd kept building in Norton Union and was getting louder, so loud the speakers resorted to using a bullhorn. Professor Fred climbed up on a table, tested the bullhorn and, when he saw enough eyes turning his way, began speaking.

"The police are among you. They are here in this room, watching you and listening to what you say. The 'Freedom of Speech' they talk about is a sham. Your efforts to change the rot in this society are going to be resisted by the establishment. You will have to be strong to change this campus, this country."

Artie walked up to Tom, Nancy and HR, hands in pockets. He leaned in towards HR and said quietly, "We're ready."

HR's eyes lit up and he said, "Got enough up there?"

Artie nodded. "Tons."

"Ok, let's go. Time to get militant," HR said. "You coming with us?" he asked Nancy and Tom.

"The Sheriff of Erie County has his men taking pictures and recording your words," the professor continued. "The arrest of the

Buffalo Nine in a place of supposed sanctuary, a church, was just the beginning."

"I'm going to stay here, HR," Tom said. "I want to hear what he has to say."

"You?" HR said to Nancy. She dropped her eyes and shook her head.

HR shrugged. "We'll be upstairs," he said, and he and Artie left the crowd.

"They started the same way in Nazi Germany," the professor said. "They blamed the Jews, the Communists for all the problems, then they started watching them, then beating them up if they resisted."

Tom heard a loud disturbance at the front of the hall, and a score of students started rushing away from the entrance doors.

"The pigs are coming!" someone shouted, and uniformed campus police, helmeted with face shields down, crashed through the doors, knocking over the tables and swinging long nightsticks. As the students fled back towards where the teacher was speaking, some picked up chairs and heaved them at the policemen. Others winged glass soda bottles, and as Nancy stepped behind Tom and grabbed his sleeve, Tom noticed several cops had stains and broken glass on their coats.

Tom took Nancy by the arms and shoved her towards a side exit.

"The repression begins!" the professor shouted. The police charged at them, swinging their clubs at anyone in their path. A student ran in front of Nancy, dropping a sign, tripping her. As Tom went to help her up, a policeman, his coat reeking of urine, started swinging his Billy club on them. Once, twice, the blows landed before Tom managed to grab the weapon.

"Motherfucker!" Tom shouted, trying to wrench the club away. "She didn't do anything! Get the fuck off..." he said as the officer pulled the stick free of Tom's hands and jabbed him as hard as he could in the gut. Tom fell on top of Nancy and the policeman kicked them both and went forward towards the screaming teacher.

77.

The next night when Nancy came into the apartment, HR was drunk and passed out in his clothes, his wet Army boots dripping on the unmade sheets. Please, no, she thought, closing the door to his snoring and sitting on the couch in the living room. She pushed the reeking bong to the side, laid down and began to cry quietly. She was just about asleep when the front door opened, and Tommy entered. She kept her eyes closed. Tommy took his coat off and looked around. He looked at her for a few moments, then came over and lightly nudged her shoulder. She opened her eyes and wiped them with the back of her hand.

"Why don't you go to sleep in my room, the sheets and blankets are all clean," he said. "I gotta talk to HR when he gets up anyway."

"Ok." She got up silently and went into Tom's room. Looking out at him, she said, "Is it ok for me to close the door? He's been mean lately when he wakes up."

"Sure, close the door. You're ok in there."

Tom looked around the apartment and took in the bong, the stained rug, the dust all over the tables and TV. He remembered the home on Cordova that always smelled of the Murphy's Oil Soap his mom used and how the sunlight glinted through the windows she washed with ammonia and wiped down with old newspapers. I'm going to have to get some stuff from the store to clean this apartment, he thought. This place is getting bad.

78.

Lt. Marty Meegan looked at the range's schedule on the clip-board and saw the rest of the afternoon was empty. Checking his watch, it read five after three. Too early to go home, he thought. Hell, go upstairs and shoot the shit for half an hour or so, then take off. Locking the door to the range, he headed for the stairs and heard a lot of raised voices. As he got to the 3rd Precinct's desk on the first floor, he saw about thirty patrolmen, all with helmets, nightsticks and gas masks, some with tear gas launchers.

"All right, we're here, how the hell are we supposed to get to the campus?" shouted an older patrolman.

"Who the hell's in charge of this operation?" said another.

"All hell's breaking loose up there, and we're standing here with our sticks up our ass," a third patrolman said in front of the desk.

Meegan went up to the desk, where Mike Yammarino was the Desk Lieutenant.

"Mike," Meegan shouted over the noise, "what the hell's going on?"

"There's another riot up by UB. This time they're coming off campus, tearing everything up down Main Street. They told all the men to muster here for riot duty."

"Who's in charge?"

Yammarino made a face and pointed with his pen at a white shirted man with captain's bars on his collar.

Beasom, he thought. Brogan was right. He couldn't pour piss out of a boot.

"Captain," Meegan said. "What have you got for transport?"

"Right now, we're awaiting word from Public Works. They're supposed to be arranging something."

Shit, Meegan thought. "Cap, you got a helmet and Billy?"

Beasom nodded to his equipment sitting on the desk's edge.

Picking them up, Meegan shouted over the din, "Ok, guys, follow me!" and went out onto Franklin Street. Spotting the red No. 15 bus at Franklin and Swan, he led the posse of policemen to the door of the bus and rapped on it with the nightstick. The driver froze wide-eyed, then opened the door.

"Police emergency, pal. We gotta use your bus. Let's get your passengers off."

"But..." the confused driver started.

"Right now, Mr.... Carey," Meegan said, checking the driver's ID badge.

The muttering passengers got off, and the policemen got on. Standing by the driver, Meegan said, "Head straight up Main to UB, Mr. Carey, I'll tell you where to stop."

When they got close to the campus, Meegan bent down to see ahead. A few hundred yards south of the campus, he spotted a line of police and saw a yellow cloud of tear gas just ahead. "Stop here," he said.

As the police trundled off the bus, Meegan went up to a Captain standing by a battered police car.

"I brought reinforcements, cap," he said to the Captain, who was rubbing his eyes.

"You're just in time, Meegan. We've got eight men on the way to the hospital already. Deploy these men across Main and we'll start moving forward."

"Yes, sir." Meegan waved his nightstick laterally across the street and the crowd of bluecoats fell into line with their compatriots from the 17th Precinct.

214

"Man," one of the 17th Precinct patrolmen said to Meegan. "These assholes have been throwing rocks, bottles, all kinds of garbage at us."

"Screaming 'Kill the Pigs,' smashing windows, tearing up cars," said another.

"All right, take it easy boys. Start moving forward when the tear gas flies, and in a line. Nice and easy," Meegan said, donning Captain Beasom's gas mask.

Ca-chunk, ca-chunk sounds alerted the crowd as tear gas canisters flew at the demonstrators, and the police line moved forward.

Meegan heard a muffled "Now!" from the man next to him, and half a dozen patrolmen ran ahead of the line, swinging their nightsticks. Demonstrators coughed and screamed as the police played catch-up on the demonstrators. Meegan caught up with the charging men just in time to see a blonde-haired girl fall to the ground, coughing and covering her face with a handkerchief. A policeman to his left kicked her aside and swung his club at a youth in an Army jacket who fell on top of her, shielding her. A blonde-haired kid, his hair parted in the middle, threw a half brick that bounced off the policeman's helmet, shouting "Off the pigs!" Meegan grabbed the kid and threw him down, then swung his stick against the kid's shins as hard as he could. The kid rolled over on the street, curling up in a ball, and the police kept rushing forward, driving the crowd in every direction.

A few hours later, Tom heard the phone ring. He took the ice pack from Nancy's side and said, "Try flushing your eyes with cold water again," as he picked up the phone.

HR shouted, "You gotta be here, man!"

Tom heard a crowd in the background chanting, "Com-u-nism!"

"We're at McShane's!" HR yelled. "Everybody's here! This is the beginning of the revolution, Tom!"

"HR, Nancy's hurt. She's still beat up from the demonstration at Norton yesterday and now her eyes are all tore up from the tear gas today."

The crowd noise drowned out whatever HR said, and then the line went dead.

79.

Around midnight the following night, HR looked at the bomb and compared it to the diagram in his hand. Perfect, he thought. He put the bomb in the cardboard box and said to Tom, "You ready for tonight's mission?"

Tom exhaled and said, "Yes."

"Don't worry, Tom. We put the bomb in their lab at night, it blows up when there's nobody there, and nobody gets hurt, just the damn Defense Department project gets wrecked. Then, maybe the university and these so-called scientists will get the message and stop this Themis Project."

Tom followed HR silently to the car and watched him put the box in the trunk at the front of the VW Bug.

"I'll drive, HR."

"Can you handle this?" HR asked.

"Yeah, I know the transmission's got some problems. I can work it."

"No, I mean this mission, man. You know how many people got killed in Vietnam today by American bombs? Hundreds. You and me, man. We're taking the fight to the streets, real action, not just words. I mean, how can you know that, know it's wrong, say we're against it and do nothing? You can't just stand still!"

"I know, I know. After the way the cops hurt Nancy..." Tom said, shaking his head. He grabbed the keys from HR and started up the battered VW.

As they drove slowly up Main Street, HR pulled a small tinfoil package out of his pocket and opened it carefully on his lap.

"Artie got me this," HR said, bending over and snorting up the white powder. "I've been saving some of it for a special occasion. Want some?"

Tom shook his head, downshifted, and the car shuddered.

"Damn. Don't break down now, baby," HR said, patting the dashboard.

"Is the bomb safe in there? I mean, can it go off if we shake it too much?" Tom said.

"Stop worrying, man. I got this all figured out." HR looked at his watch and wiped his nose. "Just right. The demonstration at Hayes Hall should be starting now. Nobody'll be near Sherman Hall."

As they drove onto the campus, the bells in the clock tower of Hayes Hall began ringing continuously and a crowd had gathered in front of the building. Tom pulled up to a silent Sherman Hall and stopped by a side door.

"And for my next act, this handy screwdriver," HR said, pulling the flat-head screwdriver out of his coat pocket. As he gathered the box out of the trunk, he whispered, "Stay put. This won't take five minutes."

Tom looked around as HR walked up to the side door, put the box on the ground and forced the lock. He gave Tom a thumbs up and disappeared inside the darkened building with the box. Tom could feel his heart pounding and heard the demonstrators chanting, "Pigs off campus! Pigs off campus!" as sirens approached Hayes Hall.

"C'mon, HR, c'mon," he said, staring at the door as a Buffalo Police car's lights flashed in the windows of the lab building. Tom ducked down as the car roared past the Volkswagen. After it passed, HR came out and jumped in the car.

"Holy shit, man! That wasn't the campus cops! Now the Buffalo Police are coming on campus! Let's park the car across Main and get to Hayes!"

"What about the bomb? Is it all set?"

"Yeah, man, set to go off at 2:00 a.m., when we're long gone!" HR said as Tom carefully dropped the car into first gear, hoping none of the Buffalo police would recognize him.

No turning back now, Tom thought.

The next morning, Professor Woranowsky stepped out of the campus police car, took out his keys and unlocked the front door to Sherman Hall. Did the janitor leave the lab door open? he thought as he entered the room. Looking around, he spotted the cardboard box on the counter and thought about the news reports of earlier bombings.

"Officer! Somebody broke in last night! There's a box in the laboratory!"

Half an hour later, Lt. Keith MacIntyre of the Arson Squad pulled up to Sherman Hall and looked over the fire engine and the black-coated men with the charged hose line, the campus policemen holding back gawkers, and the white shirted captain talking on the radio.

"What do we have, cap?" MacIntyre said.

"Definitely a device, Keith. Looked like it was wired to a clock."

"Ok," MacIntyre said. "We've got to get these people back another fifty feet at least, cap."

MacIntyre waited while the campus police moved the crowd back, checked the perimeter again, and took off his sport coat and tie. Taking a small canvas bag of tools with him, he entered the building and looked for any wires or other packages in the hallway, then the lab. No secondary devices, he thought. They aren't up to that yet.

He looked inside the box. A pipe bomb, he thought. Clock set for 2:00. Loose wire, hah! He carefully bent the loose wire away from its contact on the clock, tore a piece from a roll of electrical tape with his teeth, wrapped the wire, then slowly disconnected the other wire from the blasting cap and wrapped that as well. He cut the wires to the battery, then looked all around the box. Taking a breath and slowly letting it out, MacIntyre slid a putty knife underneath it and tilted it up ever-so-slightly. Crouching down with a flashlight, he looked under the box. Nothing. All right, put this baby in the truck and get it outta here.

As he walked the box outside with his eyes on the ground before him, he noticed out of the corner of his eye the TV cameras aimed at him. Shit, he thought. If this gets on TV, Margie will go batfuck when she sees it.

HR was still sleeping when Tom turned on the noon news.

"Today, Buffalo police defused an explosive device placed in Sherman Hall on the U.B. Campus sometime last night. Alerted by physiology Professor John Woranowsky, Arson squad commander Lt. Keith MacIntyre of the Buffalo Police examined the bomb, successfully defused it and removed it from the building at eight o'clock this morning."

Tom watched as the camera zoomed in on the middle-aged figure gingerly carrying the cardboard box across the campus lawn to a Chevy Suburban, where he placed the box into a concrete cylinder on the back of the vehicle and covered it with a heavy tarp.

That's Mr. MacIntyre, Tom thought. He used to play catch with me when he came over for dinner.

"Hey! HR! You gotta see this! The bomb!" Tom said, pointing at the TV, where the bomb truck was driving off in a procession of police cars with flashing lights.

"Huh? What? What the fuck, man? It didn't go off! One of the wires must've shook loose from that rattle-trap car ride. Damn!"

80.

When she got off the plane in Buffalo, Mary Ellen looked around the terminal. Same place, renovated a little. She got her bag and jumped in the cab and rode the short distance across Genesee to the Executive Inn. Well, this is new, she thought. Once in her room, she called Buffalo Police Department Headquarters.

"Buffalo Police Department, Patrolman Mathes."

"Can you tell me where Detective Brogan works?"

"Pat Brogan? He retired. I think he works for the DA as an investigator now."

Oh shit!

"How about Louis Constantino?"

"Captain Constantino? Where you been, lady? He retired too, several years ago. Got himself elected sheriff."

Sheriff?

She made arrangements to meet with Todd at the lawyers' office the next afternoon and ordered room service.

The next morning, Mary Ellen tied up her hair and put a scarf over it, donned her sunglasses and raincoat and took a cab downtown. She got out at Eagle and Pearl just after nine and walked to the front steps of the County Hall, watching the workers, taxpayers and license seekers come and go. When the crowd thinned out, she went into the County Clerk's Office and requested the transaction records for the last year of the properties that Yarborough and Correlli had been seeking.

She carefully examined the transaction records. A few were to a Top Flite Construction Company, a couple to a Theodore Engler, a couple to a Falcon Real Estate company and a few more to some Polish names, one of them Elzbeta Owczarczak. Jazz's campaign manager was Owczarczak, the guy who took the fall for him back when they were skimming pinball money, she thought. I wonder if Yarborough knows about this? She thought about what to do with the information. More insurance for me, if nothing else, she thought, and asked a clerk to make copies of all of them.

Checking her watch, she saw it was 12:45. Time to get over to the lawyers' office in the Brisbane Building.

"I'll be back to pick up the copies later," she told the clerk, who nodded. Donning sunglasses and scarf, she walked the few blocks to the Brisbane Building, stuffing her "disguise" in her purse when she got in the elevator. Randolph Todd was waiting for her along with two lawyers (Lauria was the happy one, Peck the one who worried, and Lafonara was in court, she was told). The deposition was straightforward and took less than two hours. Todd escorted her to the first floor and outside.

"We can't thank you enough for your trip up here, Miss Anderson. In fact, myself and the members of the law firm here would like to offer you dinner at the Buffalo Yacht Club and a boat ride on the Niagara River this evening. Miss Anderson, I think this area is a very pleasant region, and I think it's just too bad we weren't able to work with the local government on this project. I hope you'll..."

"Unfortunately, Mr. Todd, I don't think I can accept your offer this evening. I've really got to get back to my hotel," she said, glancing at her watch, "so I can get in contact with my office before the close of business today."

"I see, Miss Anderson, I see. When it's your own business, there's no end to the work to be done." His voice trailed off as she strutted across the square, her red hair tossing in the breeze.

Pat was stacking the witness statements for a construction site accident when his stomach growled. Looking up, he saw the bullpen clock read 3:40. Damn, skipped lunch. Hot dog from the vendor out front will be perfect, he thought, dropping the papers into the Out box.

"Be back in half an hour," he announced. "Anybody want anything from the dog man? Chips, maybe? Pop?"

A few muttered "no's" and "I'm fines" sounded over the perpetual rattling of typewriters as he left. When he got out front, a look around showed him clear skies and he thought a little people-watching on the steps was in order. He walked down to the vendor on the sidewalk, ordered a dog and was squeezing mustard on it when he glanced up back towards the Hall's front entrance.

Mary Ellen saw him, and he saw the red hair. He blinked, tilted his head to the side, then his eyes looked away while he concentrated. He looked again, and she glanced over the vendor's shoulder, giving him the smallest of smiles. She kept Pat in the corner of her eye as she went by, hoping he'd stay right there.

Pat turned and said, "Helen?"

She stopped and smiled, reached out and touched his hand for a second. "It is you, Pat."

"What... I...?"

"I'm in town on business."

"All these years. What happened to you?"

"So much to say... can we meet? Soon?"

"Sure, of course. I..."

She closed her eyes, smiled and said, "Not at Frank's."

His face lit up at the memory, and he said, "Oh no, it's a dump these days."

"Well, how about the bar at the Executive, this evening?" she said. "I should be free by 8:30."

"Ok, 8:30's good."

She touched his hand again and smiled. "I've so much to tell you." A cab honked in the street. "I've got to go. Until then."

Pat stood there, wondering if there were such things as ghosts. Where did she come from? What was she doing at the hall? Her slightest touch after all these years – electricity. He looked out onto the street, but she was gone.

"The Executive Hotel," she told the driver, who looked in the mirror and nodded.

Think fast, she thought. He called me Helen. He hasn't got your new name, he doesn't know where you're staying. He doesn't know anything about the new life you've got in Houston...but he's a cop and can find out. He could destroy everything you've worked for. Looking out the window at the stores, she ordered the driver, "Stop over there, at the Radio Shack. Wait here." Inside the store, she looked over the tape recorders, settling on a cassette recorder with a microphone. This will do it, she thought with a sigh of relief, reading the directions on the way back to her room.

81.

That night, Pat wrestled with the idea all the way driving back from work. He had called Rita and told her he was working late and would get dinner out. He could see her in his mind on the other end of the phone, slightly miffed that her husband wouldn't be home for dinner, but not suspecting he was meeting with another woman. What the hell, having a drink after almost twenty years. Find out what happened after she disappeared back in '53. That's harmless. Yeah, sure it is, pal. You know what you were feeling when you saw her, heard her voice, and it wasn't about a change of scenery. Eight-thirty at the Executive Bar. Six-thirty now, lots of time to get out there. Stop in at Bickleman's and get a drink, think this over. Looks quiet out here now, none of the students were out waving signs, no tear gas. Check in with the boys at the bar and see what's happening in the neighborhood, maybe get a sandwich.

Tom looked in HR's room and saw him snoring in his clothes and reeking of beer. He kicked HR's foot hanging over the end of the bed.

"Hey! You gonna make it?! We got a mission tonight, remember?"

"Nahhh," HR snarled, and rolled over.

"Big revolutionary," Tom said, shaking his head. Going into the kitchen, he picked up the keys to the VW on the table and spotted a note on the table that made him smile. *Doing our laundry, got your Army coat. - N.* Tom went to the closet, snatched out a pleated parka and pulled it on. He went to the sink, filled the wine bottle with gas from the gallon can, carefully pouring the volatile fluid through the funnel HR brought from the VW's trunk. He put the cork back in the top securely and the strip of rag and lighter in his coat pocket. The bottle fit neatly in coat's inside pocket and didn't seem to show. Tom took a deep breath and thought, This is action, not words. Who's the revolutionary now, HR? He locked the apartment door behind him and walked down the steps with his hand on the railing. No time to be clumsy now, he thought. He got in the car, adjusted the coat so the bottle was to one side and slowly drove up to North Buffalo.

Just to be safe, Pat pulled around the back of the bar and parked the car. He went through the back door past the bathrooms and spotted several regulars at the bar, voices raised.

"Those sons of bitches dinged up Kupinski's new Buick on Main Street right in front of the dry cleaners," said Frandina. "He'd just bought it from Bartlett's down the street less than a week before!"

"Yeah, but he got even with them last night," said Viola through a cloud of cigarette smoke. "I heard he took an old shotgun of his, waited in Sander's doorway until the rioters started coming down Main and filled their asses with buckshot. Oh shit! Hi Pat... we were just talking about what some guys would LIKE to do to those damn commies from UB."

Pat shook his head and stepped up to the bar.

"Schmidt's draft?" the bartender asked, tossing a cardboard coaster in front of him.

"Sure, Harley, and see what these three vigilantes will have, too."

They all laughed and quieted down while Harley backed up their drinks.

"You got anything to do with this, Pat?" Frandina said, jerking a thumb towards the nearby campus.

"Nah," Pat said. "Left all that behind when I went to work for the DA."

"It ain't right," Devine said. "We pay for the school, these kids shut it down and wreck it. They even fixed the clock-tower so it would ring constantly the other night, screwed the works up totally."

"Yeah, shut the school down completely, too," added Tyrzinski. "How are they going to handle grades and tests? How are the kids who want to learn going to graduate if this keeps up?"

And makes them eligible for the draft, Pat thought.

"What really gets me," said Frandina, "is the little pricks are waving commie flags and shouting 'NLF will win!' National Liberation Front, my ass. They're nothing but a bunch of traitors!" the Korean War veteran steamed.

Pat thought about Rory bleeding in the jungle, torn apart by a communist mine.

"Lemme have another beer, Harley," Pat said, and stared at the bar.

"That one's on me, Harley," said Frandina, remembering Pat's boy.

Pat finished his beer, left a tip and headed for the back door. What the hell, he thought. Go talk to the redhead. No harm in that.

Tom went around the streets Merrimac, Heath and Englewood, looking for the right parking spot. Not too close, where somebody would see him drive away, not too far away, so he could get away quick. Perfect, he thought, spotting an empty spot on Heath, aimed west. I'll do it, and when it's done, drive down Heath, right on Mildred, left on Englewood and be out of the neighborhood.

Tom parked the car, checked his pockets and headed for the alley behind Main. Third building in from the street, he thought. That's where Dupont and the other recruiters have been holding their interviews, in the old Chicken Delight store. Spotting the targeted window, he saw no lights were on inside. Good, no one's there, no one will get hurt, he thought as he pulled the Molotov cocktail from inside his coat.

Pat was digging for his keys when he heard feet scraping on the pavement ahead in the dark. He looked forward and spotted someone with long hair in a parka pulling something from a coat, then heard the click of a Zippo. In the lighter's flame, he spotted the bottle with a rag fuse, pulled his weapon and shouted, "Stop! Buffalo Police!" and fired two quick rounds, his eyes trying to focus in the dark. The figure turned to him.

"TOMMY!" he screamed as his son's shoulder exploded with blood. The boy dropped to his knees and grabbed at his shoulder as the bottle clinked on the concrete and rolled away. Stuffing the gun in his pocket, Pat ran to Tom, his hands clutching the shattered limb as the boy moaned, "Dad?...dad!" Pulling him up, Pat hauled Tom to his car and opened the door, shoving the wounded boy inside. Driving away with the lights off, Pat thought, What to do, where to go? Any hospital will know it's a gunshot and get the BPD involved. The gun doctor, out in Amherst. He's gotta help me.

Turning the headlights on, Pat drove behind University Plaza and parked. Tom rocked back and forth, his teeth clenched. Reaching in the back seat, Pat yanked a shirt from the gym bag there and then gently pulled Tom backwards against the seat.

"Lemme see that shoulder, son," he said as he slowly parted the shredded clothing over the wound. He folded the shirt and pushed it on the torn flesh, blood pulsing out of the bullet hole.

"Hold that tight, Tommy. Real tight."

"Dad... the bomb. I was…"

"It doesn't matter, it doesn't matter. Hold that bandage tight and stay out of sight while I make a phone call," and Pat was off, wiping his hands on his pants. Spotting a phone booth in the driveway to the empty back parking lot, he turned so passersby wouldn't spot the blood on his clothes. He fumbled through his wallet, looking for the doctor's card. What'll I tell him? I just shot my son. He was about to throw a firebomb. This is insane. I've got to get him help. My boy is hurt, and I did it.

The phone rang. C'mon, man, answer. Please be home, my boy's hurt.

"Kraft residence, Francis speaking. May I help you?"

"Hi, is your dad, the doctor, home?"

"Yes, who should I say is calling, please?"

"Pat Brogan from the DA's office."

"Just a moment, please."

C'mon, c'mon, Pat thought as he heard muffled voices in the back.

"This is Dr. Kraft..."

"Doctor, this is Pat Brogan. There's been an accident. Can you help?"

"Well, certainly. What sort of accident? Have you called the ambulance yet?"

"It was an accident with a gun. We're right in your neighborhood and wonder if you could take a look at it first."

"Well, yeah, I can, I guess. Why... why don't you call an ambulance? How badly are you hurt?"

"It's not me, it's my son. If you could just take a look at him... I'll explain when we get there. Please, doctor."

"Well, ok, Pat. I can take a look at him down at my office. You know where it is, right?"

"Yeah, we're right nearby. We'll be there in just a couple of minutes. Thanks, doc."

Kraft hung the phone up slowly, thinking about what he had just committed to, where his keys to the office were. What's going on here? Why doesn't he want to go to the hospital? A tingle of trepidation about his next few actions ran through him.

"Marian?" he called to his wife.

"Yes?" he could hear her over the noise of the TV. Good, he thought, she and the kids are watching Bill Cosby on TV in the living room.

"I'm going to meet a couple of guys to show me a new pistol. I'll be back in a couple of hours, ok?"

"All right," she said, with her voice full of disdain. "You're not going to the range tonight, are you?"

"No, no. A detective friend just wants to show me it, and we'll be down over at his place for a little while."

Kraft drove to his office, fumbled for the keys, took a deep breath and opened the office door. Turning on the lights in the examination room, he looked around. No nurses, no staff, what the hell am I supposed to do? he thought as he gathered lidocaine, cotton, Q-tips, peroxide and Mercurochrome. Vitals, I'll have to check them myself. Dammit, what did I get into here?

Headlights showed through the office blinds as Kraft spread sheets over the examining table. He heard the back door crash open and looked out into the hallway. There he saw Pat helping a young man clutching his shoulder into the exam room. He pointed at the table and Pat nodded, guiding a long-haired youth breathing through clenched teeth, holding him by the elbow and around the waist.

Tom sat down on the bench.

"Get that jacket off him," the doctor ordered, reaching around for his scissors and cotton bandages.

Tom grimaced as the coat came off. The doctor sliced away the shirt, matted with gore, blood still oozing from the hole below the clavicle.

"What type of round?" Kraft asked, looking at Tom's back and finding the exit wound. He handed Pat a small trauma pad. "Put that on the exit wound," he ordered.

"What kind of round was it?" the doctor demanded.

".38 from a Detective Special," Pat replied, looking straight at the doctor.

Then, to Tom, Pat said, "What the hell were you doing in that alley, anyway? And with a…"

"Ohhhhh," Tom moaned as Kraft probed the wound's trajectory with a long Q-tip.

"Shit, I need an emergency room crew," Kraft said. "This isn't right. Pat, hold these trauma pads over both wounds, now. You can talk later." Then the doctor put his fingers on the boy's trachea, then the wrist, and moved the stethoscope around the chest and back as Pat held pads over both wounds. What was he doing with a Molotov cocktail? Pat thought. When he had finished his examination, Kraft muttered, "I'll need something to cover the wound… Pat! Go out in the kitchenette and get me the roll of Saran Wrap that's on the counter next to the refrigerator."

"Saran Wrap?"

"Just do it. It'll work."

When Pat returned, Kraft nodded towards the table behind him and Pat put the roll of plastic wrap there.

"Now, give me that syringe on the left, Pat," Kraft said, pointing at a tray. He jabbed the wound with it, then said, "Now the other one."

As he depressed the second plunger, he saw Tom looking at it.

"One's lidocaine, the other's epinephrine. One's a local analgesic and the other constricts the blood vessels and helps keep you from going into shock."

"Great. Didn't feel a thing," Tom said, squeezing his eyes shut.

Applying cotton balls and gauze soaked with Mercurochrome to absorb the seeping blood, Kraft said, "Well, the good news is, it's through and through, no damage to the lungs or other organs. The bad news is, it'll take a lot of stitching and hurt a great deal. Then, there's the possibility of infection. He ought to be in a hospital," he said, inserting a small drain tube into the wound.

"I know doc, I know…" Pat paused for a few seconds, looking at his son, then said, "he was fooling around with a gun, and it went off. I don't want to get you into trouble, doc, but it would mean a lot if we could keep this quiet." Tom stared at his father and Pat met his eyes.

"Well, I can suture the damage and treat him for pain and infection," Kraft said, "but this will take some careful following up, and whoever does it will be bound to ask questions."

"I know, I know, doc, but it's important that he gets taken care of here. We can follow up later, in Canada."

Both Tom and Kraft looked at Pat with surprise.

"We gotta get Tommy outta here. There's a place, I think, we can get him to rest and recover, up in Canada. Doc, can I use your phone?"

"Uh, yeah, sure, there's a phone in the front office."

"Don't worry, Tommy, the doc knows his stuff. We're gonna take care of you," Pat said, hesitating to leave his son. Tom nodded as the doctor reached for the suture kit.

82.

"I've got it, dear," Wachter said, reaching for the phone from his worn easy chair and carefully putting down his book.

"Inspector, it's me, Pat Brogan."

"Well, hello, Patrick. Good to hear from you. How..."

"Inspector, I need a favor. I hope you can help me."

"What's wrong?" the inspector said.

"There's been an accident and I need your help."

"What is it, Patrick?"

"Can we come by your house? I can explain better there."

"Yes. The light will be on by the side door."

"Thanks, Inspector. I remember the driveway. Can you leave the light off?"

Wachter hesitated, then said, "Very well, I'll be expecting you." What the hell did Brogan do this time? he thought, slowly hanging up the phone.

Pat exhaled deeply, leaning his head against the wall. Good thing the Inspector never changed his number, Pat thought, shaking his head. He thought for a moment, then dialed the next number, praying Lou would be home.

83.

Mary Ellen sat at the bar and looked at her watch. Five to nine, she thought. Where is he? Her foot tapped on the bar rail and she took a small sip of her Seven and Seven. What if he doesn't show? Was he tracking me down this afternoon? Is this a setup? Someone might be searching my room right now. She noticed the guy with the silk handkerchief and matching ascot had moved around the bar to sit directly across from her. To hell with this, she thought. She called for the bill and returned to her room, checking to see if anything had been disturbed. Looks the same, she sighed and pulled her suitcase out of the closet. When she was almost finished packing, she looked under the bed at the cassette recorder. Leave that as is, I'll pack it just before I leave for the airport in the morning.

84.

"You want to what!?!" Lou shouted, then repeated it quietly. "Pat, this is nuts. What the hell happened?"

"I'll explain when we get there, Lou. Please."

"Alright, alright, Pat. Is everyone ok?"

"He will be, Lou, he will be."

Pat pulled into Lou's driveway and looked around. Tommy was rocking back and forth. "Stay here, Tommy." Tom nodded silently, his eyes shut.

Looking out his back door, Lou whispered, "What the..." as Pat trotted up the back steps into the kitchen.

"Jesus, Pat, that's Tommy," he said, looking at the car. "What the hell happened?"

Pat explained the evening's events, then his plan to get the boy over to Canada and hidden in Wachter's cottage.

"Tom knows some people up there." Pat hesitated, then said, "Draft dodgers. People who help other ones go underground. He won't be in Bertie Bay long."

"If you get caught... if we get caught, it'll mean the end of our careers, everything. You know that, right?"

"Hey, Wachter helped bail us out before and nothing happened, remember?"

They both smiled slightly, and Lou rapped him on the shoulder. "Let's take a boat ride, partner." Just then, Bitzer came into the room, put her glasses on top of her head and placed her hands on her hips.

"You will need help with the boy and docking the boat. Best we move quickly now."

"Hey, wait a minute..." Lou said.

"I have experience smuggling people across borders, remember?" she said, wagging her index finger at Lou.

Lou climbed into the front seat of the car as Pat started the engine. Tommy's eyes opened and he looked up as the sheriff turned around and his wife got in and sat next to him. He shook his head as Lou said, "Don't worry, Tommy, we're gonna take care of you."

Bitzer took an oversized jersey from a paper bag she carried. "This will hurt, Tommy, but we have to get you in this shirt to cover up the bandages and blood." As they drove towards Grand Island, she helped him into the blue Bills jersey, the young man cursing quietly and moaning. Pat slowed the car to a crawl as they drove onto the marina's gravel parking lot, and both he and Lou stared into the darkness.

"Weekday night in the fall, should be nobody around," Lou whispered. They got out of the car, and Pat held Tom around the waist as they went across the lot and over the wooden bridge that led to Lou's slip. They clambered aboard the Hungarian Rhapsody, and Bitzer guided Tommy into the cabin as Lou fired the engines up and Pat went forward to cast the lines off.

As the engines settled into idle, a man scrambled out of the cabin of the boat docked next to them, buckling his belt.

"What... sheriff, it's you... Uh, I didn't expect anyone out here tonight."

Pat and Lou turned their policemen's eyes on the boater.

"I was working on the engine. Had a couple of beers and laid down for a while. Don't want to drive home drunk to the wife, you know."

A woman sneezed inside the boater's cabin.

"Good, Everett. That's being responsible," Lou said as he put the boat in reverse and backed out of the slip.

Pat smiled as they pulled out into the river. "He won't say anything, that's for sure," Lou laughed.

Bitzer's voice came from within the cabin. "Men are such pigs." Pat shook his head, thinking about where he might have been. *I was going to meet Helen. I'm just as bad as that guy. Then, I shoot my own son. I almost killed him! Have I destroyed my marriage, my family? What the hell is the matter with me? This is insane! I've got to make this right. Now, I've got to get Tommy to these...these damned draft dodgers in Canada.*

Ninety tense minutes later, they were idling off the silent Canadian shore. "We gotta be careful here, Pat, it gets awful shallow really quick around here."

Tom pulled himself up out of the cabin, Bitzer guiding him from behind.

"I can walk it in from here, Mr. Constantino."

"Tommy! Can you walk, son? You won't be able to make it alone. It's about a quarter of a mile to the inspector's cottage."

"I'll make it, dad. I remember how to get to Mr. Wachter's. Just give me the keys."

Pat looked at Lou. "I'm gonna walk him there. His people will be there soon."

Lou nodded. "You better change your clothes, Pat. If anybody spots you covered with blood like that, they'll think you're part of the Manson family."

Bitzer handed him the paper bag she'd brought. As Pat changed, Tom sat heavily in the stern.

Lou put a ladder over the side, and Pat climbed over the side, shoes tied around his neck, feeling mud beneath his feet as the cold water rose to just below his waist. He helped Tom down and looked up at Lou. "I'll be back as soon as they come get him."

Bitzer tossed him the package the doctor had given them, and another she had brought. "More clothes. Bandages, too"

"That's my girl. Thinks of everything," Lou said.

As they waded towards the shore, Pat remembered the boys in matching red trunks diving off his shoulders here. This can't be the same kid I saw with a firebomb in the alley, Pat thought.

"You always took us out where it was deeper... so we could dive off you," Tom said.

"Remember cooking hot dogs on the beach?"

"And marshmallows."

When they got ashore, Pat stopped and listened as he helped Tom with his shoes, then they began walking along the silent lane.

"If the Canadian cops stop us, keep your mouth shut. Let me do all the talking," he said, thinking how he would explain the wet clothes, the wounded boy, and his pistol with two expended rounds.

"Cops? You always said they were to be called policemen? Remember?"

"That was before I was smuggling an illegal alien into a foreign country."

When they got to the cottage, Pat pulled out the brass skeleton key and unlocked the door. Once inside, Tom dropped into an over-stuffed chair and Pat brought him a big aluminum cup full of water.

"You gotta drink lots of water to replace the plasma you lost," Pat said.

Tom nodded. "You learn that in the war?"

Pat looked through the kitchen cabinets and found some cans of soup and vegetables as Tom nodded off in the overstuffed chair in the living room. Good, sleep, son, Pat thought. You're wounded. And I did it, I shot my own boy. Stop, damn it. Gotta feed him, get him to safety. Let's see, turkey rice soup. Good, here's a pan, I'll heat this up for him and keep getting him to drink water.

Looking out in the living room, Pat saw Tom's chin resting on his chest. The nodding head jerked up and he said, "Where's the phone, dad?"

"The phone. That's out there, on the table next to you. You got the numbers you need?"

"Yeah, I know them. I'll call them now."

Pat closed his eyes. "Tommy, I shot you. My own son, and…"

"It'll be ok, dad. Remember how you used to tell us about the soldiers who got shot and came back to your unit? I'll be ok, I can handle it."

Pat looked into his son's eyes and put his hands behind his neck, holding his head. "You've got to. Your mom…"

"I'll call home when I get to Hamilton. Let me call these guys." After a brief call, and at his father's urging, he ate some soup and drank more water. He nodded off again, and Pat checked his watch. Ten-thirty.

Six hours later, Tom moaned and picked his head up. The young man looked at Pat through bloodshot eyes.

"Dad, I'm hurtin'."

"I know, son, let me help." Pat walked over to the chair, pulled his sleeve up and jabbed his arm with a dose of Demerol that Kraft had given him. After the drug had eased into Tom's system, Pat gently pulled the jersey off, then brought the medical gear over on a TV tray. He removed the Saran Wrap and gauze and wiped up the wound area around the Penrose drain the doctor had inserted with peroxide-soaked cotton, as lightly as possible.

As he wiped, Tom winced and said, "You done this stuff before, huh, dad?"

"Yeah. Yeah. Once or twice."

After Pat re-bandaged the wound, he reached up and felt Tom's forehead. Phew, not hot.

"Ok," Pat said. "Remember, any sign of fever, you have to go to the hospital immediately, if not sooner. Oh, yeah, and Guelph."

"Guelph?"

"Yeah, Guelph. When you go to the hospital, go to Guelph. A lot fewer questions there than in Hamilton."

"They should be here any minute now," Tom said, standing up. "I'll be ok, dad," and they hugged for the first time either could remember.

They heard the sound of a Volkswagen outside. Do all these guys drive Volkswagens? Pat thought.

"I'll stay in here, Tommy. You go."

"Dad..." Tom hesitated in the doorway. "I love you," he said, not remembering the last time he'd said that to anyone in his family.

"I love you too, Tommy." There's hope for us yet, Pat thought.

Bitzer took the wheel and Lou came over to Pat, staring at the fading shoreline from the stern. He put his hands on his friend's shoulders and said, "He's gonna be alright, Pat. He's tough, like you. He's young. He'll figure things out. It's not as easy to figure things out these days for kids like him. So much trouble."

"Yeah. Yeah. I hope so..." Pat shook his head. "My boys' lives are wrecked, Lou."

"Stop that horseshit, you dumb Mick. They're both alive. Rory's going to get better, and Tommy," he said, jutting his chin at Canada, "will be back someday. What you gotta think about now is Rita. She's gonna need you more than ever now, Pat... and Wachter. He's going to kick our asses good when this is all over," and they both laughed as Bitzer kicked the speed up on the boat, taking them back to the marina.

85.

As Pat came into the house through the back door, he checked his watch. 6:15. Rita came running down the stairs in her bathrobe before he closed it behind him.

"Pat!"

"Yeah, it's me."

"Are you ok? What's wrong? It's almost 6:30!"

"There's been an accident... it's Tommy, but he's going to be ok, Rita."

"What happened? Is he hurt? Why didn't you call me!? Where is he?"

Pat exhaled and then said, "Yes, Tommy's been hurt, but he's going to be alright. He's going to heal up. He's going to be up in Canada for a while. We took care of him."

"Pat, this is crazy. What the hell happened? What is he doing in Canada?"

"Rita, you gotta trust me. Tommy got hurt in an accident, the doctor fixed it and he's gonna be ok, but he'll be staying up there for a while."

"Is Tommy in some kind of trouble? What happened?"

"Everything's going to be fine. If anybody calls for Tommy, last you heard, Tommy's at his apartment."

"Tell me what happened! What happened to our son!?"

"He got shot. In the shoulder. It was an accident..."

"How did he get shot!?"

"I... I shot him." Rita put her hands over her mouth and staggered back against the stove. "It was in the alley behind Bickleman's. I was going to my car. It was dark. I saw someone about to throw a Molotov cocktail..."

"Oh my God," she said, dropping to the floor. "How could you shoot our boy!?"

Pat rushed over and held her. "I didn't know, I didn't know it was him. I took him to the doctor's. He fixed the wound, gave him penicillin. Lou and I, and Bitzer, got him across to Canada, to Inspector Wachter's cottage. Some draft dodger guys came and got him. He can get to a hospital there."

She cried out through the tears, "What about the bullet? Is it still in my boy? He's in pain! God! What have you done, Pat?!"

Pat described his treatment at Kraft's office and in the cottage, and she calmed down a little.

What would she be saying if I'd... he thought, shaking his head.

Pat called in sick and stood by the phone. What the hell do I do now? he thought. Rita went into the kitchen and started to make coffee. As she filled the percolator with water, she started sobbing and dropped the pot into the sink. Pat went and put his arms around her, resting his head against hers. His own tears started to come as he searched for words.

"I don't know... I don't know what happened. We were fine, and the world just closed in on us. The boys were grown up, ready to go out on their own. I never thought this damn war would get us..." She's so angry, he thought. Is this the end for us?

They stood there for a long time. Finally, Rita said, "Your clothes are wet. You smell like the river."

"Yeah, I guess I do. I better get out of them and take a shower."

"I'll finish making the coffee."

They had some coffee and moved around the house in silence for the rest of the day, trying to think of what to say. Around four in the afternoon, the phone rang. Rita jumped on it.

"Hello?"

"Rita, Jon Roth from the DA's office. Can Pat come to the phone?"

"Yes, sure. Just a second." She handed the phone to him and went back into the kitchen.

"Brogan."

"Pat, Jon Roth here. How are you feeling?"

"Uhh, not bad now, Jon. Musta been something I ate."

"Good. Glad to hear it. You'll be in tomorrow?"

"Yeah, should be. Anything happening?"

"The DA's getting ready to move on these students at UB. The ones that are organizing the commotion. He wants to get some indictments ready for the Grand Jury, pronto."

"Ok. I'll be in tomorrow."

"All that trouble is spilling over into your neighborhood, Pat. You have any trouble with it?"

"No, no. Some of my neighbors got their cars tore up. The shop-keepers on Main Street are pissed off, but we're a little off Main. So far, no problems."

"Ok, that's good. Glad you're feeling better, and I'll see you tomorrow."

Pat hung up, and the silence in the house continued. He tried to watch TV, but a glance over at a closet where the kids' toys had been set him into a deeper funk. Rory joined up because of me, he thought. Duty, I thought. His turn. I can't take that back and he's crippled for life. He thought about the arguments with his father when he and Charley went off to join up, and his mother crying, and then her dying while he was away in Europe. What the hell? he thought. What the hell?

Rita touched his shoulder. "Are you hungry?" she asked.

"No," he shook his head. She nodded and went back to the kitchen. The phone rang.

"I've got it!" they both said. Pat got there first.

"Hello?"

"Dad."

"Tommy, are you ok?" he said as Rita grabbed his arm.

"I'm ok. I did like you said. A friend gave me a ride to Guelph, and the doctor in the hospital there worked on me some more. It's going to take some time to heal, but it'll be good."

Pat closed his eyes and nodded as Rita listened with her head next to the receiver.

They could hear Tom laugh through the line as he said, "I told them it was accident that happened over in the states and the police already had the reports. They just said fine and never called the cops."

Rita grabbed the phone. "Tommy?"

"Hi, mom. It's ok. Everything's going to be ok."

"Are you sure? Did they take X-rays?"

"Uh, yeah, mom, they did. They moved my arm around, too, carefully, and it hurt, but they said it'll heal."

"Did they give you any antibiotics?"

"They gave me a prescription to fill."

"Did they take the drain out?"

"Yeah, then they stitched that up, too."

"Where are you staying?

"I'm with friends in Hamilton. Look, mom, I'm going to be fine. I gotta go. I'll call you in a couple of days, ok?"

They hung up, and a thousand thoughts ran through Rita's mind. What about toilet gear? Clothes? Where is he staying? How will he live?

"I need a drink. You?" Pat asked.

"Ok. Then I'll fix some supper," she said, as she talked to Pat about how to get clothes and towels to her son in Canada.

86.

The day the sentences were handed down, Davies drove out to the Springbrook Hotel on Route 16 where nobody would know him. He settled down at the bar where he could see the TV and ordered some chili and a beer. A couple of golfers were next to him in white baseball caps, talking loudly about who had the best drive, and he slid closer to the TV when the noon news came on.

"At ten a.m. this morning, State Supreme Court Justice Ross Oberpfalz pronounced sentence on former Erie County Legislators Alfred Fort and Augustus 'Gus' Ludlow in the dome stadium bribery scandal. Both men were convicted of conspiracy in the case, and Ludlow was convicted of bribery, as well. The two having exhausted their appeals, Judge Oberpfalz sentenced Ludlow to three years for the conspiracy conviction, and an additional three years on the bribery charge, to be served consecutively. Fort was sentenced to a three-year term. The two were taken into custody by County Sheriff's Deputies and will be transported to Attica Correctional Facility where they will serve their sentences."

Davies watched the gray uniformed deputies handcuff their prisoners. He saw his keeper, Vince, overseeing the procedure, and Fort's wife was crying in the background. When the announcer came back on, he said, "In related news, the New York State Board of Examiners is considering the revocation of the licenses of the architects who bribed the County Legislators..." The rest of the announcer's words were a blur as Davies finished the beer, left some cash on the bar and brushed past the golfers. He took sips from the flask as he drove back into Buffalo, and found himself in Shoshone Park, where he listened to the radio and drank until dark, thinking about how Landice had left him.

Landice hadn't said a word to him that morning, and when he came back to the hotel after the day at court, she was sitting on the bed in front of the TV, legs crossed, one hand holding the other elbow, cigarette doing a slow burn at an upright angle between her fingers. She looked at him silently as he took in the room, his clothes scattered about and two suitcases, hers, in front of the bed.

"Charley finally moved out of the house. The lawyer says it's mine now. I'm moving back there, and out of this…dump," she said, waving the cigarette around, ashes falling on the rug.

"What about us?" he said. "The plans we were making…" A knock at the door interrupted him.

"That'll be the front desk to get my bags," she said, standing up and crushing out her unfinished smoke. "I'll give you a call when I'm settled in and we can talk about it."

"Hey, wait a minute, Landice. You don't want to leave it like this…"

She walked past him and opened the door. The kid at the door looked in, but stayed out in the hall.

"Take the two suitcases to the canary yellow Monaco in the back lot," she told the kid. Seth thought about saying something else, but the words didn't come.

"Goodbye, Seth. I'll give you a call," she said, and was gone.

When the sun was well down he drove to the lot behind the hotel and looked to see if anyone was waiting for him. Seeing no one, he went in the back entrance and slipped up to his room. He fumbled with the key and tossed it on the dresser, then fell across the bed. He noticed the call light was blinking on the phone. Maybe it was Landice calling, he thought, and dialed her number. It rang and rang and he finally gave up, falling back on top of the comforter.

87.

For several days after Mary Ellen's return from Buffalo, the staff at Anderson Accounting were walking on eggshells. The boss was silent as she stomped in and out of the office and Billy's most important job was making sure he delivered the Buffalo newspapers from Killian's Newsstand as soon as they arrived. Day after day, he brought the papers in, and Mary Ellen would look up from her calculator and worksheets to snatch them.

What is Pat doing? She thought. The papers say those two politicians were convicted and sent to jail, and Yarborough's filed suit against Erie County. Will I have to testify? This suit could go on for years.

After a week, she called the detective agency she sometimes used to investigate would-be clients and had them look into Brogan. When the report came back that he was married to a nurse, had two children, one a student, the other a soldier, she calmed down.

He'll never look for me. Ships passing in the night. And if they want testimony, I'll send Billy or Terri.

88.

Brogan looked through his inbox and found a thick package addressed to him with a blurred return address and a Houston, Texas, postal cancellation. Curious, he opened it up and found copies of real estate transactions in the Town of Lancaster, Erie County, NY over the last two years. He started to read through them, finding the names of the purchasers highlighted. He also recognized the name Owczarczak and wondered if a little digging into the principles of the more generic titles might reveal some interesting connections. After reading through them thoroughly, he knocked on the DA's door.

"Hey chief, I think I've just received an anonymous tip. You should take a look at this," Pat said, placing the papers in front of the prosecutor. After reading through them, Butler tossed his glasses on the desk, pushed his chair back and put his feet up on the stacks of paper before him. He rubbed his eyes, then joined his hands behind his head.

"Patrick, sometimes the fates are kind to us and we don't have to raise a finger for justice to be served. Whoever was behind those inside purchases in Lancaster can eat the taxes on a lot of windblown fields in the country from now until doomsday. Beats trying to prove the fix was in for those bums and that probably hurts them more than any prosecution we could muster."

89.

Rita pulled the laundry out of the dryer in the basement, put it on the table and began folding the shirts that Tommy hadn't taken over to Mariner Street. We can get these over to Tommy in Canada, she thought. The doorbell rang and she stopped, closed her eyes for a moment and went up the stairs. She looked out the dining room window and saw a girl wearing an Army jacket looking down with her hands in the pockets. Pretty girl, she thought, seeing her tousled dark blonde hair and long eyelashes. Maybe a friend of Tommy's, and she hurried to answer the door. The girl was turning to go when Rita opened it.

"Can I help you, Miss?" The girl stopped and turned.

"Is this the Brogan house?" she said, still looking at the ground.

"Yes. I'm Rita Brogan. What can I do for you?"

"I'm looking for Tom Brogan. Is he here?"

"No," Rita said slowly, "no, Tommy's not here. Are you a friend of his?"

"I'm one of Tom's roommates. I was wondering if you've seen him?"

"I haven't seen him today, Miss... Miss?"

"My name's Nancy Molla. Do you know where Tom is?"

"Would you like to come in, Nancy? It's getting chilly out here," Rita said, rubbing her upper arms.

"Uhh, ok, I guess," Nancy said, hesitating, then following Rita.

"C'mon into the kitchen, Nancy. Would you like a drink? I've got some pop in the fridge here."

"Ok," she said, smiling. "Are you his mom?"

"Yes, my name's Rita. Have a seat Nancy, here, let me take your coat," she said, looking at it closely. This is Tommy's jacket, she thought.

"We haven't seen Tommy in a few days, Nancy. Is everything ok?" Rita asked, thinking, This girl looks pale. I wonder...

Nancy sipped the bubbling drink, closed her eyes and nodded. "I haven't seen Tom since Sunday, that's all. I thought maybe he might've come here."

"No, he hasn't been by here in a while," she said, remembering Pat's advice about keeping quiet about Tom's whereabouts. "Are you ok?"

Nancy rubbed her forehead. "Just a little tired..." She sat up straight and arched her back. She took another sip of 7 Up and looked at the floor.

"Are you hungry, Nancy? I've got a roast in the oven and we'll be having dinner in about an hour. It's just my husband and me at home now, and we've got plenty."

Nancy swallowed, touched her lips and said, "Can I use your bathroom?"

Rita got up and opened the door to a room off the hallway. "Sure, Nancy, here's the powder room right here." Nancy followed her swiftly and closed the door. Rita returned to the kitchen table and sat down, listening to water running in the sink and the faint sounds of the girl vomiting. A few minutes later she came out with the back of her hand over her lips.

"Are you sure you're ok, Nancy?"

She closed her eyes and nodded.

After a long pause, Rita said softly, "You're pregnant, aren't you Nancy?"

Nancy nodded and started to cry. Rita reached out and took her hands. "It's ok, it's ok. Is the baby...?"

251

Nancy nodded again and cried. Rita got up and went to her and put her arms around the girl. "I don't know what to do..." Nancy said.

"It'll be ok, it'll be ok," Rita said, a thousand thoughts rushing through her mind.

"Where's Tom?" she cried.

"He's gone away for a little while, but he's not far. He won't leave you, Nancy. Does he know you're pregnant?"

Nancy shook her head, the long hair falling over her face.

"Have you seen a doctor yet?"

She shook her head as the tears stopped. Rita handed her a box of tissues.

"Thank you."

Rita pulled her chair around to sit close to the girl and took her hands.

"Do you have a doctor?"

She shook her head again. "I haven't seen a doctor since I left my folks' house."

"Where are they, Nancy?"

"They live in Rochester."

"Have you called them?"

"Nooo," she said, thinking of the silent banker and his waspish wife.

90.

"Pat?"

"Yes, Rita," he said, absent-mindedly watching TV.

"I met Nancy, Tom's roommate."

"Oh?" he said and changed the channel.

"She came over to the house yesterday."

"Uh-huh."

"She's going to have a baby."

"What's that bum HR going to do?"

"She says it isn't his."

Pat sat up straight. "How's that again?"

"She says it's Tom's. Nancy says HR didn't want her around any-more, and Tommy looked out for her, then... things happened."

"What about her parents?"

"Nancy and I talked a long time, and she says they don't get along. I convinced her to call them. I listened while she talked to them. I could hear someone screaming at her. She must have cried for ten minutes after they hung up."

"Does Tommy know?"

"No, she just found out herself. She hasn't seen a doctor since she came to Buffalo. We have to do something."

Pat looked at her, then blinked several times in silence. "I guess... I guess she could stay here for a while until we can figure things out."

Rita rushed over and hugged him.

"I prayed about this all last night," she said. "She says she'll be all packed up tomorrow night," and she rushed upstairs to start fixing Tommy's room.

"What the hell just happened?" Pat said. "A grand-baby, and a daughter? Daughter-in-law, I guess. And Tommy up there in Canada doesn't even know."

The next day was Saturday. Pat drove over to the apartment building on Mariner that night with a description of a girl he'd never met. When he pulled up out front, there was a pretty blonde girl sitting on the front steps in an Army jacket. He got out of the car and walked over to her.

"Are you Nancy?" he said. He put his hand out. She took it, and he helped her up.

"Thank you. You must be Tommy's dad."

"Yeah, that's me. Let's get your stuff, Nancy. Mrs. Brogan's got Tommy's room all fixed up for you."

"Uhh, my stuff and Tommy's are all packed up in the first bedroom. HR and some other people are up on the roof. They've been partying for a while."

Pat looked up at the roof and heard music and voices.

"Ok, look. Here's the keys to the car. Go and wait in the car while I get your bags. Is the apartment door open?"

She nodded and went to the car while he went into the building and loudly walked up the wooden steps to the apartment. Pat banged on the door and went in. He looked around, noticed a bag of grass and a bong on the living room table, but didn't see anyone. He grabbed a duffel bag and a suitcase from the bedroom and carried them out to the car. On his second trip, Artie was getting a six-pack out of the refrigerator as he entered.

"Who the fuck'er you?" Artie said.

"I came to get Tom's stuff," Pat said.

254

"You're Tom's dad?" Artie said, looking over the tall, middle-aged man in the windbreaker.

"That's right. I'm getting his and Nancy's stuff out of here."

As he went down the stairs, Pat heard Artie and HR talking in the stairway to the rooftop.

"What the fuck's going on?" HR said. "Tom called and said he's in Canada. He left my car up in North Buffalo, man."

"Dunno," Artie said. "This old guy's taking his and Nancy's stuff out, said he was Tom's dad."

Nancy watched Pat as he loaded the bags into the trunk. Rolling down the window, she asked, "Is everything ok, Mr. Brogan?"

"Everything's fine, Nancy. Let's get you home. You'll be fine with us."

HR and Artie came out on the front steps of the house and saw Pat slam the trunk closed.

"What the fuck do you think you're doing?" HR shouted.

"She's leaving. Tom's not coming back here."

HR started down the steps but stopped when Pat took a step towards him. They stared at each other for several seconds, then Pat nodded and got in behind the wheel.

Nancy looked out the rear window as they pulled out.

Inside the car, they heard HR shout, "You motherfuckers! You bitch!"

There was a loud crash on the street as a beer bottle shattered just behind them. Nancy spun around and saw HR screaming at them, then put her head in her hands and started crying.

"It's going to be ok, Nancy. You're all done with those screwballs. They aren't going to bother you," Pat said, handing her a handkerchief. Who is this girl? he wondered. What are we getting into, taking a stranger, and a pregnant stranger at that, into our house? Tommy's baby. What would happen if we'd left her in that house with those bums?

Nancy wiped her eyes and looked out the window. She started to say something a few times, but stopped. I don't have any family in Rochester anymore, she thought. HR didn't love me and Tommy's in Canada. She put her free hand on her stomach. My baby. Tommy's parents seem nice. Another tear dropped. When will Tommy come back? What am I doing?

Pat turned on the radio, tuned it to the FM side and hit the first button, which was the one Tommy always played. The station was broadcasting something with jazzy guitar riffs and dual snare drums working, and Pat was surprised, it wasn't half bad.

"Do you know who plays this, Nancy?"

"Uh huh, sure. It's the Allman Brothers band. It's called 'In Memory of Elizabeth Reed.' They play them a lot on WPHD."

"Hmmm," he said, and turned it up a touch. Nancy smiled just a little.

When they got to the house, Rita was waiting outside in the driveway with her arms crossed.

"Everything go ok?" she asked.

"Yeah, no problem," Pat said, unloading the trunk. "I'll take these bags upstairs now."

"All right. Come on in the house Nancy, let's get you situated," Rita said, wondering why Pat was so quiet.

When Nancy went upstairs, Rita asked Pat, "Did everything really go ok with that boy? He is her ex-boyfriend, you know."

"He had a tantrum, but there was no fight, if that's what you mean."

"Patrick Brogan, I know how that devious Irish mind of yours works. What's going on?"

"Nothing. Really. I got the kids' stuff and we left. That HR kid screamed and threw a bottle at the car and missed."

"Hmm. I'll fix us some coffee. Time for you to get acquainted with our new... daughter-in-law?"

The next day, Pat drove over to the 10th Precinct on Niagara. The Desk Lieutenant, Jim Welleshauser, smiled when he saw Pat come in the door.

"Well, Pat Brogan, how the hell are you? I heard you retired and went to work for the DA. You going tell me when your retirement party is?"

"Don't worry, Jim. Bill Murak's organizing a party for a bunch of us recently retired. The posters will be out soon. It's going to be over at Eduardo's."

"That's good, Pat. I always look forward to the war stories. They get bigger every time. So, what can I do for you today, partner?"

"Any of the detectives around, Jim? I got a location they might want to check out."

"Battin and Catroneo are back in the reserve room, Pat. They should be able to help you."

Pat walked around the desk and entered the reserve room. The two detectives were drinking coffee and looking over a machete on the table.

"You know it's a rough joint when the bouncer carries a machete," Catroneo said. "Hey, el-tee, c'mon in, see what you're missing on the West Side these days."

"Hiya, fellas. I just came by to clue you in on a house with a lot of dope in it in Allentown."

"We're all ears, boss. The problem is, most of the judges are getting gun shy about signing no-knock warrants these days," Battin said.

"Maybe I can help you there, detective. I'll tell you what to put in the affidavits, and I also happen to have Judge Casper's home number. He's a good friend of ours."

91.

When Pat went into the office the next day, the DA waved him into his office. "I've got your next assignment, Pat. Sorry to say, it's not a layup, either." He tossed a file towards the investigator. Pat flipped through it as his boss explained.

"Lou Constantino loaned me three men a while back, and I sent them with a couple of feds up to the UB Campus to check things out – dope, radicals, teachers. Most of what they did was take pictures. What I need you to do is identify the players and follow up on what they found. I don't know if we'll do much about the dope, but somebody was planning those bombings and riots up there – they were way too organized to be spontaneous. We want to figure out who the leaders were and bring charges against them. That university was in a state of chaos all last spring and now this fall again. It's fallen to us to bring order back to the campus so that it can be an educational facility, not a pot party run by a bunch of vandalizing Reds."

Pat nodded and looked through the pictures. HR, Nancy and Tom were in several. The photographs, he noted, hadn't been inventoried yet. The ones with Tom and Nancy could disappear with no one the wiser.

92.

When Pat got home that night, Rita was in the pantry putting dishes away.

"There's a letter there from Rory, Pat," she said in a cheerful tone. "He says he'll be getting out of the Army soon and he'll be able to come home in two weeks!"

Pat picked up the letter and walked into the pantry as he took it out of the envelope. Rita smiled at him and continued, "He'll need several more surgeries, but he'll be able to travel down to DC for them. He can get checkups in between from the VA right here on Bailey." She put the dishtowel down and kissed him. He put his arms around her waist and kissed her back.

"Later," she said, slipping away. "I'm going over to church for the novena. I've been saying it every week since Rory got hurt, and I'm not going to stop now."

After she left, Pat sat down at the kitchen table to read the letter.

Dear Mom and Dad,

I'm done with the therapy for my arm and leg. Spec. McKenna even got me shooting a basketball the other day. I'm not half what I used to be with one eye and a hook for a hand, and I can't move on the court, but I never thought I'd get this far. I'll tell you the truth, when I was still in the hospital in country and at Clark, between the pain, the blindness and hearing nothing but what sounded like real loud static in my head, I was ready to give up and die.

These guys here at Walter Reed, my guys in the squad, the dust-off crew, the people back in the hospital in Nam and Clark, they all gave it everything they had and brought me back. I'll never forget them, and I'll never be able to thank them enough.

Here's the real good news: they were probing around my face after this last surgery (that hurt!), and they say all the new structure is good and the grafts are taking. That means I can come home! I'll have to come back for more surgeries, and I'll have to wear an eye patch until they fit me for a new eye, and I can't talk or eat anything but mush yet, but I will. Fake teeth and everything. The hair is growing back on my left side. With the regulation haircut on the right so short, it'll be matching up soon.

Because I'm due to be discharged in two weeks, there has been a truckload of paperwork to fill out. The guys in my platoon looked out for me, and my footlocker should be coming home any time now. Some knucklehead at battalion was looking to account for my lost weapon, flak jacket, and other gear that got lost or wrecked when I got hurt — I had to sign off on some paperwork (forms DA200 and DA2823 to be precise!). Boy if that isn't the Army.

Dad, you're going to love this – a retired Colonel from your old unit – 60th Infantry – came up to visit and pinned a Purple Heart on me. His name is Colonel Matt Urban, and he's from Buffalo, too. Lots of guys have gotten decorations here in the hospital, but usually the big shots are here and gone, and that's just as well. This colonel sat down and talked with me for half an hour, mostly about places in Buffalo and people there. I found out later he won 2 Silver Stars, 3 Bronze Stars and 7 Purple Hearts.

We didn't talk about the war, but you could tell he cared. He knew what me and the other guys had been through. Made me feel like a soldier again, that we did our job, no matter what those assholes on TV say. You've been there, dad, you know. That's one thing I'll miss about this place — everybody here's been there, they understand. It'll be scary out there in the world.

When mom was last here, she told me about Tom. I don't understand what he was trying to do, I don't get what happened. I can't figure it out at all. I'm going to buy a car when I get home, and I wanted to ride around in it with him, go to the beach. It's too late in the year for the beach, and he's "out of town" like you said, but maybe next year. I miss him no matter what.

SEE YOU IN TWO WEEKS!

Your son,
Rory

Pat picked up a Polaroid picture that was with the letter. There was a guy a little older than Pat with a pencil mustache pinning a medal on Rory. Rory was standing at attention in his blue hospital robe, his one good blue eye staring straight ahead. Now there were three sets of tears on the letter. I think we're going to make it, he thought.

93.

All during Ludlow and Fort's trial, Sammy stayed at Nicole's house. He watched the news on TV, read the papers, and, after Fort and Ludlow were convicted, gave a sigh of relief that nobody had found him. *Fort and Ludlow Begin Sentences,* the Courier read. Sammy dropped the paper on the floor, picked up the phone and dialed the vending shop number.

"Where you sons a bitches been?" he shouted at Jack.

"Working, you old fool. Everybody's asking for you. Russo's been running ragged trying to keep up."

"I been sick. Doctor said don't go out."

"You OK now?"

"Fit as a fiddle. I'll meet you at the Queen's Plate. You can buy the lunch this time."

When Jack and Kevin came into the bar, they saw a wavy, gray-haired guy with glasses pointing at Sammy.

"You stole it, didn't you? You betrayed me!"

Sammy put his drink down, shifted his left foot slightly forward, and swung a right uppercut from his ankles. He headed for the door as Davies tumbled over the barstool and hit the floor.

"C'mon, boys," he waved. "They got the steak sandwich special at DiTondo's today you can buy me."

END

Acknowledgements

As with my last book, *Every Man for Himself,* I wish to thank the following people for their time, their research and their wisdom in helping me. Any inaccuracies are all mine. I hope to hear from the readers of this novel – contact me at my website: https://markhannonbooks.wordpress.com/ or the Facebook site: https://www.facebook.com/everymanforhimselfhannon/

Elizabeth Leik, for her excellent editing and guidance, Annabelle Finagin, Vanessa Gleklen and the rest of the staff at Apprentice House Press, Mary Kokoski for her editing and artwork, Dave Pfalzgraf, Michael Kaska, Mark Stanbach, Joseph Finnerty, Paul Perlman, Erik Brady, Chuck Maryan, the Staff in the Grosvenor Room of the Buffalo and Erie County Public Library, The 1030 Tech Support Services, Harry Pope, Jack Siracuse, Kevin Kinal, Harley Cudney, Ric Cottom, Matt Gryta, Brian McHale, Barry Scheitlin, Tom McCarthy, Edward Cosgrove, Jim Patz, the Staff at the Newspaper Reading Room of the Library of Congress, Peter Hubbell, Jim Neill, Marc Leepson, Steve Cichon, Peter Anderson, Captain D. Green, C.J. Black, Justin Hurley, John F. Toolen, Jack Messmer, Brian Poliner, Bill Keenan, James Leith, Robert Graber, Bill Offhaus and the staff of the SUNY Buffalo Archives.

About the Author

Mark Hannon is a retired firefighter who grew up in Buffalo. He is the author of *Every Man for Himself,* a crime novel about Buffalo in the 1950s.

Apprentice House is the country's only campus-based, student-staffed book publishing company. Directed by professors and industry professionals, it is a nonprofit activity of the Communication Department at Loyola University Maryland.

Using state-of-the-art technology and an experiential learning model of education, Apprentice House publishes books in untraditional ways. This dual responsibility as publishers and educators creates an unprecedented collaborative environment among faculty and students, while teaching tomorrow's editors, designers, and marketers.

Outside of class, progress on book projects is carried forth by the AH Book Publishing Club, a co-curricular campus organization supported by Loyola University Maryland's Office of Student Activities.

Eclectic and provocative, Apprentice House titles intend to entertain as well as spark dialogue on a variety of topics. Financial contributions to sustain the press's work are welcomed. Contributions are tax deductible to the fullest extent allowed by the IRS.

To learn more about Apprentice House books or to obtain submission guidelines, please visit www.apprenticehouse.com.

Apprentice House
Communication Department
Loyola University Maryland
4501 N. Charles Street
Baltimore, MD 21210
Ph: 410-617-5265
info@apprenticehouse.com • www.apprenticehouse.com